Brady shook his head sadly

"Trust me, Tess. The way we feel right now is nothing compared to the pain we'd feel if we... pretended it might work."

"I'm not pretending, Brady! What I feel for you is absolutely *real*."

With infinite care, he released her hands and brushed his fingers through her hair. Slowly he pulled the long locks back over her breasts and smoothed the strands until her bra and bare midriff were completely covered. For a moment he studied his handiwork, as though he'd just finished a painting, then once more he sadly met her eyes.

He leaned forward and kissed Tess again, kissed her longingly, gently... kissed her with a poignancy that did not herald any future between them.

It was a kiss that said goodbye.

ABOUT THE AUTHOR

Suzanne Ellison, who lives in California, visited the red rock country of Colorado, Utah and Arizona numerous times while working on the Living West trilogy, and developed a genuine love of the area. She hopes that readers of the Living West series will come to appreciate the beauty of the West as much as she, husband Scott and daughter Tara do.

Books by Suzanne Ellison

HARLEQUIN SUPERROMANCE

165–WINGS OF GOLD
258–PINECONES AND ORCHIDS
283–FOR ALL THE RIGHT REASONS
308–WORDS UNSPOKEN
315–FAIR PLAY
369–CANDLE IN THE WINDOW
393–WITH OPEN ARMS
420–HEART OF THE WEST

HARLEQUIN INTRIGUE

46–NOWHERE TO RUN

Soul of the West

SUZANNE ELLISON

Harlequin Books

TORONTO • NEW YORK • LONDON
AMSTERDAM • PARIS • SYDNEY • HAMBURG
STOCKHOLM • ATHENS • TOKYO • MILAN

Published October 1990

ISBN 0-373-70423-2

Printed in U.S.A.

For Arthur and Edith Clarke,
who taught me that family goes beyond blood.

CHAPTER ONE

TESS HAMILTON STUDIED the space-age curves of the steel-and-glass bank next door to the quaint old-brick hotel where she'd spent the night and sighed. "Look around you, Roberta," she ordered her tall, robust friend. "Here you have a classic example of war between preserved gold rush America and late twentieth-century architecture. It's just a matter of time before these fine old buildings are going to be a memory." As she took a step forward to brush off the dust from a plaque embedded in the bricks, her luscious waist-length blond hair spilled over her shoulder. "Founded 1866."

"I thought we signed up for this wagon train to forget about work for a while, Tess," Roberta Wheeler countered, tugging Tess toward the ancient train station on the other side of the hotel. "Can't you just enjoy this trip into the past without fretting about the future for once?"

Tess laughed. "A busman's holiday, wouldn't you say? I'd hardly call a trip into the past a way to 'forget about work' for either of us."

Tess had met Roberta when the two of them had been plunked into the same college dorm room by accident as freshmen, but from then on they'd chosen to room together, on campus and off, until Tess's wedding shortly after she'd finished graduate school. Nowadays Tess worked for Historic West Preservation in Los Angeles, a nonprofit organization that devoted itself to rescuing and renovating old ghost towns and landmarks that were about to be buried by the sweep of progress. Roberta, an American history professor in Arizona, thrived on any book, costume or artifact that captured the essence of the old west. It was Roberta—always up for a challenge—who had heard about the Rocking T Wagon Train Adventure and cajoled Tess into spending a week in the Four Corners area with her.

Not that Tess wasn't game for a new experience, especially one that took her deep into the country she'd come to love. But Roberta had been raised on a Texas ranch where Conestoga wagons from her grandparents' time held an honored position near the still-occupied bunkhouse. Tess, on the other hand, had been born and raised in New York City, where prairie schooners were not exactly part of everyday life.

"Okay, maybe that was a poor choice of words," Roberta admitted, running a brisk hand through her short, dark curls. "What I mean is, let's have a good time, okay? I left my troubles in Tucson, Tess, and I thought you'd left yours in L.A."

Tess flashed her friend a quick smile. "No troubles in L.A., Roberta. I left them all a few years back."

Roberta returned the grin and didn't ask her friend to elaborate as they strolled through the parking lot toward the brightly painted clapboard station. Of all the friends who had watched Tess live with the strain of her ex-husband's volatile career and even more volatile nature, Tess knew that none understood her past heartaches better than Roberta. And none of them understood with any greater certainty that she would never again get involved with a man who expected her to take second place to his dreams—no matter what they were.

"'Slow Joe Loco,'" read Roberta as she stared at the rustic hand-painted sign above the station house. "Is that the original name of this place?"

"As a matter of fact, it used to be called the Colorado Fireball," declared a pretty redhead slipping in through the door on their right. Her petite frame and freckled face made her look like a twenty-year old, but the confidence of her tone and the tiny smile lines that framed her mouth revealed her maturity. Tess, who was thirty-six, decided that the woman was at least her age and probably ten years older.

As the redhead unlocked a side door, disappeared and instantly reappeared behind the ticket window, she continued, "The train was renamed for my husband, Joe."

Tess envied the woman's richly satisfied smile; she didn't need to ask what condition *this* marriage was in. "I take it he's . . . a rather laid-back sort of person?"

The redhead laughed so hard her strong white teeth showed. "The opposite. He was positively hyperactive as a child."

Tess didn't quite know what to say to that. She couldn't think of a man she knew who'd been part of her life for more than a year or two. "It must have been nice growing up in such a small town," she commented almost wistfully.

Roberta rolled her eyes in a look that said, "You've got to be kidding!"

Too late Tess remembered how desperately Roberta had struggled to escape her own cloying rural past.

But apparently the redhead hadn't had the same problem, because she replied cheerfully, "Oh, I didn't grow up here. I know what Joe was like as a child because I was his sixth-grade teacher."

Roberta's mouth dropped open. "You were his..."

"It's a long story," she declared energetically. "With a *very* happy ending, I might add."

That's obvious, Tess thought. *What I'd give for a husband who made me glow like that!*

Before the conversation could grow awkward, the redhead said, "I'm Mandy Henderson and I help Joe run this place in the summer. How can I help you two gals?"

Tess, who knew that Professor Roberta was still struggling with the notion of marrying one's student—let alone a student one had taught at the age of twelve—decided to step in and take charge of the arrangements. "I'm Tess Hamilton, and this is Roberta Wheeler. We're here for the Rocking T Wagon Train Adventure. The letter Roberta got said we should meet the ranch van here."

"You're in the right place," Mandy assured them, then took a second glance at Roberta, who was sporting a floor-length calico dress with a Mother Hubbard apron and a sun bonnet with eighteen-inch straps tied under her chin. "And in the right garb, I might add."

Tess, intending to stay cool and casual as long as possible, planned to leave her sturdy riding clothes in her duffle bag until she reached the ranch. Even if she could have endured wearing a floor-length dress in the staggering desert heat, she would never have arrived on the Rocking T dressed as Roberta was. Roberta thrived on being different—downright odd, at times—and gathering a crowd around her. Tess, on the other hand, had no use for the limelight that Roberta craved. She was not a shy person, but neither did she like to flaunt herself.

"You're in for a marvelous week," Mandy exclaimed, her sunny smile a vote of confidence in and of itself. "Everybody who spends a week on the Rocking T says they'd love to come back again."

Tess flipped a long strand of hair out of her face and asked, "Have you taken the trip yourself?"

"About a dozen times. Actually Brady used me as a test case in the beginning. He wanted to get a woman's perspective on things. I think he made a few adjustments on rest breaks, privacy and bathing accommodations after my input."

While Tess was thinking, *What a thoughtful fellow this Brady must be,* Roberta said, "That's Brady Trent, the wagon master who wrote to me?"

"Wagon master, owner, wrangler extraordinaire and genius who thought up the whole thing and talked my husband into it." Her tone was tender as well as proud. "Brady is . . . well, he's a very special person. Family, really, to Joe and me. You couldn't be in better hands out there."

"Out there?" Tess repeated, gazing to the orange and purple cliffs to the south where it was obvious that few boots had ever trod.

"Well, out in the red-rock country. No sensible person goes off in the desert without proper equipment and somebody who knows what he's doing. Especially now that . . . well, especially now."

Before Tess could ask what she meant by that cryptic comment, a young couple with four bouncing little ones arrived, dominating the conversation for several minutes. Eventually Mandy Henderson was able to get a word in edgewise, suggesting that everybody waiting for the ranch van might like to visit the Slow Joe gift shop. As they ducked inside to the quaint single room—a showcase of old train prints, train trinkets, train note cards and other train-related gifts—she asked Roberta, "What do you think she meant by 'especially now'?"

"She probably meant that it's June, Tess, and as hot as Hades out there."

That seemed like a reasonable explanation to Tess, so she pushed Mandy's mysterious words to the back of her mind, and forgot all about the remark when the Rocking T van arrived a few minutes later, driven by an old geezer who could have galloped right off the set of *Rawhide*. As he limped down the van steps and ambled toward the Slow Joe lobby, Tess studied the salt-and-pepper beard that drooped halfway down his chest and the felt Stetson, which looked as though it had been run over by a herd of stampeding longhorns.

"That's probably Brady Trent," Tess declared. "Somehow I thought he'd be a little younger."

Roberta chuckled. "I don't know if he's any younger, but I know he's not Brady Trent."

"Why do you say that?"

"Because I've lived with cowboys all my life, Tess, and that van driver *is* one. The owner of the Rocking T would look like an educated rancher, not a bunkhouse drifter. My guess is he's lucky that this Trent fellow took him on. He's probably too old to work anywhere else, and if he's done any rodeo work, he's probably got a dozen half-healed bones and has trouble moving when his arthritis acts up."

"Poor old fellow," said Tess, who liked the old man's generous whiskered smile. "That's a terrible way to live your life."

Roberta grinned. "I bet he wouldn't change a single day of it. In this day and age being a cowboy isn't something you do because you can't do anything else. It's something you do for love."

"Love of what?" asked Tess, then wished she could have swallowed the words as she remembered the great love of Roberta's life—horses—and a dream that had been shattered with a vertebrae-cracking show-jump fall at the age of seventeen. It was only through sheer chutzpah that Roberta had ever learned to walk again, a confession she'd once made to Tess when she'd tearfully admitted that after nearly twenty years, she'd never yet found the courage to mount another horse.

"I don't know if I can explain it to a city person," Roberta answered slowly, a dark sobriety coloring her normally upbeat tone. "But if you grow up with ranch dust on your feet, you can't ever shake it off completely." She shrugged with good-natured embarrassment. "Look at me. I went crazy living with cowboys. In high school I thought they were going to ruin my life. And once I dragged myself through college, what field did I choose? American history. *Western* history, no less. And where do I go on my vacation?" She gestured toward the magnificent red-rock country all around them. "Like a homing pigeon. It's an addiction. I can't make any excuse for myself."

Tess grinned at her friend and patted her warmly on her shoulder. "Oh, come on, it's not such a bad addiction as these things go. The fresh air is good for you."

Roberta laughed. "May I quote you at the end of the week? It'll be interesting to see how bright-eyed and bushy-tailed you are after five days on horseback."

"Now don't you start treating me like a greenhorn, Roberta," Tess admonished her friend. "You know I've been riding every weekend for two months just to warm up for this."

Roberta covered her mouth as she began to cough in a manner that bore a suspicious resemblance to laughter. It was a sore spot with Tess that Roberta always reminded her she was a tenderfoot. Granted, she'd grown up in New York and now lived in L.A., but her heart was in the primitive country of the untamed west. She, at least, was willing to make a go of it on horseback, which was more than Roberta was going to try. It was the one weapon Tess knew she could have used to win any argument over her western credentials. . . and the only weapon, out of love for her friend, that Tess would never resort to.

"Head 'em up, move 'em out!" the old geezer behind the wheel bellowed suddenly, as though his passengers were a herd of longhorns. "If you want to make the Rocking T by sundown, let's get a move on!"

"Sundown!" Tess exclaimed. "I thought it was only an hour or two from here."

A tall sandy-haired man in engineer overalls, trotting through the gift shop on his way toward the van, stopped to give her a wink. "Ragweed Willie just wants to get you into the spirit of things, ma'am. You'll reach the Rocking T by noon."

"Thank you," she replied, watching the attractive fellow hop up into the van to greet the older man.

"It's him," opined Roberta.

"Brady Trent?"

"Nope. Joe Henderson. He acts like he owns the place, and he's married."

"How can you tell?"

"Ring on his left hand and the same 'Wow-life-is-good-to-me' smile that redhead at the ticket counter is wearing."

"You sound disappointed, Roberta. I always had the impression that you were too busy to worry about whether or not a good-looking fellow was single."

Roberta grinned ruefully. "I'm not too busy to notice. Just too busy to do anything about it. At least until somebody really special comes along."

"Give it time, Roberta," Tess said gently, then realized that she'd chosen exactly the wrong words. At thirty-six, Roberta had had a great deal of time to meet the man of her dreams. And though she'd dated some over the years, she'd told Tess that she'd never truly been in love...never found that incredible someone who could turn her life upside down.

Tess had already had her life turned upside down once, and she wasn't at all sure that she wanted it to happen again. Oh, deep in her heart she knew she'd love belonging to some heaven-sent fellow, but she no longer believed that such a match was in the cards for her. There had been a time when she'd believed that Nathan—an actor, or so he believed—was the perfect man for her, and she'd given up everything that mattered to her—her home, her career, most of her friends—to follow him blindly from job to job, city to city, dream to dream ad nauseum. Finally she'd had enough. One day she'd told him, "If you move again, you move alone."

A few weeks later he'd done exactly that, leaving Tess with nothing to show for her eight-year marriage but a heart that was a lot more fragile these days because of its poorly mended cracks. It would take a great deal of love—and a great deal of confidence—to risk getting tangled up with someone else. If and when it ever happened, Tess was determined that it would be with a man who put her at the absolute top of his list of priorities.

Under no circumstances would she ever again allow herself to be an understudy for the part of wife.

As she followed Roberta on to the van, she noticed Joe Henderson deep in conversation with the old man—Ragweed Willie, Joe had called him—and though his voice was low, his eyes looked very tense. Once or twice she caught a phrase like "warn Brady" and "not much time." It made her uneasy. Even though Mandy Henderson had insisted that they couldn't be safer with Brady Trent, there was a lot of dry and empty land between the Slow Joe Loco and the Rocking T.

"Roberta," she said softly, "do you think something's wrong?"

"Umm?"

"Look at Joe's face. He looks pretty unhappy about something."

"He's got a right to be happy or unhappy. It's *his* life. Honestly, Tess, you don't even know the man. Maybe he always looks that way."

"I don't think so. He sounded worried about something in particular."

"The Indians probably attacked the last wagon train," Roberta suggested with a smile in her voice. "We're in Ute country, I think. Maybe Navajo."

Tess straightened indignantly. "I'm serious, Roberta. You don't need to make fun of me."

Roberta grinned. "Oh, come on, Tess. You're a city girl and I'm a Texan. I can't help spinning a tall tale or two."

Less irritated than relieved, Tess returned her friend's smile. As Roberta settled down in the seat and closed her eyes, Ragweed Willie glanced at Tess in the rearview mirror and asked, "This your first wagon-train trip?"

"Yes, it is. I'm really looking forward to it."

He nodded; even his whiskers bobbed up and down. "Ain't no outfit better than th' Rocking T. I've worked on half a dozen. I oughta know."

Tess smiled at him by way of the mirror. "How long have you worked on the Rocking T, er, Willie?"

"Four years now. I been with Brady right from th' start. I was workin' fer an outfit in Wyoming when him 'n' Joey Henderson come on a wagon-train ride at th' end a th' season. I could see right off that Brady knew more 'bout horses than any young whippersnapper I ever seen, so I volunteered t' come out here when I heard he was startin' up a wagon train hisself."

Interested in the life of such a modern day nomad, Tess asked, "Do you stay on the ranch during the winter or move on when the wagon train isn't operating?"

"Oh, Brady lets me live on the ranch whenever it suits me. He don't leave much come snowfall—don't want to, for that matter—but ever' now and then he needs somebody t' tend th' stock 'n' such like, an' he cain't do everythin' by hisself."

"You mean he lives out there alone?" Tess asked, awestruck. She hadn't really given much thought to Brady Trent's life before, but she'd assumed, somehow, that he was the scion of some multigenerational western clan—Ben Cartwright running a modern day Ponderosa. It was hard to imagine anyone living all alone in the rustic country they were now traversing. "Doesn't he have a family?"

"Not anymore," Ragweed Willie offered garrulously. "Been divorced fer years. Used to have a pretty li'l wife, though. I never met her. First snowfall come an' she was off like a shot. Lost his baby girl, ran back to her folks in New York. Brady don't talk about her much an' what he got t' say ain't good."

And he probably doesn't like his employees to talk about her to Rocking T guests, either, Tess surmised. But she made no comment. Instead she asked, "What's the most exciting thing about the Rocking T wagon train?"

Willie laughed. "You mean other than the trouble with the local Injuns?"

She knew he was kidding—at least she thought he was kidding—but his words were an ominous reminder of Roberta's. Tess was well acquainted with the sad history of Native Americans, who had been abused, hunted and cheated by cowboys and cavalrymen and ultimately restricted to minuscule amounts of their former lands. Many of the elder ones still clung to the old ways, but Tess knew from personal experience that countless others had taken a vigorous role in the American mainstream in all professions. It was hard to imagine the Sioux girl she'd known in college or the Cherokee lawyer who'd handled her divorce as troublesome hatchet-wielding "Injuns."

Out of curiosity she asked, "Is there a reservation near the ranch?"

He nodded. "Three. Ute due south, Jicarilla Apache to the east, Navajo everywhere else for a day's ride after that. But they all wander into these parts a lot."

"Well, it's hardly the 1800s, after all," she countered a bit defensively. "They've got as much right to visit this area as anybody else. It's not as if they're a danger to anyone."

Ragweed Willie was silent for a moment, then he declared conspiratorially, "I reckon the danger is just different now."

"Oh? How's that?" Despite her rationale, Tess tightened. Nowadays Native Americans defended themselves with politics, not bows and arrows. No Four

Corners tribe had done battle in more than a hundred years. *Surely he's pulling my leg,* she told herself. *There's no Indian trouble out here!*

"Well, I probably shouldn't say nothin', but . . ."

Tess raised her eyebrows, encouraging him to go on. If he wanted to tease her, the least she could do was be a good sport about it.

"Them Injuns ain't got much, ya know. I mean, th' ones what still live on th' reservation. Some of 'em get t' stealin' what they can. And last summer some Utes thought it'd be a good idea t' ride out here in war paint an' coyote skins an' scare th' wagon-train guests inta givin' up their belongings. That's why Brady tells ya'll t' leave yer 'valyabuls' a' home."

Tess stiffened. She still thought he was kidding—wasn't he?—but it made sense that helpless tourists could be robbed by modern day Native American marauders as well as any other kind of thieves.

Over the course of the journey, she listened to Ragweed Willie ramble on about Brady, his own lifetime in the saddle, and life on the Rocking T. Roberta, bonnet slightly whopperjawed, dozed peaceably beside her, oblivious to the mesmerizing view all around her.

In Tess's opinion, the red-rock country was absolutely spectacular, with its staggering pink and purple cliffs, lumps of primitive buttes in multiple shades of red and orange, and an endless expanse of rust-colored sand that swept across the southwest. She couldn't get enough of it, but by the time they passed an old wagon wheel broken to look like a "rocking T," several people in the back of the van were starting to complain about the length of the journey.

"Well, folks, we've just arrived on the Rocking T," Ragweed Willie announced, unable to disguise the pride in his creaky voice. "The wagons are circled just over that next ridge—" he pointed to a ragged butte that was barely visible in the distance "—and the boys ought to be driving in the remuda any time now."

"What's a remuda?" asked a woman in the back.

Roberta, who up until now had been snoring, answered in a deep Texas drawl, "The re-myooda is th' herda horses that'll pull them there wagons, ma'am. We cain't git t' Californy if'n we don't got mules an' oxen an' such."

Tess rolled her eyes. Roberta loved street theater and dropped into her Texas cowgirl act—or whatever other role suited the moment—at the drop of a hat. At times, Tess found her demonstrations a bit disconcerting.

"You shouldn't talk like that," she whispered. "Ragweed Willie will think you're making fun of him."

"Ragweed Willie is not a grammarian," Roberta replied, arching her eyebrows dramatically. "As long as I'm nice to him, he won't care how I express myself."

Tess wasn't sure she agreed, but before she could pursue the subject, the van lumbered over a rise and a trio of hard bumps in the dirt road. On the open prairie ahead of them rested a circle of Conestoga wagons.

"Roberta, look!" Tess burst out. "It's like...it's just like I always dreamed it! A real wagon train! Don't you feel like we've just gone through a time travel machine and lost a hundred years?"

"Closer to a hundred and fifty," Roberta replied nonchalantly, but the sparkle in her hazel eyes gave away her true feelings. "I'll be damned," she added as they drew closer. "He hasn't made slick imitations or even doctored these up with paint. They look like the real thing."

Tess grinned. She glowed. She shook herself like a dog right out of a bath. Even at a distance she recognized the authenticity of the massive wooden wagons, splintered and grayed with age. Most of the wheels were relatively round, but one had apparently been mended with a branch and had a piece of flat rim, which she knew would be felt by passengers every time it hit the ground. Even the canvas tops, which didn't billow but hung limply, were yellowed and patched.

The literature for Brady Trent's Rocking T Wagon Train Adventure, which Roberta had forwarded to Tess, had stressed that every attempt had been made to reproduce the original experience—including guest participation in chores and repairs. Unlike many wagon-train tours that towed along portable bathrooms and kitchens, this one was supposed to be utterly rugged. Like the original pioneers, the travelers were supposed to "make do."

"It's absolutely terrific, Roberta!" Tess gushed. "I'm so glad you picked this ranch! Who wants padded wagon seats when we can be jostled around just like the pioneers?"

"Says she who's going to be on horseback," Roberta commented dryly. "Maybe these guys will make you ride bareback for a week so you can feel what it was like to be an Indian back then."

Tess shuddered, wondering again if Willie was just pulling her leg about the reservation thieves. "I never understood how they did it. Didn't they ever get sore?"

"I'm sure they did. Then again, so did the cowboys who lived in the saddle. You don't live on a ranch if you're interested in physical comfort, Tess."

As the van lumbered to a stop and the passengers eagerly clambered off, several began to complain about the powerful heat, a jolt after the air-conditioned ride. But Tess paid no attention to the shimmering desert temperatures. She was too busy studying a massive cloud of dust rolling speedily toward the circled wagons.

"What's that?" she asked Willie as he hauled himself out of the driver's seat and groaned a bit as he stretched.

"Brady and the boys, I reckon," he answered nonchalantly as several pairs of horse legs became visible despite the swirling, murky air. "Don't you worry none. One a' them wild ponies'll be jist right fer you."

It was hard for Tess to imagine that *any* of the horses heading in their direction would be rideable. All of them were galloping hell-bent for leather toward the wagon train. There were twenty or thirty head, with only four cowboys—and at least half a dozen yapping hounds—steering them toward an opening between two of the wagons, which were about twenty feet apart.

"Ayee-haw!" one of the men shouted, shaking his Stetson at the nearest horse. Another man whistled. A third called "Giddup, giddup!" Only the fourth, a tall man whose turquoise bandanna was drawn tightly over the lower half of his face, remained silent as he galloped behind the herd.

It was a breathtaking sight, one that alerted all of Tess's senses. She could smell the dust—she nearly choked on it!—and could actually feel the ground rumbling from the force of so many hooves. Beside her the other tour guests stopped their grousing and hovered breathlessly in tiny clusters. Every set of eyes was turned toward the galloping remuda. Not one person glanced away.

For the next few minutes, chaos reigned in the makeshift corral of wagons as the horses plunged inside. But once the horses began to settle down, Turquoise Bandanna swung down to pull some sort of a rope over the opening between the two wagons, which were far enough apart to serve as a gate. He looked even taller on the ground than he had in the saddle, and he walked with a beguiling bow-legged stride. Tess only had a moment to enjoy the view of his taut backside—clad in snug jeans and framed by wide leather chaps—before he leaped back in the saddle and galloped toward the tour van with the other three cowboys thundering along by his side. Roberta started humming the opening theme to *Bonanza*, but Tess was too entranced to reprimand her.

At the moment her eyes were on that turquoise bandanna, whose owner casually slipped it off his mouth as he swung off his buckskin gelding and called out a cheery hello. Like the other men, he was dressed authentically, right down to his twin holsters, pointy-toed boots and silver-rowel spurs.

Two of the cowboys appeared to be in their mid-twenties; their wide, cheery mouths and heavy brows marked them as possible kin. A young one, clearly in his teens, was sunny-haired and bright-eyed. He rode his horse well, but he looked a bit overwhelmed by the sight of the crowd . . . as though he didn't know what all these strangers were doing in the middle of his private "I'm going to be a cowboy when I grow up" dream.

But Tess didn't focus on the three younger men. They might as well have vanished. It was the cowboy on the right—the one with the bandanna who'd tied the rope of the makeshift gate—who held her spellbound. The closer he got the better she could see him, and the better she could see him the more she liked what she saw.

He had sky-blue eyes and broad, quietly muscled shoulders; he had thick black hair, which curled around his plaid collar and teased the rim of his cowboy hat. His long sleeves were rolled up to the elbow, and a huge bronze buckle with a Rocking T brand drew her eye to his low-slung belt.

He looked...well, he looked terrific—like every woman's dream of the perfect cowboy hunk. Deeply tanned, he seemed naturally virile, a man whose carriage radiated strength of every kind.

A good-looking man Tess could have ignored; hunks, after all, came a dime a dozen. But nobody, she was willing to bet, had ever patented this fellow's smile. It covered the whole lower half of his face. And where those curving, wide lips stopped, laugh lines took over, fanning out from keen, happy eyes. There was a joy inside the man that poured out of every virile pore.

The moment Roberta spotted him, she said to Tess, "The boss has spent his life in the saddle. He's the real thing."

"Oh, yes, he *is*!" Tess agreed, feeling a curious wobbliness in the vicinity of her heart. It took no genius to realize that this was not a man who'd been hired on for the summer, a man who might just as well earn his living doing other things. Any fool who looked at Brady Trent could see that he *was* the Rocking T, and this regal, barren land was the only place he wanted to be.

"Wearing real six guns, no less." Roberta chuckled, as though this authentic detail was the most important aspect of his appearance. "I reckon we don't hafta worry none 'bout them wild Injuns after all, Tess."

Tess nodded. She smothered a sigh. Despite her earlier tension, the Utes were now the last thing on her mind. From the moment she'd laid eyes on Brady Trent, she'd known that her "valyabuls" were in safekeeping on the Rocking T.

But she couldn't say the same for her heart.

CHAPTER TWO

BRADY TRENT TIPPED his hat to his latest group of greenhorns, making a quick assessment of the ones who would need special care. Off to the right stood one sullen teenage girl, her arms stiffly crossed, her lower lip pouting. *Parents forced her to come. Would rather spend the summer on the beach,* he tentatively decided. *I'll get Ira to brighten her up.*

Ira was the sixteen-year-old son of his best friend and business partner, Joe Henderson, without whom Brady would not have been running the Rocking T. Ira was also a special pal of Brady's in his own right. He was a determined youngster who had started helping out on the ranch at the age of twelve and, to everybody's surprise, now carried the same weight as any of the other men.

Near the van stood an elderly woman, tugging on a broad-brimmed hat in defense of the sun. She was surely the plucky old gal who'd written, "My grandchildren tell me I'm too old for this, but ever since I heard my grandmother's stories about coming west in a wagon, I vowed that I'd do this someday." *There's somebody after my own heart,* Brady had decided, encouraging the octogenarian to give it a shot.

There was one other couple that worried him, a pair of newlyweds. When he'd called the wife on the phone in response to a request for more information, the husband had answered and made it clear that the last thing he wanted to do for his summer vacation was pay for an opportunity to get dirty and sore. Brady had almost hoped that he'd talk his wife out of coming, but in the end she'd won the battle. Now, scanning the faces, he found one frowning, disgruntled thirtyish man. To his right stood a young woman sporting well-worn jeans and western boots. She was glowing.

So was the other gal, the long-maned palomino beside the brunette in period dress. That would be the history professor, Roberta Wheeler, and her historical preservationist friend. He nodded in silent approval of Roberta's outfit, and then, for no good reason, let his gaze drift back to the blonde.

She was beautiful. Her delicate, heart-shaped face said "model," and her small but elegantly curved frame said "Pick me up and carry me home." Her ludicrously impractical blond hair flowed around her shoulders as fluidly as the famous hair of Lady Godiva, making Brady wonder—for just a moment—how it might look spread out on a pillow case. Her lively eyes matched her pale blue cotton gauze shorts and equally impractical matching camp shirt, both of which he knew would be red within the hour from the dust that coated every nook and cranny of the Rocking T. Her feet, protected only by strappy sandals, which the rocks would shred in an hour, were already the color of rust from the few seconds she'd been off the van.

He knew the type. He'd had more than one guest who radiated romance and lacked common sense. This one looked like a city gal who'd never been on a horse and couldn't imagine the painful welts that came from riding in shorts. She'd probably brought along a hair dryer and would spend the first night looking for a plug.

He didn't have time for more than a cursory glance at the other two dozen guests before he began his welcoming speech. It varied some, depending on the time of year, but basically his goal was to get everybody into the spirit of things and warn them of the genuine risks associated with traveling in this part of southwestern Colorado.

"As you know, this is desert country. Water was scarce when the pioneers came through here, and it's still more precious than gold. We need to save every drop. We've got one pond on the west side that hasn't dried up yet, and we ought to reach it tomorrow afternoon in time for a late-afternoon swim. For those of you who think two days is a long time to go without a bath, remember that the pioneers often went weeks without enough water to spare for anything but drinking. Even the diapers had to be scraped off and air-dried."

A nervous giggle swept through the crowd.

"Now, all of us here at the Rocking T—" he introduced Ira and the two Jenson brothers, Jeb and L.T. "—want you to have a real good trip. But I know that you all chose the Rocking T because we run one of the most authentic wagon-train tours in the country, so we don't want to spoil things by babying you. If an axle breaks, we're not going to run into town and buy another one. All of us—" he grinned at the gangly crowd "—will tackle the problem with the materials at hand. Like the settlers who came through here, we're just going to make do."

He didn't point out that there wasn't anywhere he could go to get another axle anyway. And with equipment as old as his—which was partly by necessity, partly by design—breakdowns went with the territory. The first time he'd had a problem on a tour, he'd expected the guests to be upset, but to his surprise and pleasure, they'd been absolutely tickled by the aura of authenticity it provided and the chance to brag about their resourceful repair to their friends. One women had even asked at the end if he'd "staged" the broken wheel incident—the highlight of her trip!

Nobody ever asked if he staged the trouble with rattlers or sunstroke or leeches in the dwindling pond that would vanish by the end of the month, however, so he made a point of clarifying the genuine dangers on the ranch. "The only way you can get yourself into real trouble is if you wander off from the group and get lost. So, for everybody's safety and my piece of mind, our one inviolable rule is that you stay in sight of the wagon train at all times." He grinned to soften the force of his stern tone. "Any questions?"

There were a few—about sleeping arrangements and saddling up the horses, but in no time at all Brady was helping load up "bedrolls" on wagons and matching riders to the horses that now stood calmly inside the circle of wagons. Despite the burst of energy with which the remuda had come over the hill, Brady's horses were all well trained, to saddle or harness or both, and he worked with all of them on a regular basis to make sure that they didn't develop any bad habits from being ridden by guests of varying degrees of skill.

In the four years since he'd been running the wagon train, he'd learned a lot about the tourist business in general and running a wagon-train tour in particular. And though he worked terribly hard at maintaining the ranch and jollying up his customers, he gave credit for a great deal of his success to Joe Henderson, who had paid the down payment for the ranch as a partner, cosigned Brady's loan for the rest, and encouraged the Slow Joe tourists, who poured in by the droves, to stay around for a few days to "complete a true western vacation" with a trip on a wagon train. Without Harold Dobson's historic hotel adjacent to the Slow Joe and the joint advertising the three businessmen did, there was no way Brady could have gotten enough business to keep a wagon train going on such a remote piece of real estate.

At the moment, the tourist trade was pretty solid for both Joe and Harold. Brady, who was still paying off his initial start-up expenses, cleared very little profit even though his business was improving by leaps and bounds every year. He'd actually managed to accumulate a small surplus the previous season. According to his calculations, in another eighteen months—at the five-year mark he and Joe had agreed upon—he would actually have enough profit to start giving Joe more than pin money. It was vitally important to Brady to believe that someday he *would* be able to reward Joey's incredible loyalty with more than gratitude. Joe had three kids, one of which would be starting college in a few years, and though he never discussed his financial state with his friend, Brady was certain that he would welcome some extra Rocking T cash.

His only real concern about the health of his wagon-train enterprise was that the historic ambience of downtown Redpoint was slowly being cheapened by the influx of modern buildings. Several of the old landmarks—the library, a schoolhouse, and an old saloon—had recently required renovation, and their owners had been unable to get local loans. One by one, each owner had been forced to sell—or tear down his building and replace it with a modern one. The mishmash of styles worried Brady, as did his fear that sooner or later, building and safety codes would require Joe or Harold

Dobson or both to renovate. He knew that neither one of them could afford major repairs without massive financial assistance. And as the others had discovered, getting a business renovation loan in Redpoint was almost impossible to do. Mercifully, John Carleton, Joe's banker friend who had approved Brady's loan for the Rocking T, had considered the repurchase of the ranch a pure real-estate transaction.

Brady had double-checked the wagons and supervised the mount-matching of a half dozen tourists when Ragweed Willie suddenly called out behind him, "Brady, where's Sweetwater? I've got a gal here just right for our lady's mare."

Brady swallowed a chuckle. Sweetwater was the name the men used in front of the guests for the sleepiest mare on the Rocking T. Her unofficial nickname was Sissy, because she was gentle and sleepy enough for the most fragile juvenile rider.

"Sweetwater threw a shoe just before we started saddling up, and we left her back at the corral," Brady informed Willie reluctantly, referring to the ranch headquarters that included the tiny cabin he'd built for himself. "How about Calypso?"

Calypso was a rather stylish black pinto who was a lot more horse than Sweetwater but performed quite well under a skilled hand. If Willie had a moderately experienced rider in mind, Calypso would be fine. But if they had another tenderfoot to mount, he'd have to do some shuffling.

Ragweed rolled his eyes and mouthed the words "New York," which, to a man of Brady's perspective, pretty much said it all. He had a bone-deep grudge against New Yorkers. He knew it was unfair and irrational, but he'd given up trying to be rational where his ex-wife was concerned, and Claudia hailed from New York. Claudia also represented everything he most disliked about big city women—big city people, for that matter—and the mere sound of a New York accent was enough to trigger the half-faded pain of her abandonment several years ago.

"I think we better put her in a wagon," Brady told his assistant, assuming the worst. "We can't afford any trouble on the trail."

As soon as the words were out of his mouth, he spotted the petite female trailing Ragweed and had to stifle an inner groan. It was that radiant Lady Godiva, grinning jubilantly and all but skipping toward him as she studied her potential mounts.

He'd already sized her up during his welcoming speech, and he didn't need a second look to help him make his decision about Calypso. There was no way on earth that he was going to risk a guest's neck on a horse that was too hot for her to handle. Lady G. was simply going to have to ride a wagon seat, and he intended to tell her so.

But he knew he couldn't just bark out a command and expect her to obey, so he took a moment to enjoy the feminine view while he led up to it. "Howdy, ma'am," he greeted her in his best western drawl. He tipped his hat for effect. "I'm Brady Trent, ramrod of this outfit. And you must be—"

"Tess Hamilton," she declared in an accent that anybody in America could have pegged as born and bred New York. There had been a time in Brady's life when he'd had no prejudice against the sound, just a healthy curiosity about the different ways people talked. But that was before he'd lost Claudia, before he'd lost the baby. Before he'd sold the ranch in desperation to follow his beautiful blond wife back to her parents' mansion in Manhattan. Before he'd groveled and begged for a year and finally come back to Redpoint as a single man.

He tried to stifle the sudden urge of antagonism he felt for this stranger who'd done nothing but remind him of his loss. It wasn't Tess Hamilton's fault that she was blond, beautiful and spoke like the woman who'd crushed his heart. But it was her fault that she wasn't dressed for riding...that she had, in fact, completely ignored the rules of proper ranch clothing, which he'd so painstakingly outlined in the brochure he'd given up dessert in order to pay for.

"Well, it's a pleasure to meet you, Tess," he lied with professional cheer. "Willie here says you'd like a nice friendly lady's horse."

To his surprise, those blue eyes met his with a straightforward, assertive glance that bore no resemblance to the vacuous stare he'd expected.

"I'd like a horse with some pizzazz," she answered. "I've done a lot of riding, so I don't want a broken-down mount."

Brady's lips tightened just a bit. "None of my horses are 'broken-down,' ma'am. Each and every one is like family to me, and—"

"I'm sorry." Her tone was surprisingly gentle and held just a hint of regret. "I'm sure that all of your horses are wonderful. All I meant was that I've read that on trail rides there are some horses that have no spir—I mean, that are baby-proof. You know the kind I mean—that have long since forgotten how to trot. I know you need horses like that for inexperienced riders, but I'm not one of them."

Brady's brief irritation fled as he listened, but now he had to contend with the rising corners of his mouth. As calmly as he was able, he drawled, "And what sort of experience have you had on horseback, ma'am?"

She answered proudly, "I used to ride every Saturday in Central Park, and now I ride on the beach in L.A."

"In Central Park?" He almost gagged. Central Park was bad enough, but on the *beach*? It was just too "California" for words.

"Yes. Central Park is in New—"

"I've been there, ma'am."

"You have?" She sounded genuinely surprised. "It's hard to imagine a wagon master in New York. Surely you weren't there on business."

Surely my reasons for going to that concrete jungle are none of your affair, he wanted to snap. Instead he said softly, "No, ma'am, I wasn't there on business."

Her eyes met his with a curious glance. "I take it you didn't like it very much."

Brady tried to control the surge of anger that shook him—not anger at this pretty gal but anger at the other one…the woman who had snapped his heart like a tiny twig. "It wasn't a pleasure trip," he forced himself to reply. Then he gestured to Calypso, who was cheerfully rubbing her neck against the New Yorker's fingernails.

"This mare isn't a handful, exactly, but she's not a beginner's horse," he said straightforwardly, getting tired of beating around the bush. "If she knows she's packing a greenhorn, she'll try to spend the day sneaking mouthfuls of galleta and blue grama grass. If she'd got an old hand on her back, she does what she's told."

The blonde nodded, then pressed her face against Calypso's cheek and cooed. The pinto did not respond, but she did not attempt to pull away.

"I think I can handle her," Tess declared. "If that's all right with you."

It wasn't all right with him, not by a long shot. But he knew that if he told her so outright, she'd fight him. At least, that's what Claudia would have done.

He debated with himself for a moment, then lied diplomatically, "I'm sure you could handle her, Tess, but the truth of the matter is that I think you'd be miserable in about ten minutes of her saddle rubbing against your legs. And the stirrups will blister your ankles in no time."

For the first time, Lady Godiva looked hurt...almost bewildered by his words. "Why, Mr. Trent," she retorted, suddenly going formal on him, "what do you take me for? I dressed for town this morning, but I've got a pair of jodhpurs and riding boots in my duffel bag. I expected to have a moment to change before I mounted up."

This time Brady did smile, and it was all he could do to keep from laughing. Jodhpurs and English boots on the Rocking T—well, now, that was something new! On the one hand, it seemed ridiculous. On the other hand, if Claudia had ever tried even that much of a compromise...

"Okay," he relented. *What the hell. Maybe she does know how to ride. I'll give her ten minutes, fifteen tops, while I watch her like a hawk. If Calypso hasn't dumped her by then, she's on her own.* "Why don't you give it a shot. No dressing rooms out here, but there's a cluster of ocotillos over there that might give you a bit of protection. Just keep an eye out for rattlers and Indians."

She laughed—a beautiful, from-the-heart sound that took him by surprise. She sounded...sincere. Friendly. Gracious. All of the things that Claudia was not.

She studied him cautiously as she asked, "You are kidding, aren't you?"

Brady tried not to chuckle—surely she didn't think he was serious about Indians!—as he told her as much of the truth as prudence required. "Not about the rattlers." There really *were* rattlers out here—all over the place—and it was important that his guests think of them as a genuine threat to safety. As to the Indians . . . well, they were part of the game. Granted, in the past he'd had two or three guests fail to realize that the Utes that trailed the wagon train were led by Harry Painted Hat—a Ute plumber who was a childhood friend of Brady's hired to jazz things up a bit—but so far Brady had always ferreted the nervous Nellies out early in the ride and privately clarified the situation so they didn't linger in genuine fear. At the rate things were going, he imagined that Tess might turn out to be one.

But she didn't press him about the Utes again. In fact, she asked no other questions except one.

"Should I take Calypso with me? I mean, am I in charge of her for the duration of the trip? Feeding her, brushing her down, that sort of thing?"

He was stunned. No guest had ever wanted to go *that* far before. "Uh, Tess, I don't think that's necessary," he stonewalled, suddenly feeling very protective of his little pinto. "Just don't ride her too hard and let me know if she gives you any trouble. In my book 'adventure' means fun. Don't feel you have to prove anything on this trip. Don't be too proud to ask for help."

Tess raised her chin and stared at her. "I don't expect to have any trouble, Brady. I told you I could ride," she insisted. "And I don't have any stubborn macho hang-ups, so I'll have no trouble squawking if I get in over my head."

He realized then—or rather, he realized again—that he was making assumptions about Tess Hamilton that had nothing to do with *her*. So far he'd assumed she couldn't handle a gentle horse, lacked common sense, and was ruled by stubbornness and pride. It wasn't normally his habit to judge people on so little evidence, and he found himself struggling with a moment's remorse.

"I'm sorry if I...stepped on your toes, Tess," he managed to tell her, amazed at his verbal clumsiness. Joe, who was never afraid to point out his flaws, often assured him that diplomacy with guests was one of his virtues. But somehow, Brady couldn't get a grip on the conversation with this small-boned beauty. He couldn't begin to treat her with tact. Even now that he realized he was floundering, the best apology he could come up with was, "Please understand that my foremost job on the Rocking T is to make sure that nobody gets hurt."

As he said the words, he surprised himself yet further, because the quiet flare in Tess's eyes revealed that he'd stuck his foot into his mouth again. Though she faced him with dignity, her stiff lips confessed that she'd already been hurt on the ranch...by *him*. She'd arrived more eager than any other one of his guests, and he'd already insulted her in half a dozen ways and made it painfully obvious that she'd failed to measure up to her wagon master's expectations.

It's going to be a hell of a long week, he suddenly realized as Tess took Calypso's reins and offered Brady a beguiling view of her trim legs as she led her mount through the circle of wagons toward the ocotillo clump he'd told her to use as a dressing room. *Five days of that gorgeous hair, five days of New York memories, five days of surprises from a woman I've pegged all wrong.*

Five days of wondering why Tess Hamilton's quiet dignity had stripped him of both common sense and tact.

BY THE TIME the wagon train stopped for lunch, Tess was moderately bruised from the long unaccustomed hours on horseback, but she was proud of herself. She *had* remained in the saddle for half a day in the blazing desert sun while Roberta had jostled and bounced along in the wagon's shade. In some small measure, Tess felt as though she'd conquered the west. She also felt as though she'd scored a small victory over Brady Trent.

It had been painfully obvious that he thought she was a greenhorn of the most inept and whimpering kind, and there was no way she could pretend that his estimation didn't hurt. She would have been disappointed if she'd failed to meet the expectations of any dyed-in-the-wool westerner, but it was especially galling that the man in question owned a fourteen-karat smile, which he seemed eager to bestow on everyone else but her. Although the wagon master had ridden by to ask about Calypso almost hourly—stopping once to check the mare's girth—he had remained decidedly distant all morning. He was courteous and concerned about Tess's welfare, but not by the flicker of an eyelash did he indicate that he found her the tiniest bit attractive.

It's just as well, she told herself as the cowboys circled the wagons into a defensive posture for lunch. *I'd be out of my mind to fall for a hermit like Brady Trent.* Granted, he seemed to be far too sociable to make a good recluse, but if he really lived out here alone through every winter. . . what else could she call the man?

And yet, she understood why he loved the vast, open landscape. It was not empty; it was teeming with life. Oh, the serviceberry wasn't as green as an elm in the spring, but its gnarly branches and thorns held their own kind of beauty. Roadrunners weren't as delicate as hummingbirds, but they were no less fascinating, and the occasional antelope or tuber-eared jackrabbit was enough to set any city girl's pulse to pounding.

The sights and sounds of this rich, red desert were more than enough to thrill any Four Corners visitor, but Brady had planned a week full to bursting with pioneer activities as well. His theory seemed to be that nobody had fun unless everybody got to participate—which meant work—and right from the beginning he set up a schedule that parceled out the jobs. Not only had several men—and Roberta—taken turns learning how to drive the teams that pulled the wagons, but several of the guests had drawn K.P. duty for the first meal. Tess was one of them.

"Take heart, sweetie, at least it's not just the women," eighty-four-year-old Trudy Lincoln told the glowering teenage Eagleton girl, who looked as though she'd been condemned to ten years hard labor. "If the men didn't have to cook or clean up, then we'd really have to squawk."

Tess appreciated the old gal's gumption, especially after spending a good deal of her morning trying to cheer up young Sandy, who had determinedly complained about everything from the get-go. Once Brady had ridden by while Tess had been enthusiastically explaining the pioneers' motives for taking such risks to settle in a new area—making it clear that she was honored simply to be allowed to trail in their memory—and she cringed when she saw him watching her. About the last thing she wanted Brady Trent to think was that she shared Sandy Eagleton's propensity for whining.

It was Ragweed Willie who taught them how to prepare a frontier wagonside supper. First they had to make a fire—which took a good twenty minutes in and of itself. Then they had to fill up buckets of water from the barrel on the back of the chuck wagon. In deference to modern-day sanitation, Brady allowed each guest to use a tin cup with an identifying number scratched on the bottom. Those who preferred to rough it shared a dipper. Everybody got a tin plateful of canned beans and half-burned steak that the six members of the lunch crew managed to produce, and Willie told everybody to give them a round of applause.

"Wonderful, ladies," Brady declared with a wink, then smiled at the two men who'd been part of the crew. "And gents. Doesn't it feel good to know that you'll be free tonight while some other tired souls are working up dinner?"

"I'll be dead by tonight," complained Peter Wilkinson, the young man whose wife had insisted that he take the trip. "I'd be playing shuffleboard right now if we'd gone on that cruise."

"Anybody can take a cruise," Tess chided him. "At least anybody with money. But how many people can say they've experienced a piece of history in country like this? I think you're missing the big picture here."

Roberta laughed. "You tell 'em, Tess." She grinned at the complainer. "Don't ever start preaching the values of modern life around this girl if you value your ears. She'll spend the next six days telling you how great it was in the olden days. She lives with one foot in the last century. If you're not lucky, she'll drag you right back there with her."

Tess was about to point out that Roberta's feelings about the past were not much different from her own when she noticed that Brady, off to one side, was staring at Roberta thoughtfully. In fact, he seemed to be staring at Roberta the way Tess wished he'd stare at *her*.

"At least in the old days the men didn't have to cook and wash up," Peter whined. "I don't even do dishes at home. And I'm on vacation!"

That was enough for Roberta, who instantly launched into action. Bolting up on the tongue of the nearest wagon, she raised one hand high in the air and cried out Susan B. Anthony's famous quote, "Men their rights and nothing more, women their rights and nothing less!"

"You tell 'em, sweetie!" yelped old Trudy with a dramatic shake of her fist.

A couple of other women smiled, as though they figured that Roberta was part of the tour, and in her long, pioneer woman's dress and bonnet, she did look like she was living her part. Tess, of course, had seen Roberta take on some dramatic persona at the drop of a hat dozens of times, so she was not surprised to see her transform herself into the famous suffragist now. Nor did she have to guess what was going to happen next. She'd heard Roberta give her dramatic Susan B. Anthony speech countless times. She'd actually helped her memorize it in college.

"The history of our country the past hundred years has been a series of assumptions and usurpations of power over women," Roberta began in a powerful, unwavering tone, "in direct opposition to the principles of just government acknowledged by the United States at its foundation!"

After that she was off and running. For the next five minutes, not a soul moved as she expounded on the denial of rights of nineteenth-century women. All of the guests—and even the cowboys—seemed entranced. Especially Brady.

Finally Roberta thundered her dramatic finish: "We ask justice, we ask equality, we ask that all the civil and political rights that belong to citizens of the United States be guaranteed to us and to our daughters *forever*!"

Everybody clapped, even the men who tossed out a few obligatory, good-natured boos. Brady, grinning, marched forward to help Roberta down from the wagon tongue, easily lifting all five foot ten of her as though she were a porcelain doll. Tess had never seen a man handle fiesty Roberta quite like that before.

"Congratulations, Miz Anthony," he exclaimed, though Roberta had never identified her role by name. "I've never heard you give a finer dissertation."

Roberta grinned. She spoke Tess's very thoughts out loud when she replied, "I'm flattered, sir. It's not often that I'm recognized by cowboys in this part of the world."

There was something in Brady's smile—real but yet restrained—that told Tess that while he loved Roberta's demonstration, he did not appreciate her surprise at his historical knowledge. In a quiet tone which subtly revealed how much he valued his background, he revealed, "A Dartmouth boy has plenty of time to read when he's wintering in the desert all alone."

Dartmouth? Tess repeated to herself. *This born and bred cowboy went to Dartmouth?*

She realized that it should not have surprised her. Despite Brady's charming western drawl, his grammar, unlike Willie's, was clearly that of an educated man. And Roberta, after all, had grown up on a ranch and had conquered the halls of higher education. Why should it be different for Brady Trent?

She realized that she was secretly pleased by Brady's revelation. Although many things about a man mattered more to her than how many years he'd spent in school, Brady's education—and his obvious pride in it—only increased her admiration for him. He, like Tess herself, had found the best of both worlds in a career that embraced both a formal urban education and a firsthand knowledge of America's past. She longed to tell him all they had in common. She wanted to let him know that even though she didn't flaunt herself the way her best friend did, she shared Brady's keen historical interests, too.

But Tess had no opportunity to communicate her feelings to Brady, because for the next half hour—while she joined the rest of the K.P. crew in washing up with primitive tin tubs and buffalo hide washcloths—Brady perched on the back of the chuck wagon and talked to Roberta about the west.

BRADY LET both the horses and the guests rest until the peak of the heat had passed for the day. Fortunately darkness came late in the summer, so he planned on several more hours of travel before they camped for the night. But they'd only rumbled westward for maybe forty-five minutes before Ira, in the lead, pulled his teams to a halt and clambered up on the running board, waving for help. For the next hour, most of the group took another rest break in the meager shade while Brady, his crew and four of the men—and Roberta—worked on an axle that had split into two.

"I think you need to nail it back together," suggested one man.

"We've only got a dozen nails t' hold us 'tween here'n Californy," Willie told him. "Besides, th' wood's split. Them nails'd only fall out by tomorrow or th' next day."

"I think we should cut down a tree and carve a new axle," suggested one of the older men. "Isn't that what the pioneers would have done?"

"On the Oregon Trail," squeaked young Ira, "where they had pines and cottonwoods lining the mountain routes. But if you find a tree strong enough to serve as an axle within a hundred miles of here, sir, you're a miracle worker."

"You men amaze me," Roberta, or Susan B. Anthony—at this point Brady wasn't sure which one to expect—loftily declared. "You think wood is the only solution to anything. Hasn't it ever occurred to anybody to take a set of harness reins, soak them, wrap them as tightly as possible around the old axle to hold it in place? By the time the leather dries under this sun it'll be as hard as stone." She slapped her hands smugly. "Didn't any of you big strong men ever think of that?"

Brady grinned. He *had* thought of that; in fact, he'd done it before. And he knew it would work—at least for a while. But half of the fun of the wagon train was ferreting out solutions just like this. Not for anything would he have told the men—let alone fiery Roberta—the best way to proceed.

"It's your idea, Miz Anthony," he goaded her cheerfully. "Carry on as you see fit."

In a matter of moments Willie had sacrificed the oldest set of reins and Roberta had started soaking them in a makeshift wooden tub. In the end, two of the guests and L.T., the taller of the two Jenson brothers, set about wrapping and tying the reins while Brady spent some time jawing with old Trudy and sent Ira to cheer up

Sandy Eagleton, the sullen teenage girl. He'd noticed how much of the morning Tess Hamilton had spent with her, and though the New Yorker's painstaking efforts to cheer up Sandy had surprised and heartened him, he didn't think that a guest should have to take on any of the burdens of the staff.

Actually he'd expected Tess herself to be a burden—*his* burden—and he'd expected Calypso to toss her off. Worse yet, he'd expected her to keep riding on his tail all day, asking naïve and pointless questions, trying to melt him with those beautiful blue eyes and that enticingly sensuous veil of hair. Mercifully she'd kept her distance; he'd hardly seen her all day. Now he wondered why. And to his surprise, it bothered him. Telling himself that keeping track of his guests was part of his job, he glanced around the wagons until he spotted a long braid near the black-and-white pinto. While the other guests were resting in the shade, Tess was watering her horse.

An hour later, after the repairs were done, Brady gave the order for everybody to mount up again. After commending Roberta for her foresight, he declared in his most wagon-masterly tone, "Everybody in this wagon is going to have to get out and walk till we're sure it'll hold. Can't risk the extra pressure. Who wants to saddle up for the next hour or so?"

At least six people who had started the day in the wagon asked for a gentle mount. But outspoken Roberta—brave, crusty, and obviously well acquainted with leather—just got out and walked. A few minutes later, when mounted Sandy squealed, "He bit me! He bit me!" It was Roberta, just a few feet away, who picked her dusty skirts up off the ground, trotted a few paces and grabbed the mare's bridle.

"He is a *she*, and she did no such thing," Roberta told the girl bluntly. "She was just blowing at a fly. But if you keep sawing at her mouth like that, she's liable to toss you off. I sure wouldn't blame her."

"I suppose *you* could ride her better?" challenged the girl.

To Brady's surprise, Roberta's thorny bravado seemed to slip. Her complexion whitened.

"I was just trying to help," she said more gently. "She's a good horse. Just give her her head."

It was precisely the advice that Brady would have given—minus the tongue-lashing that preceded it—and it did not surprise him that plucky Roberta knew her way around a horse. What did surprise him was that even after the girl dismounted in a huff, Roberta did not climb up on old Sugartooth. She took the reins like a halter lead and sweet-talked the old mare as the two strolled along together, but she made not the slightest attempt to mount her, even when her blond friend rode up a moment later.

There was something almost protective in the way Tess hurried to Roberta's side, and for the first time Brady wondered if—despite Roberta's general hoopla—Tess might be the stronger of the two. He had obviously been wrong to assume that he'd be spending most of this trip keeping the beautiful woman out of trouble, listening to her whine, trying to solve make-believe problems with make-believe solutions while she complained about trail dust and lousy food and the oppressive heat. The first day was almost over, yet she'd done none of those things. She had kept in the background, staunchly done her chores and unobtrusively cared for her horse. She had not, in fact, behaved like a greenhorn at all.

Brady tamped down the nudge of guilt that reminded him of how he'd burst the bubble of her eagerness that morning. He'd never seen a guest more excited about the Rocking T Wagon Train Adventure...at least until he'd pulled the rug out from under her by accusing her of being ill prepared. It had been a long time since he'd seen anybody in jodhpurs, but he had to admit that they looked great on Tess. In fact, now that he studied her from behind Calypso, he had to admit that just about anything would look good on that shapely tush.

Her no-nonsense single braid seemed to change her image, and he found himself curiously longing for the uncurbed feminine look that had earned his private nickname for her when they'd first met. *Lady Godiva,* he repeated to himself, liking the sound of it. *I wonder what she'd do if she ever heard me call her that.*

On the heels of that thought came another perplexing one—a startling vision of Tess as the real Lady G., who'd ridden through the village of Conventry bareback and bare bottomed six hundred years ago, with only her endless tresses keeping the townsfolk from seeing all there was to see.

He shook himself sternly, blinked twice, and focused on the distant buttes ahead. *Desert mirage,* he decided. *I've been out here so long I'm starting to see things.*

It was a lousy explanation for the vision, and it did him precious little good. Hours later, as they pulled into camp at the end of the day, he found himself scanning the group for the enticing woman who had remained in his mind all afternoon. When he finally spotted Tess, she was still dressed in jodhpurs, but her braid had come loose and her palomino mane was flowing provocatively around her head.

As though it were beckoning to Brady.

CHAPTER THREE

IT WAS NOT QUITE DARK when Tess strolled to the camp fire where she'd been told that everyone gathered each evening for some sort of group activity. Roberta, busy making notes in her journal, promised to be along shortly, which was just as well with Tess. She was secretly a bit annoyed with her friend. Although Roberta had always been bold and outspoken, it seemed to Tess that she'd been too sharp and flamboyant today...at times almost rude. On top of that, she felt that Roberta had hogged entirely too much of Brady Trent's attention after lunch. And even though Tess had given Roberta no sign that she was intrigued by Brady—and she certainly had no reason to believe that Brady returned her interest—it still hurt to think he might be attracted to her friend.

As it turned out, Tess was the first guest to reach the camp fire, and she found Ira, Willie and Brady involved in a subdued conversation clearly meant for their ears alone.

"My dad must be really worried to send you a message like that, Uncle Brady," she heard the boy say while she was still a few steps away. "He's always telling me that the church is really important because it's the oldest building in town and it's right across the street from the Slow Joe."

"I know, son," Brady answered softly, his own voice throbbing with a note of uncertainty she had never heard him use with the trail guests. His drawl had all but vanished. "I'm not sure what we can do about it, either. We can't buy it, that's for sure. All we can do is hope and pray that my dad will give the Board of Trustees a refurbishment loan before that damn Buck-A-Cluck chain makes a bid on the church land. God knows, nobody in the congregation wants to sell the building if there's any other way to keep a roof over our heads."

"Jake's got to approve it! It's his own church! He and Arleen were married there," Ira pointed out.

Brady's strong shoulders seemed to hunch. "I'm his own flesh and blood and he didn't loan me a penny when the chips were down," he replied morosely. "Dad's not one to let sentiment get in the way of dollars and cents."

It was the first time Tess had ever seen Brady look anything but cheerful, and she realized, as she had not before, that the public wagon master persona was only half of the man who stood in the shadows before her. Despite his joyful pride in the Rocking T, clearly he was no stranger to sorrow.

Ira's young face glowed earnestly in the camp-fire light as he commented, "Well, we've got two other banks in town, after all."

"Sure we do. But if Dad turns the church down, they're likely to follow suit. Those three guys are sort of like a club," Brady answered tensely. "Joey told Willie that Oscar Reynolds is going to make a loan application to my dad sometime this week."

Ragweed Willie, chomping on a twisted lump of Indian rice grass on the other side of the fire, shook his head. "Ol' Oscar's awastin' his time. Jake knows what th' church can spend better'n th' Board a Trustees. If he was gonna help out, he woulda said so by now." He glanced uneasily at Brady. "No offense."

Brady shrugged. "I don't speak for my father."

By this time Tess felt awkward about intruding on the conversation, but she didn't see any graceful way to turn back. Fortunately the Wilkinsons arrived about that time, and she entered the friendly camp-fire circle with them.

"Ah...good evening, ladies. Peter." Brady tipped his hat in Tess's general direction. For just a moment his eyes met hers, but he quickly glanced away.

So much for that. Even when Roberta's not with me, I'm invisible to him, she decided. Determined not to let it get her down, she plunked down on a rock next to Ragweed Willie, who promptly started telling a colorful ghost story, stroking his chest-length silver beard at key dramatic moments. By the time he was done with his tall tale, the camp-fire area was full, and L.T. Jenson had tugged out a guitar and started to sing "Red River Valley." He was halfway through when Ira suddenly jumped and squealed, "What's that?"

Everybody froze. "I didn't hear anything," said Peter Wilkinson.

Neither did Tess. At least she didn't hear anything out of place. The nearly silent night wind was brushing the squawbrush and cliffrose that clutched at the hope of water beneath the dry red sand, and tiny animals—collared lizards, midget rattlers, spadefoot toads, perhaps—scurried out from their daytime retreats. Far away—too far to cause a moment's fear—she could hear the breathy scream of a cougar.

It was wondrous. It was desert. It was still.

But Willie was looking solemnly at Brady, and Brady was solemnly looking back.

"Could be anything," said Jeb Jenson, as though he, too, had heard something menacing. Something that Tess had not. "Go ahead, L.T."

L.T. went back to his song and led the group through a second one before one of the camp dogs started to bark.

This time Brady stood, glancing toward the far ravine. "Anybody see anything strange this afternoon?" he asked.

"Like what?" plucky old Trudy asked, her thin lips curved in a grin. "Indians?"

Brady didn't smile. He told the dog to hush, then sat back down. "Keep singin', L.T.," he ordered tersely.

This time the cowboy started singing "Sweet Betsy from Pike," and Roberta, who possessed only a modest alto voice, insisted on doing a high soprano harmony, which Tess felt spoiled the song. She knew she was being petty, and hated herself for it. After all, Roberta was her dearest friend in the world, and she'd really looked forward to taking this trip with her. It was silly to be so riled up over a man who probably had no interest in either one of them.

L.T. and Roberta made it through one more number before the dog started up again, and this time several other dogs joined in the chorus. At once Brady was on his feet, and even Willie bolted stiffly upright. His gun hand resting on his holster, Brady slunk into the darkness almost furtively. A moment later Tess heard a rustle beyond the campfire a mixture of hooves on rocks and metal clanking. Her heart did a cartwheel or two before she heard Willie call out, "Well, what do we have here?"

A moment later an old geezer right out of the pages of yesteryear stepped into the firelight. He looked twice as old as Willie, and he sported a real beard that hung down his chest. Wearing a patched Civil War army jacket, deerhide pants and knee-high moccasins, he led a tiny burro laden with a pick, a shovel and a mining pan.

It was his miner's gear, more than his outfit, that assured Tess that he was part of the wagon train tour. Nobody in his right mind or out of it could make a living mining with only a burro for company in this part of Colorado...in this century or the last. Still, it was a nice touch, and she enjoyed the old man's performance enormously.

"Another train headed fer Californy, huh?" he asked, taking in the spellbound group around the fire. "Y'all goin' cross th' Sierra 'fore winter sets in?"

"Yessir," said Ira, when nobody else spoke up. "We hope to get settled in at Sutter's Fort before the snow flies."

The old geezer shook his head. "Y'all'll never make it over th' pass by then. Not in them there heavy wagons. You'd be wise to leave everythin' to the Utes an' go th' resta th' way on foot."

"The Utes?" Sandy Eagleton squawked. "You mean there really *are* Indians out here?"

"'Course there are Injuns out here, girlie," he exclaimed with an overly dramatic slap on his knee. Dust spattered upward from the light contact. "What'd you expect to find in the desert?"

"I...I don't know," Sandy sputtered, then glanced around at the group. "My dad said this was going to be fun," she declared resentfully.

"And it is," said her father. "We're in good hands, Sandy. Relax. This is all part of the show."

They all chatted with the ancient miner for another half an hour. He told stories about missing mountain men, wandering ghosts and even a mythic camel left-over from the U.S. Army's ill-fated nineteenth-century Camel Corps. Tess had heard many of the tales before, but it was one thing to read them between the covers of a book—another to hear them from the lips of somebody who might actually have been there.

The only thing that marred her pleasure was Brady's continued absence from the camp fire. She had assumed that his hasty departure was part of the miner's show, but based on that rationale, he should have returned by now. Was it possible that he really had heard something unexpected out there in the endless desert darkness? Could that gun-on-hip reaction have been a genuine response to some perceived danger? Tess didn't consider herself particularly neurotic about personal safety, but a lifetime in New York and L.A.—and the memory of several very frightening episodes in both cities—had made her wary.

By the time the old miner said, "Thank ye kindly fer th' grub" and wandered off in to the night, Tess was tired and ready to turn in for the night. She was one of the first to leave the camp fire—Roberta was still entertaining the others with a spirited rendition of a Carri Nation temperance lecture Tess could also have delivered if she'd been inclined to make a spectacle of herself—so the rest of the camp seemed quite empty as she walked toward her sleeping bag alone.

A sudden rustle, like footsteps in the dark, caused a momentary bullet of fear to ricochet through her. Again she wondered where the boundary was between Brady's scheduled historical drama and the reality of modern life in the red-rock country. She was actually considering slinking back to the camp fire to ask if all this Indian talk was, indeed, just talk, when Brady himself materialized beside her out of the darkness.

"Oh!" The word came out as a tiny squeak. "It's you."

He favored her with his megawatt anything-for-the-campers smile. She knew he would have smiled that way at anybody, but it wrenched her heart just the same.

"You were expecting someone else?"

She shook her head. "I wasn't expecting anybody. I just thought I heard something out there."

"Well, you did. You heard me saying goodbye to our unexpected guest."

She relaxed just a little, hoping that Brady hadn't guessed she'd been afraid. "He's really quite knowledgeable," she informed him. "Where did you find him? Just a local old-timer, or does he run a museum?"

Brady smiled mysteriously. "He's just an old miner drifting through these parts tonight, as far as I know."

Tess couldn't stifle a moment's disappointment. She knew that Brady had hired the "miner," and he knew that she knew it. In fact, there wasn't a single person in the camp who didn't know it. But Brady's role—his part in the game—required that he keep up the pretense. Only to somebody special would he reveal the truth. And his very appropriate courtesy reminded Tess that she was no one special to him. A paying guest. No more, no less.

"Good night, then," she said quickly, eager to escape before he realized how much she wanted to talk to him.

But as she took a quick step away, his deep, rich voice drifted back to her. "Tess?"

"Mmm?" She couldn't keep the flutter of hope out of her voice.

"Uhh . . . did Calypso work out for you all right?"

She tried to hide her disappointment, but it wasn't easy. "She's fine. No troubles."

"Good." He sounded surprised, if not relieved. "Do you suppose you could get your buddy into a saddle tomorrow?"

Tess met his eyes and marveled at the quiet understanding she read there. *He knows,* she realized quickly. *He knows she's afraid. He may not know why, but he knows that Roberta's no greenhorn. He might even know that for all that bravado and public confidence Roberta shows, inside she's terribly lonely.*

And just as suddenly, she realized that Brady's attentions to Roberta today might have been entirely in the line of duty. Moreover he had to be an exceptionally sensitive man to understand that Roberta, for all her crusty exterior, was a vulnerable woman who needed a lot of attention.

"We'll have to see," she suggested with false energy, refusing to reveal Roberta's secrets. "She's not really dressed for riding, you know."

"Nonsense. She's dressed the part of a pioneer woman. Those hardy gals had to ride under every condition."

"Sidesaddle," said Tess, who'd ridden that way and knew how terribly difficult it was.

"Naw. Not out here. All the rules of society got broken when the first petticoat crossed the prairie. Some of the women out here even wore pants." He grinned beguilingly. "Why just today I saw a woman ride a horse wearing jodhpurs."

He was teasing her, but gently now, and this time it didn't hurt. Instead she felt a breath of genuine friendliness from him.

Tess returned his fetching smile as she reported proudly, “I guess they did the trick, because I didn't have any trouble staying on your horse.”

“Touché.” His grin grew wider. “Maybe we'll rope you a wild mustang tomorrow. How does that sound?”

Tess's eyes widened, and she was about to say, “Oh, I think Calypso will do just fine” when she realized that he was still teasing her.

“Maybe I'll rope one myself,” she answered with moxie. “And break him by sundown.”

“It's a deal,” Brady agreed, reaching out to shake her hand. “Would you break one for me while you're at it?”

Tess struggled for some witty off-the-cuff remark, but the sudden touch of Brady's callused hand threw her off guard. She knew he meant nothing the least bit personal by the gesture—surely—but that didn't change the fact that his skin triggered flashes of lightening up and down her arm.

“I'll break the whole herd if it'll make you happy,” she heard herself reply.

Suddenly his smile sobered, and Tess's stomach flip-flopped as she realized that she'd revealed too much in her clumsy joke. All too soon she felt his hand slip out of her grasp.

“Two will be fine, Tess,” he said so seriously that she couldn't even laugh. “One for each of us.”

The quiet tone of the last word tugged at her senses and filled her with hope. But before she could utter another syllable, Brady had tipped his hat and gone.

JAKE TRENT LEANED BACK in his swivel chair and listened attentively to Oscar Reynolds, the earnest, double-chinned chairman of the Pioneer Community Church Board of Trustees. He had known Oscar for some forty years, and it seemed odd to be having this strained conversation with him. Granted, Jake often did business with fellow church members and friends; in fact, he'd done business with Oscar himself, who had borrowed money to buy a new house not long ago. But this was different. And not just because it was going to so awkward saying no.

"So there you have it, Jake," his old friend finished warily. "Most of our people are sort of holding back right now, waiting to see what'll happen next. But once they get the word that it's a go, I'm sure they'll dig into their pockets. We'll get what we need. I'm sure of it."

Jake was sure of it, too; that wasn't the problem. The problem was that the figure Oscar believed the parishioners could raise was less than half of what the project was likely to end up costing. He did not know, as Jake did, that anybody who started refurbishing an old building instantly encountered a never-ending collection of long-buried problems: primitive, substandard wiring, rotting old boards, termite ridden supports—the list was endless. And each glitch slowed down construction, especially with a largely untrained, volunteer work force. After a while, the church members' enthusiasm for the project would dim and the work load would fall on the shoulders of a few devoted souls who had their own lives to attend to. Men like Oscar worked full-time and had families. The most they could muster would be ten hours a week, less in the winter when dark fell at the tail end of the afternoon.

Oh, it *was* possible for a project like this to succeed, and Jake knew that a church pillar like himself with no good reason to say no ought to bend over backward to help his fellow parishioners make a go of it. But the church renovation was part of a whole climate of historical hysteria in town that frankly, had him worried—as a banker and as a father.

His only son's business hinged on Redpoint's reputation as a little piece of western history. And that business—a pipe dream, which was in Jake's opinion, merely an adult version of cowboys and Indians for a boy who'd never grown up—was bound to collapse of its own weight sooner or later. When it did, Brady would have to sell the ranch—for good, this time—and kick his addiction to the Rocking T once and for all. Then, and only then, could he get on with his life.

As far as Jake was concerned, that day couldn't come soon enough. That ridiculous chunk of red rock had already cost Brady his wife and child and any sort of decent career. Jake no longer fantasized that Brady would some day take his rightful place beside his father at Trent Savings and Loan, but he couldn't give up his belief that a boy as bright and able as Brady—not to mention hardworking—would sooner or later decide to make something worthwhile of his life. Any career, in Jake's opinion, would be a better bet than running a wagon train!

He knew that the same hold-on-to-the-past-come-hell-or-high-water philosophy that guided Brady's life was the force operating in Oscar Reynolds now. The old man's eyes were guarded but hopeful as he studied his old friend and church brother. Shame made Jake turn away.

He knew he ought to consider the church restoration loan based on its own merits, without regard to the menace to local banking posed by the historical renovation trend...or to the direct connection between his son and that local movement. But there were, after all, only two things in Jake's life more vital than his friends—his family and his bank—and both would be affected by the answer he ultimately gave Oscar.

"You know it's going to cost more than this, Oscar," he pointed out gently, trying to be fair. "With a project like this, you can only start out with a ballpark figure at best."

"If it costs more, we'll raise more money," the other man averred, his fleshy chin wobbling with sincerity.

"Oscar, I've never thought of you as naïve. I know this old building means a lot to you, but—"

"It's not just an old building, Jake! It's our history! My grandpa's name is carved on that list of founders in the basement! So is one of Joey Henderson's great-uncles! This was the first church—the first building still standing—ever erected in Redpoint! Doesn't that mean anything to you?"

Feeling guilty, Jake grumped, "It means it's an old, ugly building that needs a lot of work. Wouldn't you like to worship in a beautiful new building for a change? Aren't you just plain *tired* of sitting in that dark, musty sanctuary?"

Oscar sat up quickly, and Jake knew he'd gone too far. But he was voicing the valid opinion of about half the congregation. Many of his customers had made similar comments about the old hotel, the livery stable-turned repair shop, and even the Slow Joe—which some considered a health hazard because of the coal smoke, and an eyesore. Jake had never thought of the train that way because it belonged to Joey, and Joey had made it a smashing success. Tourists rode trains in the twentieth century, after all, especially when they were accessible. But wagon trains in the middle of nowhere . . .

"Oscar, I can't make you any promises," he decreed reluctantly, "but I'll study your proposal and give it some thought."

Oscar's eyes met his for just a moment, as though the other man knew that his promise was only a favor to an old friend, not a reason to grasp at hope. The trustee shook Jake's hand as he rose, holding on a fraction too long.

"Please, Jake. Do it for all of us." He paused a moment, then added softly, "Do it for your son."

ALL THE NEXT DAY, Tess had the powerful sensation that the wagon train was being followed. Twice she glanced back to see a bit of dust, a pair of pony heels flying, a feather sticking up from a human head. She knew—at least she thought she knew, that the Indians, if indeed there were any, were part of the tour, like the old miner had been the first night. But these Indians—if indeed they really were Indians—never came in close, never joined the wagons or "attacked" them. It was the furtiveness of their motions that made her uneasy.

At lunch she confided her concern to Willie, who'd listened solemnly and promised to report her observations to the boss. The boss himself, she'd long since realized, seemed to be making himself scarce. Although Tess had spotted him a dozen times since sunup, he'd always been at a distance . . . or heading the other way.

A more suspicious woman would think he was avoiding her, Tess thought when they saddled up again after lunch. *But surely he's just exceptionally busy today,* she told herself.

As she rode along among the other mounted travelers—not wanting to stray from the pack with the "Indians" nearby—she mentally replayed her last encounter with Brady and tried to determine what his feelings for her might be. She did her best not to dwell on *her* feelings for *him*. She had no idea where they had sprung from, or why he affected her so deeply. She only knew that shutting him out of her mind was proving to be quite difficult.

It was also quite difficult to pretend that her whole body didn't jerk with panic when she heard a sudden wild beating sound no more than a yard away. Calypso obviously heard it, too, and an instant later the little mare was bolting across a nearby muddy stream in naked terror.

It took only a moment for Tess to realize that she was not under attack by the Utes or some wild animal. The noise was caused by a bevy of scaled quail, startled by the unfamiliar presence of a human. Calypso soon realized it, too, and she quickly eased back into a nervous walk under Tess's steady hand. Tess patted the horse and congratulated herself for her judicious handling of a potentially dangerous incident. *So there, Brady Trent!* she thought smugly. *And you thought I couldn't ride!*

But her pride was short-lived. Even after Calypso settled down, her gait remained choppy. Afraid the horse was limping, Tess quickly dismounted to check out her hooves. Three of them looked just fine, but the right rear one was missing a shoe.

"So what am I supposed to do now?" she asked Calypso, who closed her eyes and rested on three shod feet and the shoeless toe. "I bet it's not good to ride you this way, but I sure don't want to get left out here all alone."

"Trouble, Tess?" called Trudy, who at eighty-four, was still able to hold her own in the saddle. She was already a dozen yards away. "You want me to get one of the crew?"

Tess nodded, grateful that one of the wagon-train guests had noticed her predicament so she didn't have to make a fool of herself calling for help. She wished that Trudy had relayed the message with somebody else and volunteered to stay with her, but Trudy, urging her quiet steed into a hearty jog, was already hurrying toward the body of the wagon train.

As the Conestogas rumbled away from her, Tess realized that the oppressive heat of her shadeless location was the least of her troubles. The one thing Brady had impressed upon all of his guests was that they must never wander out of sight of the wagon train. And that was without even knowing that Indians—or some sneaky people—were trailing the Rocking T group.

"He warned me," she told Calypso, who now looked sound asleep. Only her tail swished, batting flies in the sun. "He said I didn't know how to handle a horse out here. He's going to blame me for this. I'll bet there was something I should have done."

As it turned out, a horse and rider galloped toward her in a matter of minutes, rushing from the still-visible wagon train. The rider, as it turned out, was Brady, and tension marred his handsome face as he hurriedly dismounted.

To her surprise, when Tess tried to hand him Calypso's reins, Brady's strong hand closed over hers, and he appeared to be in no hurry to release her. She held still for a moment, certain that he would let her go, but when his grip seemed to tighten, she reluctantly met his eyes.

"What happened?" he asked in a hoarse whisper. "Trudy said you and Calypso were in trouble back here."

He looked so concerned that Tess assumed he thought she'd truly harmed his beloved pinto. "I think she's okay, Brady. Just taking advantage of the situation to rest. I got off the second I realized she'd thrown a shoe and she hasn't taken a step since. I didn't know if it would bruise her hoof or anything." Nervously she met his piercing gaze. "I'm sorry. I've been just as careful as I could be. But a flock of quail exploded out of the sage right in front of her and she sort of went nuts. I only lost control of her for a minute, and she calmed down right away. But after that she was limping." She pointed miserably to the leg in question. "She's missing a shoe."

As Brady's grip gentled, Tess realized that he was trembling slightly. Tess was trembling, too—afraid that she'd lost the few steps of progress she'd made with Brady last night, afraid that he'd take away Calypso and make her ride in the wagon.

He was silent so long that she was sure he was reining in his temper. But when he spoke, his words took her by surprise. "My God, Tess, did you honestly think that my first concern was for the horse?"

She tried to look away, but she could not. The eyes that held hers were too blue; the masculine hand that grasped hers was too warm. "You said I was out of my league out here, Brady. You told me I was a greenhorn."

Slowly he shook his head, then surprised her further by reaching out with his free hand to touch her chin. His eyes overwhelmed her... beautiful eyes, blue eyes, as warm as the desert sun. He studied her with a mixture of longing and regret, which made no sense to Tess.

"I owe you an apology," he revealed in a near whisper. "I didn't really give you a fair chance to prove yourself before I... mixed you up in my mind with someone I used to know from New York. Someone who didn't take to the Rocking T. I guess I expected you to be a lot like her, Tess, and that was unfair of me."

Tess wasn't sure what to say. It was the most personal, honest comment Brady had made to her since they'd met, and the only one that hadn't been accompanied by a western drawl. At the moment he sounded more like an ivy league professor than a cowboy.

"The truth is, you've been a trooper on this trip. You've handled Calypso very well and you've never complained. More than once I've heard you bucking up somebody who lacked your stamina. I misjudged you right from the start, and quite frankly, I'm glad I was wrong."

Tess was glad, too, and she was glad that he kept holding her hand. Granted, her fingers were tucked under the reins and it was possible that he'd simply forgotten they were there, but the warmth of his callused skin made it impossible for her to ignore the lingering contact.

"It's...okay, Brady," she answered softly. "I'm sure you see all types out here."

"All types," he repeated in a near whisper, his warm breath brushing her loose strands of hair.

Tess's eyes flashed open then, and she studied the face of the man who bedeviled her, reading there the harnessed longing she'd so desperately hoped to see. "It's hard to imagine," she answered slowly, "that you could enjoy living alone out here all winter. Don't you ever get lonely?"

His gaze never waivered. "Terribly."

"So why do you live this way?" she asked, taking a tiny step closer, feeling his fingers stretch out to cover her jumpy wrist pulse.

"Open your eyes," he admonished her, gesturing with his shoulder toward the staggering sight of red buttes to her left. Squawbrush dotted the plain below it; proud pinon pines graced the top. An eagle cartwheeled toward the crown of the tallest tree as Brady finished reverently, "It's worth any price."

She followed his gaze, studied the mountain, then met his eyes again. His expression was so fierce that she was frightened that she really had angered him. She struggled for something lighthearted to say. "At sunrise, I'm sure I'd agree with you. By midafternoon, I'd be hard-pressed." She said it with a smile, but the smile didn't seem to work on Brady, who looked more tense than ever. "It's magnificent country," she continued conversationally, losing heart. "I'm glad I got a chance to see it."

Slowly he released her hand, then broke off their shared gaze. "And you'll be just as glad to get back to the beach in California," he replied as he squatted to check Calypso's leg.

The comment was benign and straightforward, but Tess had the distinct feeling that somehow she'd gravely disappointed Brady Trent, and not just because she liked the weather in L.A.

CHAPTER FOUR

BY THE TIME Brady had assessed Calypso's situation—the muddy stream had sucked off the shoe when the mare had ploughed through it, but her hoof was fine—the wagons were a good distance off. He and Tess could have galloped for ten minutes to catch up, but he saw no good reason to weary the horses under such intense sun, and he didn't want Calypso to work hard until she was reshod. Willie could handle anything that came up before the wagon train made camp for lunch. Besides, after the way Brady had rather pointedly ignored Tess during her first two days on the Rocking T, the least he could do was give her a little personal tour time to make up for it.

It's only good business, he told himself. *I wouldn't want a tour guest going back to L.A. with bad things to say about the Rocking T.*

But good business had nothing to do with the tiny jump in his solar plexus when he'd grabbed the reins and accidentally gripped Tess's fingers. And good business had nothing to do with the fact that he'd made it difficult for her to snatch her hand away.

Now, as the two of them rode side by side through the mesmerizing desert, Brady asked casually, "So what is it you do, exactly? I know your work has something to do with museums, but that's about it."

Tess chuckled. "Actually it has nothing to do with museums, except in the sense that museums seek to preserve history and so do I. I'm a warrior in the battle against encroaching twentieth centuryism."

"And well armed for it, I'm sure." He grinned at her, and her eyes sparkled as she grinned back.

"Actually the thrust of H.W.P.—that's what we call Historical West Preservation—has more to do with historical buildings and sites than artifacts," she explained, "though sometimes they're involved."

"You mean H.W.P. tries to save landmarks, refurbish old schoolhouses, that sort of thing?"

"Partly. Sometimes we work on a grander scale, trying to save entire historic districts or even entire villages or ghost towns. Basically we just try to provide whatever services are necessary to get the job done. Each group or individual who contacts us has some specific target in mind. Often the people involved just know that something is too special to lose, but they don't have any idea how to save it. It's my job to figure out the best approach and craft a plan. The folks involved still have to execute it."

Brady was entranced. "That sounds really intriguing, Tess. I wish we had something like that around here. We've been losing our best historic buildings one by one even though we've done our best to save them."

"Have you ever really tried to save them in an organized fashion?" she asked bluntly. "A lot of people just bemoan the loss of a building after it happens, but that's not a very effective approach."

Brady studied her seriously, his thoughts on the old saloon, which had recently been leveled for a fast-food restaurant near his dad's bank. They'd all complained about the sale, grieved over its possible destruction, yet all he and Joe had done was write a letter to the *Redpoint Register*. At the time, it had seemed like a lot. Now it seemed like nothing.

"Well, I guess we don't really know what to do. One by one we've lost our old buildings. Right now we're trying to get a refurbishment loan for our church. It's the oldest public building in Redpoint, and we'd like to save it, but if we can't get funding the congregation will have to vote to sell it before it's condemned for safety reasons. The price for proper renovation is simply astronomical, and the local bankers take a dim view of preservation, I'm afraid."

To his surprise, Tess's eyes glowed as she automatically slipped into her professional persona. Her voice took on a sophisticated, intellectual tone. "We tell people never to mention historical preservation to a bank when they're trying to wangle a refurbishment loan. The key is 'enhanced business revenues' due to increased trade and tourism. Money sells everything—even money."

Brady grinned. He'd have to remember that. Certainly the preservation angle wasn't going to help Oscar and the rest of the Board of Trustees get a loan from Jake Trent or any other banker in town. All of them had turned down other worthy causes, even when the private businessmen involved were lifelong friends. Or—in Brady's case—family.

"It helps if you know something about the local bankers. Sometimes they're more receptive to one angle or another. If they're actively involved in a given organization, sometimes a little pressure from the national group can be amazingly helpful." She glanced at Brady, smiling now, getting into the spirit of Redpoint. "You must know the bankers in a town that size. Are they committed to anything in particular?"

Brady grimaced. "Sure. The owner of Trent Savings and Loan is committed to proving that his only son is an idiot for becoming a wagon master instead of a banker. He's opposed to just about anything that smacks of the past."

The words came out more sharply than he'd intended, and he swallowed abruptly as he met Tess's worried eyes.

"I'm sorry that came out so...bluntly, Tess. I love my dad. Don't get me wrong. But we're...well, we're at loggerheads over the ranch. Have been for years. And anything in town that touches on some aspect of living western history just...sets off more sparks."

Tess didn't answer at once, but her eyes filled with sympathy. "I'm sorry, Brady. I guess I stuck my foot in my mouth on that one."

He shrugged. "No offense taken. I think you made a valid point. Frankly my concerns about preserving Redpoint are about half-historical and half-business. For Joey and me—Joe's my partner, the guy who runs the train—the history of the area is an important part of the product we're selling. And I think it is for Harold Dobson, too." He glanced at her, noticed the way her blond hair had tugged out of the braid and was blowing in the breeze. "He owns the Redpoint Hotel."

Tess nodded. "I met him when I stayed there the night before I came to the Rocking T. An enchanting inn, but...in need of some reparation, if I may say so." She smiled, as if to reduce the effect of any inadvertent sting.

"I know," he answered soberly, "and so does Harold. I think he's putting off making improvements as long as he can because it's so hard to get a loan." *Or maybe he's just going to ignore the problem until he's old enough to retire,* he thought, worriedly. The last time he'd seen Harold the older man had seemed weary, almost worn down. And he'd mentioned twice in the same conversation that he had nobody to pass the business on to when he got "old."

"If your friend ever gets around to making repairs," Tess suggested, "he might want to focus on the business end of things when he applies for a loan. In fact, if you have other merchants in the downtown area who advertise some aspect of history, or sell historical artifacts, you might gather them together before anybody else applies for a refurbishment loan."

Brady studied her thoughtfully. "You've really given me some good ideas, Tess. Thanks a lot."

She grinned. "Glad I could be of service."

"You like your work, don't you?"

"I love it," she admitted. "Every time I'm called out to see a ghost town or an old store or a lone sod house on the prairie, I imagine that I'm actually living in 1789 or 1836 or whatever. I can almost hear the old voices talking around me. I get chills."

They shared a smile that went beyond courtesy...a smile of two people who both knew the mystical magic of the past. "I've got a ghost town on the Rocking T," Brady heard himself confess, though it was something he'd never mentioned to a wagon-train guest before. The structures were too fragile to survive a herd of tourists picking up old boards and dragging off bottles, and he'd deliberately planned a trail for his tours that never came in sight of Silvergold. Yet he knew, with absolute conviction, which he could not explain, that Tess Hamilton would not injure his shanties or reveal his secret to the other guests. "It's over that eastern ridge, not too far from my home."

She glowed. He could see the anticipation building inside her. "Oh, Brady, I'd love to see it," she confessed, her enthusiasm quiet but barely restrained. "I don't suppose there'd be time before the trip is over?"

"I doubt it," he answered honestly, knowing that a private trip to Silvergold with this enticing female was neither professional nor wise. Yet the edges of her mouth drooped in such obvious disappointment that he tacked on, "Maybe I can take you some other time, Tess. Some other time when you're back this way."

But he knew that after Saturday Tess Hamilton would never set foot on the Rocking T. Not if he could help it.

TESS DIDN'T SEE Brady much after they caught up with the wagon train, which was just as well, because their conversation had left her confused and full of longing. Despite his determined efforts to keep her at a distance earlier, he'd been open about his father and his concerns regarding historic Redpoint; he'd even told her about his ghost town, something she was sure he wouldn't reveal to just anybody.

Who had he meant, she wondered, when he said she reminded him of someone he'd known in New York? His wife, perhaps? Some other woman who'd chosen city life over him? In any case, it was obvious that the reference was not a compliment. But revealing the whereabouts of the ghost town was.

She was still thinking about Brady, and the feel of his fingers on her wrist, when she slipped into the natural spring near their evening camp. For two whole dusty days she'd been looking forward to this swim—bath and hair wash, actually—and the sight of a natural pool of water, cool and beckoning, was almost more than Tess could bear.

"Ah," she moaned as she sank to her shoulders in the baby lake, tightly clutching a sample-size vial of shampoo, "now I can go on living."

Roberta, clad in a turn-of-the-century shoulder-to-knee swim dress, laughed as she followed Tess in. "Aw shucks, Tess, at home we only filled th' tub from the river onceta week on Sattiday night an' we did jist hunky-dory."

As the red dust washed away and her hair splayed out on the surface, Tess felt as though she'd died and gone to heaven. "Next time you decide to drag me on a wagon train," she told her friend, "let's do it in the spring, okay? Or maybe late October?"

"Somehow I have a feeling that I won't be along on your next wagon-train tour," Roberta countered as she breaststroked along next to Tess toward the middle of the lake. "Aren't you planning on taking a Rocking T trek of the three-would-be-a-crowd kind?"

Tess tossed her a startled glance. She didn't think she'd given anybody a good reason to think she was interested in Brady, and she certainly didn't want him—or the nearby guests who were also swimming—to overhear Roberta's comments. "Not so loud, Roberta, please!"

Roberta shook her head. "Nobody can hear me, Tess, and nobody is listening, anyway. Unless you count the Indian that just ducked behind that tree."

"What Indian?"

An astounded chuckle was Roberta's only reply.

Exasperated, Tess splashed her. "Honestly, Roberta, don't you ever grow tired of teasing me?"

"Nope. Never." She grinned from ear to ear as they started to tread water in the deepest section of the lake. "It's what I live for. You remember in college when I short-sheeted your bed six nights in a row before you finally remembered to check before you got in, and the night you did was the first night I didn't do it? So the next night you *didn't* check, and that was the night I stuffed your sheets with hay?"

"I remember." Now, in hindsight, it did have a tinge of humor to it. At the time, she'd been more angry than amused. "I certainly hope you've outgrown that sort of thing, Roberta. As for the Indians, you heard Willie say that they really *are* causing some troubles around here. Not old-fashioned scalping or anything, but taking advantage of our isolation to rob us."

Roberta rolled her eyes. "Have you ever known a real Indian, Tess?" she asked.

"As a matter of fact, I have. More than one," she was glad to say.

"Then you ought to know that the ones who leave the reservation don't want to call attention to themselves and the ones that choose to stay don't want any trouble. If these local Utes were desperate enough to hassle tourists, which I sincerely doubt, they'd be out here begging for handouts, not mugging tourists. Either way, they'd never wear traditional war-party clothing while they did it, even if they might at some other time. After all, no criminal wants to get caught, and the clothes would be a dead giveaway."

As she unscrewed her small shampoo bottle, Tess asked, "So what's your point? I imagined those Indians I saw back on the trail?"

Roberta rolled her eyes. "No, you didn't imagine them. I saw them, too. We were *supposed* to see them.

That's the whole point! They're not *real*, for Pete's sake. They're part of the Rocking T program. Even if they're Indian by blood, I'll bet you dollars to doughnuts that Brady paid them to stalk us."

"Why?" Tess asked. "Why would Brady want to scare his own guests?"

Roberta grabbed Tess by the shoulder and shook her gently. "Get with it, girl! It's not supposed to be *that* scary. It's like going to see an adventure film! We're supposed to be *pretending* that we're on a real wagon trek in the 1800s. So we need Conestogas, horses, and Indians! You're the only one who got scared enough to report the 'danger' to a member of the crew! Though I doubt it was the hottest topic you discussed with the wagon master while you two were nursing along that shoeless mare this morning."

Roberta was teasing—loudly—and Tess knew that the only way to get her friend to hush was to tell her the truth. Despite the hoopla Roberta generally made in public, when the chips were down, Tess knew she could count on her friend's discretion.

"Roberta," she said gravely, eyes squaring off with her friend's, "it's really important to me that you stop teasing me about Brady in public."

Roberta's smile dimmed. Her expression softened. Then she said almost gently, "You've really got it bad, don't you, Tess? I don't recall seeing you so wound up about a man since you first met Nathan."

Tess ducked under the water once more, then started to soap her hair. She couldn't quite face Roberta. "Is it . . . really so obvious?"

Roberta nodded. Then she added, "But just to me. And probably Brady."

Oh, dear God, I hope not! Her heart thudded. Again she met Roberta's eyes. "Does it...bother you? That I'm interested in him, I mean?"

Roberta's eyes narrowed for a moment. She looked confused. "You mean, am I jealous that you'd rather spend your time on this trip with him than with me?"

Tess smiled, suddenly certain that she had nothing to worry about as far as Roberta was concerned. "No. I was afraid that you might want to spend more than a little time with Brady yourself. He seems to...well, chatting time with you."

For a moment Roberta stared at her as though she'd lost her mind. Then she laughed out loud. "Tessie!" she burst out, careful this time to keep her voice low. "You done thought that fine-lookin' trail boss had eyes fer li'l ol' *me*?"

"You know, Roberta, there are times when you are downright obnoxious," Tess growled, half seriously.

"I know. And it's so much fun! But honestly, Tess, I can't resist playing cowpoke with a real live cowboy. You ought to know by now that Brady Trent is the last kind of man I'd fall for. I've had enough cowboys to last me for a lifetime. I think Brady's a real nice guy, but I wouldn't ride off into the sunset with him if you paid me."

Tess wasn't sure whether to be angry or relieved. "You were flirting with him yesterday," she said accusingly, just to get it off her chest.

"Of course I was flirting with him! I have to keep practicing to keep my skills sharp. If I ever actually stumble over a man I really go for, I don't want to be so rusty that I forget how to act."

Tess considered suggesting that maybe Roberta's problem was that she never *had* learned how to act with men. They always welcomed her as "one of the guys" but when it came to romance, they seemed to back off. Tess secretly thought her friend was just too tough for most of them.

Generously she said, "Someday you're going to find a man who's sick to death of pansies, Roberta. He's going to be thrilled to find a woman of solid pioneer stock."

"That's me," said Roberta glibly, or what would have passed for glibly to someone other than her best friend. "Solid as a rock."

She blinked quickly, as though to ward off some hidden pain, then met Tess's eyes again. "Now, at the moment the problem is you and What's-his-face. You know, yesterday afternoon we chatted mainly about you. I'm surprised he's been so slow to make his move."

"He hasn't made a move," Tess corrected her. "Sometimes when we're alone together he's...well, friendly...but most of the time since I've been here, he's just avoided me."

"I've noticed that." Now Roberta's tone was tinged with sympathy. "And now that I think about it, I suspect that he's just being discreet."

"Discreet? We're both divorced and we don't work together or anything. Why would he have to be discreet?"

"Tess, he's the boss here. He's running a wagon train. How would it look if he were openly romancing one of his paying guests?" After a moment's pause, she added, "Besides, I imagine that women come on to him all the time. Part of the fantasy, you know. Intrepid heroine falls for dashing wagon master. Like a movie."

Tess colored and more vigorously sudsed her hair. "What you're trying to tell me is that I'm really making a fool of myself."

"No," Roberta said gently. "At least not yet. But I think the situation here is a little more complicated than boy meets girl. I think Brady would keep a safe distance from you even if he fell head over heels for you. Your best bet is probably to wait until the last day and tell him you'd like to keep in touch when you say goodbye."

"Tell him? Just straight out? You think that's subtle?"

"I didn't say it was subtle. I said it was reasonable. Frankly I think it's the only thing you can do."

Tess didn't mind waiting for Brady. She didn't even mind having a long-distance romance. What worried her was the possibility—probability?—that Brady had no interest in keeping in touch with her after she left the Rocking T...that he would, in fact, heave a sigh of relief when she was out of his hair. At times he acted as though he returned her growing feelings for him, but there were other times when he seemed impatient or downright displeased with her.

But why on earth had he mentioned his precious ghost town to her if he still thought she was a flake? She was about to ask Roberta if he'd ever mentioned Silvergold to her—a logical extension of their old west conversation—when she suddenly felt a slimy creature slither across her knee. It felt like a slug or a snail.

"Yuck!" she yelped, reaching under the water to try to brush away the culprit. But as soon as her hands settled on the fleshy creature, she felt the same sensation oozing over the soft flesh of her upper thigh.

The fat, slippery worm on her knee was somehow holding on for dear life. The one on her thigh—*Oh,*

God, it's not one! It's a whole bunch of them!—had attached itself most securely. A whole nest of the slimy creatures were feasting on her blood! And she could not pull any of them off.

Panic twisted her stomach as she started swimming wildly for shore. And as she swam, she couldn't stop from screaming.

CHAPTER FIVE

WHEN BRADY HEARD the piercing scream, he knew that one of his guests was in genuine trouble. Only once in the four years he'd been running the wagon train had a visitor been truly injured—when a teenager had tried to charge a coiled rattler, and the young man's terrified steed had thrown him in panic.

At the moment, none of Brady's guests were mounted, and all the rattlers in the vicinity of the evening camp had had more than ample time to slither away. Still, the screams persisted—high-pitched female screams—and they were coming from the direction of the spring.

It was a toss-up whether it would be faster to run the distance or ride, but since he was already mounted, he didn't give it a second thought. Galloping through the camp at top speed, he reached the spring in about ninety seconds and brought his buckskin gelding up short at the edge. In the flash of reality that greeted him, he saw a surreal scene of people—some scattering, some rushing to help—and two women in the water. One was Roberta, swimming strongly behind the one who was screaming . . . the one with soap suds covering her lanky head of hair.

It had to be Tess.

A strange twist of panic clutched Brady's innards as he hit the ground running, then sloshed through the water toward her, boots and all. His first thought was that she couldn't swim and was drowning—or had hit a pocket of quicksand—but the steady motion of her lithe body in his direction put the lie to that notion.

She was almost hysterical, but at least she was still swimming with vigor. It was not until he reached her bikini-clad body that he was close enough to see the desperation that cloaked her face under that wig of shampoo. She wasn't screaming for effect. She was absolutely terrified.

"I can't get them off!" she shouted at him. "They're all over me! Digging in! They're everywhere!"

He got it then. Leeches. Utterly harmless, but horrifying to a greenhorn who couldn't get the slimy things off her body. Brady had yielded a fair share of his blood to the toothy critters over the years and he knew how disconcerting their sudden snacking on human flesh could be. He also knew that nothing the leeches did to Tess—no matter how repulsive—could do her any lasting harm.

He also knew that at the moment, there was no point wasting his breath trying to tell her that. He swooped her out of the water, clutching her tightly to his body as he carried her the last few yards to shore. Together they collapsed on the sand, Tess half lying in his lap as she slapped and tugged ineffectually at the leeches—a good half a dozen of them—and continued to sob.

"Tess, let me do it!" he ordered her. "Just hold still. I've done this before."

She shook convulsively and tried to still her hands, but she couldn't keep them from brushing at the worms. Since he planned to pry each one loose with his pocketknife, he didn't dare let her keep poking her fingers in his way. More harshly he barked, "Put your arms around my neck and keep them there! Don't move!"

Her eyes grew huge, as though his fierce tone frightened her even more than the slimy creatures sucking on her thigh. Abruptly she stopped her squirming and followed his command, whimpering now. And just as suddenly, he gripped her with his left arm, pulling her closer and locking her in place, while he deftly dismantled the bloated creatures feasting on her leg.

"It's okay," he crooned a moment later, dropping the knife as he pulled her tightly to his chest. Instinctively he dropped a kiss on her temple. She drew a deep breath.

"I'm bleeding," Tess whispered. "Really bleeding a lot. But I can't feel anything at all."

"It's okay." He soothed her nearly naked back with his calm hands. "They have some sort of juice that makes you numb, so it won't hurt. But it'll keep the blood from clotting for about ten minutes. The best thing to do is hold still until your body's natural coagulants are working again."

He nudged a soapy lock of hair off her forehead. "Leeches aren't poisonous and they don't carry any diseases, at least not the ones around here. You're in no danger, and even if you were, I'm here now, and you know I'll take care of you, don't you?"

Tess hugged him more tightly, burying her face in his chest. She was still crying, but more softly now, and he knew she'd surrendered her panic to his safekeeping. He also knew that when it was all over, she'd be as embarrassed as hell for making this scene.

By this time they were surrounded with gawking wagon train guests, though Roberta was trying to hustle them out of the way in a very businesslike fashion. For the first time Brady was aware of the picture, they made, sopping wet wagon master and half-dressed female guest. Even now, he realized guiltily, his hand braced her thigh—soaking up the blood with his bandanna—as though it were a natural place for it to be. Everything in Tess's demeanor revealed her absolute faith in him, and only a fool would believe that she'd have responded the same way to another crew member's equally competent touch.

Slowly, reluctantly, her red-rimmed eyes met his. She looked so vulnerable, so helpless! *My God, she was nearly done in by a half dozen leeches,* Brady realized sadly. *How would she react to a real challenge out here in the blaze of August or the dead of snowlock?*

Gradually Tess got a hold of herself. Awkwardly she straightened. A heavy silence grew between them. "I'm sorry, Brady," she whispered sheepishly as she took the bandanna from him and started to wipe her leg. "I guess I went off the deep end there. I was just so startled. At first I didn't know what was on me, and even when I could see that they weren't that big, I just couldn't brush them off. I was surprised as much as frightened, I think. I guess I had no good reason to go berserk."

He smiled acceptantly, sweeping another soapy lock of hair out of her face. "I understand. You don't have to apologize." He considered telling her that what she *did* have to do was go back in the water to wash off the blood once the bleeding stopped—he didn't have water to spare back in camp—but he decided that he ought to wait awhile to break the news. Instead he deliberately led her into more casual conversation.

"Tell me about L.A.," he said, disliking the topic but unable to think of anything more safe and sterile. "Have you lived there long?"

Tess shrugged. Her eyes, still uncomfortable but no longer frightened, revealed that she understood what he was trying to do. "About three years, actually. My husband—my ex-husband, that is—moved to Hollywood to try out for a part in a TV show. It didn't pan out. When he went back to New York a few months later, I stayed."

Brady was surprised. He hadn't expected Tess to do the leaving. "You really must like L.A.," he said carefully.

She smiled, trying to buck herself up. "Oh, I love it. I love the weather, the open-mindedness, the casual attitude of most folks. I don't like the smog or the traffic, of course, and I have to avoid certain parts." Her eyes met his. "I could have been anywhere when he left, however, and I would have stayed put. There are just so many times that a person can be uprooted and dragged hither and yon after a fool's dream before she says 'no more.'"

He nodded, understanding her perspective but wondering about her ex-husband's. Had the other man's dreams been any more foolish than his own? "Do you have any children?" he asked quietly. It was a more personal question than he'd meant to pose, but somehow it came to him naturally.

Tess shook her head. "No. And I know that I'm supposed to say I'm glad, considering how the marriage ended, not to mention what an unstable father Nathan would have been. But I desperately wanted children. It was one of the reasons I was so eager for him to settle down. But I'm not too old to have children if I ever marry again."

The instant the words came out, Tess's cheeks grew red, and Brady, sparing her further embarrassment, quickly moved the conversation to safer ground.

"Joey's sort of let me adopt his kids. They call me 'Uncle Brady.' They only live with him half the time—Mandy's his second wife, you know—but I've been part of the family since they were born. You know Ira?" He waited while she nodded. "He's got two younger sisters. Lynne is fourteen now—just discovered boys—and Sally, my nine-year-old special sweetie, is about to discover braces."

Tess was watching him closely now, reading, she was certain, the great depth of love he had for Joe's kids. He didn't want her to ask the obvious question—"I take it you don't have kids of your own?"—because then he'd have to tell her about his baby girl. Or tell her it was none of her business.

Instead he said gently, "I know you're not going to be real hot on this idea, Tess, but—" he glanced pointedly back at the water "—you need to go back in for a minute or two."

Her eyes grew wide. "Brady, please—"

He shook his head. "In the first place, you need to wash off all this blood before I put on some disinfectant. In the second place, you need to finish washing your hair."

"My hair?" She looked absolutely horrified. Obviously she had forgotten about its current condition.

"You look like a queen in a turban," Brady teased her gently, trying to put her at ease. "But if you don't think you look your best that way," he gestured once more toward the water, "please go back in."

Tess moved slowly out of his lap, making him only too acutely aware of the proximity between his groin and her thighs. She had to brace herself on his shoulders to stand, inadvertently pressing her lower body close to his face. Again he had to touch her thighs, just to steady her. By the time she melted back into the water, *he* was the one who was trembling.

He forced himself to look away. For the first time he recalled his gelding, whom he'd left ground-tied by the water's edge, and he wanted to reward Buck for delivering precisely what was expected of him. But the horse, he discovered, was nowhere to be found. Neither was Roberta. But prints of dry hooves and wet human feet were clearly visible leading back toward the remuda where they'd made camp.

"Everything's all right now," he told the last few gawkers. "Why don't you go get ready for supper. Corn bread and Willie's special chili tonight."

It took a little more persuasion, but after a moment he was alone on the bank.

Tess was alone in the spring.

She was rising her hair, both hands above her head in a manner that lifted her shapely breasts to a position of inviting prominence and left the long expanse of skin between the two halves of her blue-and-white bikini delightfully bare to his view. In her reluctance to reenter the water, she'd kept very near the shore, so very little of her was actually below the surface. She stood there, half-facing him, with every exquisite female feature displayed as though she were a fine work of art.

"Woman at the Spring," he could have called the picture. He could imagine an artist stroking the lines of those curved-just-right thighs, the gracefully muscled calves and trim ankles. He could see the delicate brush caressing the curve of her breast where it was hidden by her bikini top...and where it crested in beckoning cleavage. He could see his own hand holding that brush...no, caressing without the brush that soft flesh he'd so recently felt beneath his fingers.

A sudden jolt of need swelled the masculine tension between his own thighs, and he suddenly realized that Tess wasn't the only one in trouble.

My God, I want her, he realized belatedly. *I want her so much that I'm really going to feel it when she goes.*

Until this moment, he'd looked at Tess as a woman who entranced him, but one he could ignore. But now he knew that it wasn't going to be that easy. Right from the start he'd been perplexed by her, drawn to her, struggling with feelings that he'd thought he'd buried long before.

Physically, Tess aroused him. Emotionally, she beckoned. Mentally, he knew that she was trouble with a capital *T.*

For all practical purposes, she was Claudia. And Claudia had insisted that she loved him, right up to the time she'd left him for New York.

LATER THAT NIGHT, a teenage Pony Express rider reined his half-wild mustang to a screeching stop in front of the camp fire while the Rocking T guests were attempting a singalong with L.T.

"Delivery for Mr. Trent!" the young man called out, digging into a breast pocket for a wrinkled gray envelope. "Don't have all night!"

With a great show of surprise, Brady emerged from the wagon he'd been repacking, took the letter from his "Aunt Minnie back in St. Jo," read the colorful old-fashioned prose out loud, then graciously asked if anybody would like to take this rare opportunity to send off a letter to the folks back home.

"Can't say when the Pony Express will come through again," he told them soberly. "Best get word off to your kinfolk while you can."

Tess and Roberta exchanged superior glances and tried to suppress a mutual giggle. Up until now the wagon train had, in Tess's view, been a fairly accurate portrayal of the old west, but now Brady was veering away from history to pander to his guests.

"Do I see a smirk exchanged between you two ladies?" he asked in an undertone when he observed that neither was writing a letter. "I suppose you're over here counting up the historical inaccuracies in this scenario."

"Why, I never, Mr. Trent!" guffawed Roberta. "Surely a edjicated gentleman like yerself could never make a mistake?"

Brady shrugged good-naturedly, his eyes on Roberta, not Tess. "I reckon I made a choice, Miz Anthony, not a real mistake." He grinned with that rocket-blast-off smile. "I know the Pony Express riders followed the Oregon Trail, a good two hundred miles north of here, and I know they didn't come on the scene till the wagon train era had just about come to an end."

"Really," said Roberta, in mock surprise.

Brady ignored her. "I also know that no Pony Express rider was ever allowed to remove the mail from locked oilskin pouches during his ride, and he did not collect mail from passing strangers. His lightweight saddle held four special pouches to carry everything. Vest pockets, if he had any, were only used to carry sidearms."

"Is that so?" This time her sarcasm was cheerful but pointed.

Tess wondered, at times, if other people who didn't know Roberta's gentler side got fed up with her constant teasing. Brady had never revealed any impatience with her games, but now he turned to Tess, as though she were an old friend, and asked, "Have you ever really been able to turn the tables on her? Ever brought her down a peg or two with a world-class practical joke?"

Tess couldn't help but smile. "Not yet, Brady, but I'm working on it. When I come up with just the right thing, I'll let you know."

"Well, I never!" huffed Roberta, trading in her country character for that of a snob as she hiked up her long skirts and pretended to stalk off. "If you think I came on this arduous journey to listen to coarse talk between a trail hand and a saloon gal, Mr. Trent, you are very much mistaken!"

Brady laughed and tipped his hat. His eyes followed Roberta for a moment or two, as though to make sure that she was indeed only acting. And then, having run out of places to look, his gaze came to rest on Tess.

He looked uneasy. In fact, nothing in his bearing reminded her of the take-charge wagon boss who'd so quickly dispatched the leeches on her legs just hours ago. Nothing in his expression justified her sudden memory of the feel of his body as she'd half lain in his arms.

"Are you okay, Tess?" he now asked gently. "I mean . . . really okay?"

She nodded, fighting a flush of embarrassment. "I've got a rash of tiny red wounds on my skin, but nothing I can't live with."

He nodded. "Are you sure you don't want to see a doctor? Or just . . . sleep in a real bed? I can have one of the men take you back to Redpoint in the morning . . . or even tonight if you'd rather."

Tess wasn't sure whether to be complimented by his solicitude or deeply hurt. In his welcoming speech he'd made it quite clear that once the wagon train started, only a first-class emergency would justify anybody turning back. And her little set-to with the leeches just wasn't that serious. It wasn't even on a par with a twisted ankle, and she'd bet dollars to doughnuts that if Roberta had broken both legs, Brady would have set them himself and loaded her up in the wagon.

"I...I'd never even thought of leaving, Brady," Tess told him honestly. Unable to help herself, she tacked on, "Do you...do you want me to go?"

To her surprise, Brady didn't answer right away. The aloof but polite wagon master she'd met the first day would have jumped right in with a quick denial, assuring her that he was only thinking of her comfort and safety. But now he was stalling, apparently battling with some inner conflict. When he finally spoke, she knew that he was struggling with his words.

"Tess," he said quietly, "I told you before that you reminded me of somebody I used to know." He swallowed hard. "You still do."

Despite his quiet tone, she felt as though he'd slapped her in the face. This person in his memory was obviously a louse in his estimation, a hopeless citified greenhorn. The comparison was not a compliment.

"I'm sorry," she said lamely. "I am who I am, Brady. I don't know that there's much I can do about it."

He shook his head, looking helpless and frustrated. He reached out to touch her face, but the instant his fingertips grazed her cheek—branding her with fresh fire—he pulled back as though *she'd* burned *him*. He glanced away, then bleakly met her eyes again. He jammed both hands into his back hip pockets, as though to keep them from her face.

"Tess, don't misunderstand me. It's not that...that I don't find you...pleasant company."

Pleasant company? she groaned to herself. *Talk about damning with faint praise.*

"What I mean is—" his hands came out of his pockets and flailed helplessly "—I can't see you . . . fitting in . . . on a long-term basis—"

Again he broke off. He tugged his hat down on his forehead, pushed it back and hooked both thumbs in his belt. He looked tormented when he finally burst out, "Oh, hell, Tess, I might as well just spit it out." His voice darkened with a mixture of longing, self-disgust and pain as he rasped, "Dammit, girl, you remind me of my ex-wife."

THE NEXT DAY Brady made it a point to stay away from Tess. He'd told her as honestly as he could why he felt the need to keep his distance. Either she understood it or she didn't. He felt a little better now that he'd faced the problem head-on, but he didn't intend to take any chances from here on in. After all, she was only going to be on the Rocking T for another couple of days. Surely he could resist her that long.

Unfortunately a square dance was always scheduled for the fourth night of the trek. Since the Jenson boys played fiddle and guitar and Ragweed Willie did the calling, it was up to Brady and Ira to spend the evening making sure that every unattached female had a chance to dance.

Brady had never been much on dancing, and after a long day on the trail—tiring not because of the hours on horseback but because of the strain of supervising his guests—it was always hard to get in the mood for "The Butterfly Whirl" or "Dive for the Oyster." Tonight would be even harder than usual because he'd have to dance with Tess.

She was one of the last guests to arrive for the evening's activity. She'd shucked her riding blouse and jodhpurs in favor of a cool pink sleeveless top and cutoffs that showed off her lovely legs to fine advantage. Her hair, usually bound on the trail, was loose and flowing freely. It draped past her waist, caressing her finely shaped tush.

Brady was tempted to do the same, but he steered his thoughts toward the smooth patch of sandstone that he'd designated as a dance floor several years ago. By now it was almost as level as the barns the pioneers had danced in. And some of them, he would have bet dollars to doughnuts, had danced on sandstone just as flat.

As Jeb began to rub his bow awkwardly across the fiddle strings, Brady recalled that a former guest had groused that he'd just as soon listen to a cassette recording. Brady had taken umbrage. He wasn't about to tarnish the authenticity of his wagon train with technology! Besides, how many ordinary settlers who'd traveled west had had professional musicians to provide their evening's recreation? Most of those old-time fiddlers probably played even worse than Jeb.

"I don't want to dance," grumped Peter Wilkinson as Brady cheerfully ordered all the men to partner up. "I don't even know how."

"Neither do I, but I'm not about to let that stop me! Peter, you take your wife over there—" he gestured to one corner of the square "—and I'll come over here with Trudy." He gestured toward the grandma, who grinned at him with her usual spunk. "The rest of you partner up and form squares."

Ira, bless his heart, asked the Eagleton girl to dance without any directions. At sixteen, such courage did not come to him easily. But Joe had made it clear early on that if he wanted his uncle Brady to pay him for a man's work, he had to act like a man. "No wimping out, no sassing back, no complaining, or you're coming home on the next stage," Joe had told him. Ira, as it turned out, had been the most reliable assistant Brady had yet hired. Except, perhaps for Willie.

"All jump up an' never come down. Swing yer honey 'round an' 'round!" the old cowboy pattered from his perch on a boulder near the smooth sand square. "'Til th' hollow a yer foot makes a hole in th' ground."

Maybe half of the guests had square danced before, but none of them were very good at it; then again, neither was Ira nor Brady. Still, Brady was happy to see, everybody seemed to be having a good time. As the evening progressed, the two Rocking T men excused themselves from each unattached woman after three or four dances and went on to the next. Roberta, wearing a full-skirted red gingham gown for the festive occasion, boldly asked Ira to be her partner "Because I like 'em young." Brady hoped that Tess would do likewise. But she was cut out of a different piece of cloth than Roberta; she possessed a quiet restraint that he found particularly appealing.

For nearly an hour she sat silently by the fire until Brady had danced with every other unpartnered female in the group. At last he could postpone the inevitable no longer. Giving himself a firm mental shake, he sauntered over to her side.

Tess was slow to look up, even slower to let her eyes acknowledge him. Her expression was tense, almost angry. It took no genius to realize that she was smarting from his earlier comments and his obvious attempt to keep his distance from her this evening.

"Are you ready to dance?" he asked almost brusquely, determined to hide his apprehension.

To his surprise, Tess shook her head hard enough that her long locks brushed from side to side. "I don't think so, Brady." Her tone was controlled but cool. "I've had a long day in the saddle and I'd just as soon rest."

"Nice try, but it doesn't wash," he countered politely, trying to overcome her resistance without making an issue of it. "I'd wager you think *I've* had a long day in the saddle and *I* might just as soon rest."

She smiled, but her lips were stiff. "I think that's pretty obvious, Brady. It looks like everybody's about ready to quit anyway. No point in tuckering yourself out just for me."

No audible sarcasm colored her low voice, but he couldn't hear a trace of warmth there, either. Brady couldn't really blame her for being unhappy with him, but nonetheless he felt stung by her unexpected formality.

Carefully he coaxed, "You know what they say, Tess. Last but not least. Or . . . saving the best till last. I guess they say that, too." He tried to smile, but it wasn't easy.

Tess shook her head again. She did not smile back at him. "Truly, Brady, I'm not much of a dancer," she insisted, her tone almost frosty now. "I had a good time tonight just watching Willie trip over his tongue. You don't need to worry about me. I've got no complaints to tell the folks back home."

Again he stiffened. Now she was striking close to home. "You think that's all I'm worried about? Making sure that the guests who leave here give the Rocking T good word-of-mouth advertising? You don't think the safety and pleasure of my guests means anything to me?"

Her blue eyes met his, and for a long moment—too long a moment—their gazes held. Now her anger was clearly visible; she was losing a grip on her composure. "Brady," she declared woodenly, "I'm not casting aspersions on your sincerity or your hospitality. I just suspect that under any other circumstances, you'd admit that you were tired and you wouldn't be pretending that you want to dance with me."

Suddenly he felt a flush of anger. He didn't know where it came from, unless it was the splash of memory of the thousand and one times that Claudia had said to him, "Why don't you just admit it, Brady? Why do you keep pretending that you want this child? If you did, you wouldn't take the risk of making me live out here when I'm pregnant! You don't care if you lose this baby. You don't care if you lose *me*."

"I asked you to dance," he snapped, struggling to thrust Claudia's face from his memory, struggling to see only Tess. "Is your answer yes or no?"

Tess straightened. Shock colored her face. Tension permeated every line of her delectable female form.

For a moment he was certain that she'd tell him to stick it in his ear and walk off in a huff. But then he studied her eyes more closely and found another emotion simmering below the anger. Something sad, something tender. Something that told him that if things were different, she'd follow him wherever he wanted her to go.

Suddenly, with no visible change in demeanor, she said, "Yes." Her firm breasts rose as she took a deep breath and thrust her shoulders back. "Let's go."

She sailed past him to the sandstone square, where everybody else was already paired up. Willie started calling before she had time to get her bearings, and Brady had to touch her back to turn her around, then bow to her quickly before he took both her hands—crossed at the wrist—and started to swing her around the square.

At first she barely touched him, as though she found such casual intimacy repugnant. But he knew she was angry, simmering, certain that she'd been dragged into a duty dance. He was determined to prove she was wrong. He would show her that he really did want to...well, to... *What the hell do you want to do with her, Brady?* he harshly asked himself. *Is dancing all you have in mind?*

The realization of his deeper desire hit him hard, hard enough to knock him off his stride. He stumbled and bumped into Tess, who impatiently braced his fall as though he were a clumsy oaf she'd passed on the street. Her eyes were blazing now, as if to say, *I told you you were too tired to do this.* And then it occurred to him, belatedly, that maybe that was really all she'd ever wanted to say. Maybe she did just feel sorry for him and he'd imagined the rest. After all, hadn't she shown sympathy for everybody else on this wagon train? Was it really so bizarre for her to show the same concern for him?

In a blast of confusion, Brady realized that he knew nothing, nothing at all, about how Tess Hamilton really felt about him...and that he desperately wanted to know. Suddenly it was unbearable to think that she might regard him with pity! He wanted her to crave this round of dancing, to ache for a moment to be his partner in the square.

Hell, I want more than a dance, he realized as his heart began to hammer at triple the speed of the scratchy fiddle and guitar.

And just that suddenly, he knew he was in trouble. Major trouble of the long-hurting kind.

The realization struck him in the solar plexus just as the number ended and the two of them faced each other at the tail end of a do-si-do. In an instant he found himself searching Tess's beautiful blue eyes for the same desperate longing that he was certain she could read in his own.

To his amazement and relief, Tess met his stare boldly. She no longer looked scared or angry. She looked perplexed, excited...radiant with some brand of fresh hope that he had never seen in her before. Underneath the sound of the noisy crowd's good-natured joshing, he thought he heard her whisper, "Brady?" as he reached out to touch her long blond hair.

A smile broke through his breathless lips, a smile that seemed to wrap around Tess. At least, it triggered an answering smile that warmed him from the tips of his fingers to the tips of his toes. It made him tingle. It made him ache. It made him long to reach out and touch something other than her magnificent mane, and it made him long to pull her close.

"My throat's goin' out on me, Brady," Willie rasped from his perch on the boulder, oblivious to the breathless moment he was interrupting. "I'm afeared that's gonna hafta do it fer tonight."

Around him, Brady heard the others complain, cheer and clap. Vaguely he realized that he, the boss, should have made some sort of closing statement. But at the moment, the only words he could find in his heart were, *Good God, Tess, I want you,* and it didn't seem to him that it was the sort of line he ought to shout out loud.

CHAPTER SIX

BRADY DID NOT GET a lot of sleep the night after the square dance. It was the first time in his adult life that he'd lost sleep because of any woman but Claudia, and he did not welcome the physical frustration. Nor did he appreciate such a flagrant reminder of the emptiness of his life.

He'd made a serious blunder last night, losing a grip on his feelings and revealing them to Tess. He had no intention of compounding the situation by trying to speak to her privately this morning, let alone deliberately whisking her off where they could be alone. The last thing he intended was to trot up beside her less than an hour after he got the wagons moving to mutter under his breath, "Silvergold's less than half a mile from here, over that ridge. If you want to see it, drop back a bit and I'll circle back and meet you."

Tess made no comment then, nor when he joined her behind the wagon train ten minutes later. She did not meet his eyes. Body tense, shoulders high, she simply reined Calypso to the east and trailed behind Brady's buckskin gelding, making conversation impossible.

He was desperate to know what she was feeling, desperate to touch her, desperate to look into her eyes. But even at a good clip, it took fifteen minutes to reach the abandoned mining camp neatly tucked away between the two buttes that provided the illusion of protection to the once-thriving community. Now it boasted only a dozen buildings still recognizable as such and a smattering of weathered boards and iron rims strewn along the ground. Two buildings—the jail and the bank—had been constructed of a curious mixture of redbrick and adobe, and both had several damaged walls still standing. A hand-carved sign that had once announced the Red Rock Saloon now swung precariously by a single hinge.

He was not sure how Tess would react to Silvergold. He'd only brought two women here before—Mandy, who'd found it charming, and Claudia, who'd hated it on sight. He knew that if Tess were anything less than enchanted, he'd have nothing left to worry about. He'd race her back to the wagon train and that would be that.

But Tess was clearly overwhelmed. She slowly shook her head back and forth in unabashed delight, causing her long ponytail to brush her back enticingly. As she sat pert and upright on Calypso, it was easier than ever for Brady to imagine her as Lady Godiva, clad only in that shimmering waist-length hair, which was so ludicrously impractical for a rancher's wife.

"It's just incredible, Brady," she whispered, as though the sight were too glorious to be desecrated by the sound of a human voice. "I can't believe you actually own this treasure!"

He grinned. *Damn right I own it,* he wanted to crow. *I paid for it with blood, sweat and tears and I'll be paying for it till the day I die, but by God, every inch of Silvergold is mine....and Joey's.* Technically Joe had the right to force Brady to sell the ranch at any time he failed to make the payments, and Brady knew that Joe would go hungry first. But Brady would never let that happen. If he ever thought that Joe was in serious financial trouble because of what he'd done for his friend, he would give up the ranch...though he knew it would break him. Joe was family, and Brady had been taught from birth that family came first. It seemed Jake Trent had forgotten that boyhood lesson, but his son had not.

There were other lessons he also remembered, lessons about the reality of city girls and country life. But at the moment he couldn't seem to recall them. His heart was too full of Tess's beauty, her sparkle, her grace.

She dismounted with the ease of a seasoned rider and ground-tied her horse. Her eyes shining, she licked her lips as she turned back to ask, "Is it okay if I look around? If I don't go inside or touch anything?"

Her eyes—shy, uncertain, now that they were alone—met his for just a moment. Surely she realized that he wouldn't have brought just anybody to Silvergold; he hadn't even mentioned the place to gutsy Roberta. He wanted no one but Tess to share in his private fantasy world.

"Feel free," he urged her as he dismounted from Buck. "There are a couple of buildings that I think are safe to enter, but keep an eye out for rattlers."

She grinned broadly, then scampered off to study the old church, which had been boarded up over a hundred years earlier. Like a miner mesmerized by the lure of color in a stream, Brady followed the golden hair that shone in the sunlight.

He stood close behind her, struggling not to touch her, struggling to keep his eyes on the thirty or forty wooden pews and still-standing pulpit. It was big but unengraved or adorned in any way. A spindly cross made of two uneven branches was still nailed to the back wall.

"Boy, this is in good shape!" Tess exclaimed, her smile calling out to him. "After all this time, it's phenomenal."

"I suspect it never got much use," Brady pointed out, his voice low, almost hoarse. "And it was built quite securely. The buttes knock off the full force of the storms, and we don't get as much snow here as we do on the mountainside in Colorado. That's what blocks me from leaving in the winter."

Tess sobered as she asked, "You're actually trapped out here?"

He nodded, not caring for her use of the word "trapped" but unable to disagree with it, either. "I prepare for it in the fall, just like any old mountain man, so I'm ready for the time it comes. Unless I come down with appendicitis or something, there's nothing much to worry about."

Nothing for you *to worry about,* her startled glance corrected him. *Anybody else would be scared and lonely.*

Mercifully she did not voice her views out loud, but turned and trotted on to the next structure, an old store, which had largely collapsed. In one corner Brady could still see some tins and barrels, and a piece of wood that had undoubtedly been a sign on one wall. Whatever words it had once boasted proudly were now lost to time.

"What was the population here, Brady?" Tess asked, a professional note gracing her straightforward tone. "Was it supported entirely by mining?"

"As far as I know. At its height it only had about two thousand people, about ninety percent of them men. It took me quite a bit of research to even learn that much. I'm afraid Silvergold never made much of a splash in the history books."

Tess turned to shower him with another radiant smile, a smile that made him long to touch her face. "I'll look it up when I go home. I've got access to all kinds of reference materials that most people never see. I'll send you copies of whatever I find, okay?"

Brady nodded, but he didn't speak out loud. He wanted to learn whatever he could about his ghost town, but he wasn't at all sure that it would be wise to keep in touch with Tess. And he was certain that it would be stupid to take advantage of this unique moment of privacy to let their relationship grow.

But I asked her to come to Silvergold because I wanted to spend some time alone with her, he admitted to himself. *And she surely came because she wanted to spend some time with me.*

Of course he knew that Tess loved old ghost towns, and that might have been the lure. But no ghost town could grace a woman with the jubilance that now lifted Tess's shoulders and painted her eyes with joy.

He found himself drawing closer as she slipped into the old brick jail, which still had three firm walls and the springs of a bed in one cell. The mattress, if there had ever been one, had long since been carted off...probably by animals to help feather their own beds.

"Imagine, Brady! A real sheriff tried to bring civilization here." Her voice thickened with awe; his body thickened with sensual dawning. "Real criminals slept here and probably planned a jailbreak."

She'd edged into the tiny cell and gingerly touched the bars. "It's so tiny, Brady. A man would go crazy in here if he had claustrophobia."

"A woman, too," he pointed out, moving closer, though he was still outside the cell. It seemed safer, somehow, to keep the bars between them. And yet he knew already that the bars would never be enough. "Apparently there was a notorious temperance speaker who went berserk and attacked the town drunkard and was hauled off on a charge of battery."

Tess grinned. "It was Roberta, in another life. I'm sure of it."

They shared a laugh, and then, quite suddenly, the laughter stopped. There was no sound, not even a snorting horse or a passing bird. There was only Tess on one side of the bars and Brady, a few inches away, on the other.

He did not speak. He dared not move closer, but he could not move away. His eyes pinioned her in the tiny cage, and his hands, against his will, slid up to grip the bars just inches from her smooth fingers.

"I guess it was the *Taming of the Shrew,* western-style," he told her, struggling to keep his voice even, "because the sheriff married her a few weeks later. I always wondered how he managed a romance in this musty cell."

And suddenly he knew the answer to his question, and so did Tess. When sparks flew between two people, it took no special ambience to create romantic magic. And suddenly, in the dusty portal to the past, magic abounded. Only by the keenest force of will could he beat off the sweet sugary web of romance that swung from the ceiling and reached out from the bars.

Brady swallowed hard, struggling to get a grip on his feelings. He knew there was some reason why he could not touch this compelling female, some reason why he shouldn't have brought her here at all. But at the moment, such logic escaped him. All he knew was that he was tired of fighting his hunger, tired of overriding his desire.

Against his will, his fingers slid over Tess's, covering her inviting skin as well as the dusty bars. She did not move, but her lips parted ever so slightly.

Brady took a step closer. So did Tess. The bars still stood between them, bars that spoke of all the other barriers in their lives. But just as old western jails had failed to hold so many others who defied some law or another, this jail could not restrain Brady from reaching out for his heart's desire.

His hand slid through the bars, and he cupped Tess's delicate jaw. As one finger spread out to stroke the shell of her ear, he heard her swallow a whimper. The sound tightened something deep inside him, swelling his own hunger, goading him on.

His fingers slipped through her hair to smooth her nape, and he felt her shiver as he rubbed that quiet, pulsing erogenous zone. For a moment she did not move. She closed her eyes and bowed her head, as though to give him greater access to her sensitive vertebrae. Then she slowly stepped forward until her face was pressed against the bars.

Brady felt a great quivering inside, a quivering that tightened the heart of all that was male within him. A quivering that begged release.

Dear God, I've got to kiss her, the voice of his masculinity urged him. *I can't keep pushing her away.*

His lips lowered to find hers, to join with this woman who moved him so. It wasn't easy through the bars, and the touch he finally managed—a tantalizing graze of her mouth—promised far more than it delivered, and only succeeded in arousing him more.

Abruptly he pressed himself against the bars, and felt Tess pressing against them, too. His other hand dived through the metal lines to grip her waist as her fingers seized the loops that held his belt in place and the heels of her small hands dug into his hipbones on each side of his now-throbbing body.

He kissed her again. At least he tried. But the bars blocked him again, and their lips could barely touch. In mounting frustration, he let his tongue slip out, inviting hers to join it. At once her mouth opened, and their writhing tongues hotly coupled.

A moment later Brady lost all control of the situation, all power of rational thought. Urgently he tugged her closer, pressing his body bluntly against hers. His mouth opened fully as his face shifted to deepen the tongue-dancing kiss. *I've got to have her,* a wild voice within him hollered. *I've got to have her now.*

He never found out what might have happened if they hadn't been separated by heavy bars. Because the instant he lost control, his nose smashed into unyielding steel and he yelped with sudden pain.

Startled, Tess pulled back, too, her eyes wondrously blurry and blue. She said nothing—though she was struggling for breath and still leaning toward him—but the surprise on her face shook him back to the present, back to the reality of the only future that could ever greet them.

How could I be so stupid! he silently railed at himself.

At once he released her, rubbing his injured snout. "Boy, I bet the sheriff didn't try too much of that!" he declared as lightly as he was able. "Ow! I'll be bruised for weeks."

It took him a minute to realize that Tess hadn't moved; her fingers still gripped his belt loops. In that instant he realized the full extent of his folly. He hadn't just taken the risk of breaking his own heart. He'd played foolish games with Tess's, too.

As a kid he and Joe had played a game at school called Tangle, where everybody held hands and climbed over and under each other's arms until nobody knew which end was up. That was a fair description of the way he felt right now. And by the stampede of emotions galloping over Tess's face—hurt, surprise, fury, and unmasked physical frustration—he figured it was a fair description of what she was feeling, too.

FOR OVER AN HOUR that night Tess lay stiffly on top of her sleeping bag, too hot and edgy to sleep. She wanted to walk off her tension, but she was afraid to wander out of camp, and was leery of running into Brady. He knew—oh, God, of course he knew!—how badly she wanted him. He'd kissed her; he'd pulled her close. And then he'd turned away. What more was there to say?

There were other men in the world, and when push came to shove, Tess knew she could do without men, anyway. She'd fought hard to get her career established—no thanks to Nathan—and she was certain that falling in love with anybody, especially somebody determined to live out in the sticks, wasn't likely to do her situation any good. She didn't need on-again, off-again Brady Trent. She was better off without him. Which was a good thing, since it was perfectly obvious that despite his games, he had no use for her.

So why do I feel so blue tonight? she had to ask herself. *So terribly alone? So depressed about a man I hardly know?*

It was the Utes, Tess decided. She'd spotted another one on the trail today, and even though Roberta had laughed at her again, she had mentioned the scout to Ira, who'd asked her why she kept twisting around in the saddle. He'd warned everybody in earshot to stay in close and promised to report the sighting to the boss.

The boss who pushed me away.

Tess knew that someday, back in L.A., she'd forget this afternoon with Brady, and she'd forget her Indian jitters, too. But at the moment, she was decidedly unnerved by the idea of Ute muggers lurking behind the crimson buttes. The Rocking T crew would protect her, of that she was certain. But she didn't want to go crying to "the wagon master," that distant fellow who was as nice as apple pie to all his guests. She wanted no solace from Brady Trent, the man who'd broken his own rules by taking her to his ghost town, then her heart by pushing her away.

She'd left the camp fire early, right after a stagecoach—complete with colorful western characters—had "stopped for water" and gone on its way. In her current mood she had no interest in another evening of camp fire singalongs and Roberta's dramatic displays. In fact, she no longer had interest in anything the Rocking T had to offer, except for Brady Trent.

Damn that man! I want him so much, she confessed to her pillow on the ground. *I want his hands on my face, on my waist, on my...* A hot flush spurred her middle and fanned out to her breasts and legs. How easily he'd aroused her! One touch, and she was ready...one kiss, and she'd given way! Oh, she wouldn't have made love with him completely, not so soon, not today. But it would have been different if he'd stopped because he felt he'd been rushing her. She was certain he'd stopped because he'd simply changed his mind.

She didn't know what had possessed him to take her to Silvergold; she didn't know what had persuaded him to act so aroused, so excited, before he followed his stronger inclinations and pushed her away. All she knew was that her body was flaming with need for him, and her heart felt more battered than Brady's nose after his close encounter with the jail cell bars.

The first blink of drowsiness was finally washing over her when she heard the footsteps, felt the sensation of a person crouching beside her in the dark. A bleat of terror escaped from her lips and her heart thumped a dozen loud staccatos before a rich male voice whispered hoarsely, "Tess? Are you awake?"

It was Brady. Brady with his hand on her leg.

CHAPTER SEVEN

IT WAS A MISTAKE. He knew it the instant he touched her, the instant he felt the muscles in her thigh flex and tighten, the instant she reached out both arms to cup his face.

I should have sent Ira or Willie, he punished himself. *I should have known she'd react this way.*

He'd come to her as a wagon master, not as a man, and he'd only wanted to speak to her gently without alerting the whole camp. But now her arms were pulling him down beside her, misreading his casual touch and furtive demeanor.

He stiffened just enough to stop the downward pull of her fingers, bracing himself with one hand on the earth. The clean soapy scent of her mingled with the sagey smell of the desert night; both called to him, but he desperately held his ground.

He waited tensely until she realized he was not lowering himself to her side or scooping her into his arms. It was a long, awkward wait. At last he told her softly, "I came to tell you that the Utes who've been following us are friends of mine. I went to school with one of them. I pay the guys to scare the tourists because most of our wagon-train guests feel cheated if they don't have a tall tale about Indians to take back home."

She did not move. The hands that gripped his neck seemed paralyzed. She did not pull him closer, but she did not let him go.

"Every summer we have one or two guests who take the whole thing too seriously. We try to keep an eye out for them and let them in on the secret early in the game. Ira and Willie and I have been too busy to compare notes until this evening or one of us would have clued you in earlier." He took a deep breath, struggling to maintain his professional composure. He hated to treat her so distantly, but he was certain it was in Tess's best interests, as well as his own. "On behalf of the Rocking T Wagon Train Adventure, I'd like to apologize if our teasing has caused you any discomfort."

It was the phrase "Rocking T Wagon Train Adventure" that did it. Abruptly Tess jerked back her hands as though she'd just discovered she was holding the wrong end of a branding iron. Mercifully it was dark, so he could not see the humiliation that he was certain now etched itself across her lovely face. And she could not see the self-reproach painted on his own.

As though she had never touched him, Brady continued, "My Ute friend, Harry Painted Hat, will 'attack' us tomorrow night at sundown along with some of his reservation pals. They'll be shooting rubber-tipped arrows and my crew will be firing soft plastic bullets." He could hear his own heart hammering. How he longed to tell her how much he wanted her! How he longed to pull her into his arms! His own need was escalating by the moment, and if Tess was feeling a fraction of the physical anguish that gripped him now, he knew she'd never forgive him for giving her false hope twice in the same day.

"We'll all be making a lot of noise," he finally managed to continue. "If you'd rather skip the whole thing, one of my men can take you on a ride during that time. Or you can just take a walk, if you'd like, as long as you stay close enough to see the camp."

The silence was eerie. Although she was no longer touching him, Brady could almost feel her heat, as potent as the flames of his own suppressed desire.

When she didn't answer, he concluded gently, "You know I live here alone year-round, Tess. I couldn't do that if there was any real danger from Indians or desperadoes."

Finally she snapped. He heard the anger girding her furiously courteous words. "Thank you for your concern and your information, Mr. Trent. I'd like to get some sleep now, if you don't mind."

"Of course, ma'am." He took her lead and opted for formality, brushing the brim of his hat, not certain whether she could hear the gesture, let alone see it, in the dark. When she didn't answer, his long legs straightened. His business was over, and he knew he should have just let her be. He should have just walked off.

But still she lay there, so close to his legs that she could have wrapped her arms around his ankles without even rolling over. *And what would I do if she did?* he asked himself sharply. *Would I tell her I was sorry? Would I just collapse beside her? Would I really walk away?*

But she didn't roll over, didn't reach out, didn't say another word. In the distance, Brady heard a coyote howl in preparation for the nightly hunt, and a moment later its packmates joined in. Nearby he could hear Willie rearranging the chuck wagon. L.T. was humming a song as he strummed his guitar. One of the Hanover kids was crying, and Peter Wilkinson was complaining that he couldn't get any sleep.

But the woman at Brady's feet lay utterly silent. He longed to ask her if she understood why he had to keep his distance, why he had to stay away. He longed to tell her that he would thrash tonight as sleeplessly as she, and he would not forget her when she left the Rocking T.

Then he heard her swallow a sob, and in desperation he forced himself to recall the last time he'd said goodbye to Claudia on a cold, smoggy New York morning. It was the only way he could find the strength to walk away.

IT WAS A LONG and terrible night for Tess, and by morning, she still had no idea how to cope with her predicament. Her longing for Brady Trent was unbearable, and her humiliation was complete. If she could have crawled into a wagon and hidden there for the entire day, she would have done it.

But after five days of vigorously riding Calypso, such an obvious change would have been noticed by everyone, including Brady. And she was determined not to let him see her pain. Besides, she desperately needed to keep busy to keep from dwelling on her dismal situation. Bouncing up and down on a wagon seat wasn't likely to jostle the man out of her heart.

The sun was fierce by the time Tess finished breakfast and mounted up. In fact, it seemed to be three times hotter than it had been any day since they'd started out. To make things worse, one of the harnessed horses seemed to have some sort of problem, which caused a lengthy delay. The last straw was when Brady decided to check Calypso's girth.

If he so much as cracks a smile, I'll kill him, Tess vowed when he greeted her cheerfully as though nothing had happened the night before.

"Good mornin', Tess," he said, lifting one finger toward his hat. "Calypso looks a bit puffed up today."

"I'm sure she's fine," Tess replied stiffly, pulling back her stirruped foot as far as possible from his body. "Shouldn't we be going?"

Brady took a step closer, slapping the mare's big belly as he unhooked the strap and pulled it up a good three notches. "Never hurts to check," he commented casually. Then, to her surprise, he laid one big hand on the heel of her boot and slowly tugged her leg back to its natural riding position.

Even then, he didn't let go.

Although Tess could feel only the imprint of his hand against the tough leather, the touch ignited her hopes and humiliation. *Let go, damn you!* she wanted to scream at him. *I know I'm nothing to you, but you... you... you...*

Suddenly he did let go, but only to slide his hand up her booted calf. His gaze remained fixed on the nearest wagon, but his fingers slipped above the leather and came to rest in the sensitive hollow behind her knee.

Tess held her breath, wondering how he could handle her so indifferently, as though she were part of the horse. Didn't he realize that she was a flesh-and-blood woman, a woman who responded to every nuance of his touch?

And then she felt his thumb brushing the side of her knee while his fingers closed around her fiery flesh. Slowly he pressed closer, as though to shield her leg from view. She could feel his strong shoulder against her thigh, feel a wisp of his warm breath a little higher.

Against her will, she closed her eyes. This was no accident, no imaginary vision spawned of her own longing. Brady was caressing her leg. Intimately. Like a man who knows a woman wants him; like a man who wants her, too.

She could have stopped him . . . *should* have stopped him. After all, what could it mean? Where could it lead? After last night, surely it was obvious that *he* didn't want her interest in him to lead anywhere at all. And she didn't want . . .

When his hands teased the back of her knee like that, all Tess knew for sure was that she wanted him to keep right on touching her. There and a few other places that seemed to be taking on fresh lives of their own.

Suddenly he was talking. His eyes were still on the wagon, and his voice was so low that she almost missed his words. Besides, concentration was growing difficult.

"I'm sorry if I've hurt you, Tess. And I'm sorrier than you can know that I can't—" the hand on her leg stopped moving "—get to know you better. But I can't expect my men to follow rules I can't uphold myself."

Tess took a deep breath. "Is that all it is, Brady?" she whispered, her heart suffused with fresh hope. Had Roberta been right when she'd said he was only concerned about the prudence of romancing a paying guest on his wagon train? Oh, if only he had told her! Propriety was one thing, rejection something else altogether! "If the timing's all wrong, Brady, we could just . . . put it on hold," she suggested gently. "After the trip is over—after the season—maybe we could . . . keep in touch." Even that seemed pushy under the circumstances, but she was in such turmoil that she just couldn't let the chance slip away.

But it made no difference. Though he still caressed her knee, Brady slowly shook his head.

"It's not that easy, Tess," he confessed in a low, husky tone. "I don't know how to play with a woman just for fun. When I was young I was too busy going to school, and after I got divorced, I was too busy trying to find a way to get my ranch back." With his free hand, he motioned toward the canyons with a loving gesture that seemed to say it all. *The ranch. My love. My life.* "This is all I've ever wanted, Tess. I've had to buy it twice. Once I was foolish enough to give it all up for a woman. I lost her anyway. It was the worst mistake I ever made in my life."

Stung, Tess wasn't sure how to answer. "I'm not asking you to give up anything, Brady," she urged him, feeling desperate now. "I'm just asking you to spend some time with me."

At last he looked at her directly, his eyes so beautifully blue that they almost matched the sky. "This is the only place I want to spend my time," he told her almost gruffly. "Your life is in L.A.—you love it there! *I* couldn't even stand to go there for a weekend vacation!" A hint of red darkened his neck as he released her and turned stonily toward his buckskin horse. "Our paths just happened to cross this week, Tess. Sheer luck or bad karma." As he mounted, he glanced back at her longingly one more time. His voice dropped as he finished grimly, "From here on in we're riding down separate trails."

IT WAS NOT A LONG WALK from Trent Savings and Loan to the Slow Joe Loco, but Jake did not take it often, especially in the noonday heat. Although Joe Henderson was all but family to him—nearly a second son—he didn't like spending time at the train station anymore. For one thing, it reminded him of Brady. For another, he hated getting secondhand news about his son from Joe. Worse yet, every now and then Jake actually ran into Brady at the Slow Joe, discovering by accident that he'd been staying there for a couple of days and hadn't even bothered to contact his own father. In the old days—before Claudia had cheated on Brady the winter she'd spent with Jake—he'd always stayed with his dad on overnights in Redpoint.

Today was not so different from all those other days. Certainly Jake's relationship with Brady had not improved. And since he'd turned down the church loan two days ago, he knew things were likely to be strained between himself and Joe. Yet he'd come upon a piece of news he felt compelled to share with Joey, compelled to share with his son. There was absolutely nothing they could do about it—and they would not appreciate his own part in the fiasco—but it seemed to Jake that the very least he could do was let them know.

He bypassed Joe's office and walked through the grounds to the little red house in back, which looked exactly like the stationmaster's house it had originally been. He knocked on the door, hoping to find Joe's wife, Mandy, who was less likely to grill him if he left a simple message.

But Joe himself answered the door.

"Jake?" Worry clouded his rugged features as he tugged on one strap of his engineer's overalls. "Is everything okay? Have you heard something from Brady?"

Jake shook his head, embarrassed that nowadays his visits were so rare that Joe thought the worst when he showed up on his doorstep. In the old days—when Brady was a boy—Joe had practically lived at the Trents' house on Second Street. It had been a happy time of men and boys, of shared dreams and fond remembrances. A time before Claudia, before Mandy, before Arleen.

"I came to tell you something you boys should know. It's not the end of the world, but I know you won't take it as good news. Brady's going to take it especially hard."

Joe scowled uneasily as he stood back and invited Jake in, but Jake stayed on the doorstep. "I can't come in. I promised Arleen I'd take her out to lunch. I just wanted you to know that Harold Dobson came to see me this morning."

The color drained from Joe's face, but he asked for no explanation. He knew as well as Jake did that if Harold Dobson had come to the bank and asked for Jake, the hotel was in serious trouble. And if the hotel was in trouble, so were the Slow Joe and the Rocking T.

After a deep breath, Joe said, "You told him no?" It was not an accusation, just a statement of fact.

Jake nodded. "So did Hal Palmer and John Carleton. I gave Harold a couple of hours and called them both." He didn't need to explain the significance of Harold's visits to Redpoint's other two bankers. Anybody could have predicted his actions after he'd left Trent Savings and Loan, and sooner or later somebody else would have reported the news to Joe Henderson. A couple of hours made no difference in the big scheme of things. But the fact that *Jake* had taken the time to relay the news might make a difference to Brady. Not that it would outweigh the fact that Jake had turned down Harold's loan, but it was better than nothing.

"Does he just want to redecorate or does he need major structural repairs?" Joe leaned forward, his eyes tense. "If he can't get a loan, will he have to sell?"

Jake lifted his hands in a helpless gesture. "I don't really know, Joey, and even if I did, it wouldn't be appropriate for me to tell you. As it is, I'm stretching things. Harold begged me not to tell a soul. But you know as well as I do that if the hotel folds, Brady's business will fall to its knees. I think the Slow Joe can carry on anyway, but without a historic hotel, his fly-by-night wagon-train business is for the birds."

Joe stiffened visibly. "His business is doing fine, Jake. He works like hell. Your doomsdaying won't push him under."

Jake took a step back as though to absorb the blow. "I've never accused him of being lazy, Joe. He's got gumption, he's got brains, and he's got determination that just won't quit. The only thing he's lacking is common sense."

"I see no shortage," Joe loyally insisted.

"That's because you're bitten by the same bug that he is. Yesteryear! Cowboys, Indians and railroads! The only difference is that you picked something tourists are interested in. And you don't have to live like a hermit to make your business work."

Joe did not answer at once. His eyes held Jake's in a strong, steady gaze until the older man had to look away.

"You want him to fail, Jake. You knew Harold wasn't the only one who'd take it on the chin when you turned down his application for a loan."

Jake shook his head. "I don't want my boy to fail!" he insisted. "I just know it's inevitable. I'd hate to see him make a lot of heavy investments in the ranch right now with all this hotel trouble in the works. No point in losing any more money than he has to."

"There's a lot more at stake here than money, Jake," Joe snapped. "Though God knows I've had to stretch my neck out pretty damn far to make up for the fact that you turned your back on Brady when he needed a loan."

"He always needed a loan!" Jake insisted. "He's like a gambler. That ranch is an addiction with him. He lives like a pauper, never wastes a cent and works from dawn till dusk and he's still dead broke, still all alone. Why? Because he loves the Rocking T more than anything else on the face of this earth."

And in his heart he added the words that hurt the most. *He loves it more than he loves me.*

They were words he never breathed aloud.

WHEN TESS HEARD the Ute war cry outside the circle of Conestogas that evening, she had no difficulty understanding why the sound had once struck such terror in the pioneer woman's breast. It was an eerie, high-pitched ululating cry that made her shudder even as she smiled—a luxury she could afford only because Brady had let her in on the secret. The rest of the guests scrambled to their feet and looked bewildered, even scared, before a few broad grins revealed that they understood that the impending massacre was all part of the act.

Off to Tess's left, a woman screamed, then laughed at herself when her husband joshed, "Oh, for crying out loud, Helen, it's just for fun!"

A moment later she heard phony gunfire and the thwack of an arrow as it found its mark—the running-board of the nearest wagon—but immediately bounced off.

"Everybody get down! Dive under the wagons!" she heard Brady yell as he darted dramatically through the hail of arrows, taking one in the shoulder before it, too, bounced off harmlessly in the reddish dust. "Willie, cover the east side! Ira, go circle around them to the north! I'll cover this end." He glanced around dramatically, his expression so solemn that Tess had trouble keeping a straight face. "Are any of you men armed?" he barked.

A couple of the male guests sheepishly shook their heads. One of them laughed. Roberta reached into the cook's wagon and pulled out a heavy cast-iron skillet. "If they get past you, Brady, I'll bonk 'em on the head!" she hollered, then winked at Tess.

"That's the spirit!" he yelled back, then dived under the nearest wagon as a good-looking long-haired Indian wearing rawhide pants, crude moccasins and a host of untanned animal skins around his neck suddenly galloped bareback through the camp, shrieking hideously and brandishing a huge, glistening knife.

He threw himself off the horse, rolled over and up on his feet like a stuntman, and grabbed Roberta around the waist. Tess was just close enough to her him whisper in a western drawl that didn't even hint at his Ute heritage. "For God's sake, lady, don't brain me with that thing. Brady promised me you'd be cool under fire."

Instantly Roberta threw herself into the role, pretending to whack her captor on the head with the skillet, but carefully checking her blows. "Help! Help! Somebody get this savage off me!" she screamed. "Tess, don't just stand there!"

About that time Tess realized that she had been standing perfectly still in the middle of the mock battle like an extra waiting to be called for her part on the stage. Now she flew into action, determined to acquit herself of her earlier cowardice, if nothing else.

She threw herself at Harry Painted Hat, tugging on one of his long black braids until she realized that his wig was coming off. While he grabbed the front, she released the back. Instead she seized and shook his shoulders. "Leave my friend alone!" she called out with spirit as she lightly kicked his ankle. "Get away from her!"

As Tess congratulated herself on following Roberta's lead, suddenly she realized that Brady and his Ute pal had already rehearsed this scene, or at least planned it out ahead of time. Because no sooner had she started to pound on Harry's back than Brady slithered out from under the wagon—his chest and stomach now a rusty shade of dust—and drew out an enormous knife from a sheath at his gunbelt. Up close Tess could see that it was very dull, and as the two men began to clash in what appeared to be a to-the-finish blade fight, she could tell that both were very careful to keep their knives far from each other's faces.

Still, they grunted and groaned and thrashed around—inside the circle of wagons and then outside it—as the onlookers, most of whom were now hiding under the Conestogas, gasped in alarm. At the other end of the camp the sounds of gunfire were now punctuated by the sounds of men "dying" in agony. L.T. kept hollering, "Help me! I'm hit!"

Finally Harry thrust his knife into Brady's chest—or at least it looked that way from her vantage point—and Brady moaned piteously as he staggered, then sprawled in the dirt behind a massive boulder about thirty feet away from the circle of wagons. "There's nothing more you people can do for me!" he gasped. "Follow Willie! Save yourselves!"

Right on cue, Willie crawled up on one of the wagon tongues across the circle, gesturing wildly. "Come on! Stay low!" he croaked. "Get inside!"

Tess glanced at him, amazed at the old cowhand's urgency, then gazed at Harry, who was screeching as he swung up on his pony and galloped away. When she sought out Brady's sprawled legs—the only part of him still visible from the wagons—she felt a momentary chill, as though he really were dead.

Thank God he warned me ahead of time, she told herself, uneasy with the sight of him lying there so silently now that his anguished moans had ceased. If I didn't know better I'd be hysterical by now.

Still, she was the last to follow the others to the wagon. And just as she turned to do so, she glanced back one more time. That was when she saw the blood.

It was forming a pool beside his left knee, dripping slowly from the slightly higher ground that cushioned his chest and shoulders. Suddenly her mind flashed a replay of the moment when Harry had stabbed Brady through the heart—a moment she'd been certain was only part of the game. Oh, she fully understood that he and his Ute buddy had only been playing, but they'd both been using real knives! What if his friend had made a mistake and didn't realize that his knife had accidentally done more damage than he'd intended?

Suddenly there was nothing playful about the blood dripping from Brady's still form, and nothing humorous about the certain sense of dread that seized her. All day she had battled with a tornado of feelings for Brady—anger, desire, frustration with his insistence on worrying about the future—but in that moment, all those feelings vanished. Tess could feel one emotion only—a crushing, tender terror that this very special man could be seriously injured.

"Brady!" she burst out, oblivious to the risk of humiliation as she scrambled through the darkness to his side. In an instant she saw the source of the bleeding, a coaster-size circle of blood on the left side of his chest. Panic seized her throat and shook her torso, but somehow she managed to tug off her T-shirt, the only fabric she could quickly grab to staunch the bleeding. She had just hollered, "Ira! Willie! Roberta! Somebody help!" and started to roll up the shirt when she felt one strong hand grip her wrist and another clamp firmly over her mouth.

Her eyes popped wide with fresh terror, then brimmed with tears of relief. It was Brady; Brady saving her shirt and willing her silence. Brady hoarsely whispering, "Shhh. I'm okay. It's the fake blood stuntmen use, Tess. He never even pricked the skin."

It took Tess a stunned moment to realize what she'd done. Last night she'd been certain that nothing she could ever do would embarrass her more than the way she'd reached for Brady. But now she found herself sitting half naked behind a huge granite rock, trying desperately to save a man who wasn't even remotely injured. A man who had warned her of his plans ahead of time *precisely* so she wouldn't be silly enough to get scared or interfere.

Tess closed her eyes and did not fight the tears. Mercifully everybody else was out of sight, and there was certainly no further point in trying to save face with Brady. Her humiliation was already total.

"Come on, Tess," she heard him say gently, the hand over her mouth now gliding slowly toward the first tear. "Don't be so hard on yourself. Everybody makes a mistake now and then. Frankly I'm flattered that you care that much. If I were really injured—''

''Don't patronize me,'' she snapped, whapping his hand away. ''Just lie there and act dead while I get myself together. At least shut up while I get dressed.''

It was the wrong thing to say. At once Brady's eyes dropped to her lacy bra, the one that covered her breasts with a soft gauzy fabric that did little to shield the dark circles of her nipples from his view.

Embarrassed by his blatant scrutiny, Tess tried to free her hand, the one that still held the shirt, but Brady's grip on her wrist only tightened. The hand on her face seemed to forget the tears and edged slowly, sinuously, down her cheek and the side of her neck. A moment later Tess felt his thumb gently fill the hollow of her throat while his fingers slipped beneath the silky bra strap. The heel of his hand lay perilously close to the upper curve of her now tingling breast.

She could feel her nipples stiffening, straining against the fabric as though to reach his hand. It didn't help any when his fingers splayed out and slid down until his fifth finger actually drifted inside the sheer fabric of the cup.

''Brady.'' The word was a choked gasp.

He ignored her, his eyes still on her breasts. ''You know, I've never imagined you with any fabric—'' his fingers brushed the lacy edge back and forth ''—covering your feminine assets. I've always thought of your lovely breasts covered only by your endless golden tresses.''

As though to make his point, he slowly released the hand that clung to the T-shirt, then reached up to the veil of hair that cascaded down the side of Tess's face. He tugged a silky lock forward, draping it over the breast that was not yet claimed by his hand.

"You know what I call you in my mind?" he whispered. "Lady Godiva. My Lady G. I see you dressed only in golden hair. Golden hair wrapped around a beauty who only gives herself to me."

Tess closed her eyes again, and this time it wasn't so she could cry. She took a huge, tremulous breath as the heel of Brady's hand skated ever so slowly up the feminine slope of her well-curved breast.

And then his whole hand dipped inside that veil of lace. Five callused fingers netted the turgid nipple that waited in sensual anguish beneath. Five callused fingers closed, tugged, tapped on the rigid tip until Tess had to press her lips together tightly to keep from crying out.

And then he kissed her. He kissed her as she had never been kissed before, and her cry exploded in the silence of his questing mouth. His lips claimed hers with the hunger of a lifetime, and her mouth opened to his while her tongue welcomed his inside and begged for more.

Tess readjusted her awkward position on the ground by wrapping one knee tightly around his hips. As he gripped her with his free hand and pulled her closer, she could feel his knee press between her thighs. She understood the promise of that bold touch, welcomed the invitation. Vaguely she remembered that their privacy was transitory, but at the moment they were in total darkness a good distance from the other guests, who were deeply engrossed in fending off the Indians. There wasn't time to satisfy their mutual hunger, but there was time to celebrate this moment of promise...this moment of spring-green hope.

When Brady pulled away from her mouth this time, his head dropped to her chest, and she felt the moist warmth of his lips battle the fabric as he licked her nipple with side-to-side thrusts, which drove her crazy. She dug her fingers deep into his thick hair as she silently urged him on. How she wanted to tug off that bra and throw it away! The fabric was more than a sensory frustration. It seemed to be a symbol of the fact that there was always something between them, some problem, real or imagined, that always blocked their way.

"Tell me you mean it this time," she heard herself croak in an anguished whisper, unable to bear the suspense. "Tell me you're sure you really want me, Brady, even if we can't do anything about it now."

He stopped. He did not release her nipples—one held by his deft fingers, the other mastered by his lips—but he stopped his majestic fondling. He sat there, perfectly still, perfectly silent, for a long, tense moment, until Tess uncertainly released his hair. Then he sat upright, letting his hands slide ever so slowly away from her still-yearning breasts. A moment later he moved his knee slightly back and took both her hands in her own.

"I've explained the situation, Tess. I want you—Lord knows, I want you, Lady G.—but that can't change what is. You're going home tomorrow. I'm staying right here."

Pride made her desperate. "I could come back."

Slowly he shook his head. "Only for a visit. For a night or two—for a week of this—and it could only make things worse."

Tess shuddered and clung to his hands. "I don't know how it could get any worse than it is right now."

He shook his head. "Trust me, Tess. The way we feel right now is nothing compared to the pain we'd feel if we . . . pretended it might work."

"*I'm* not pretending, Brady! What I feel for you is absolutely *real*."

With infinite care, he released her hands and brushed his fingers through her hair. Slowly he pulled the long locks back over her breasts—both of them this time—and smoothed the strands until her bra and bare midriff were completely covered. For a moment he studied his handiwork as though he'd just finished a painting, then once more he sadly met her eyes.

He leaned forward and kissed Tess again, kissed her longingly, gently...kissed her with a poignancy that told her, an instant before he let her go and marched stiffly back to the circled wagons, that it was not a kiss that heralded any future between them.

It was a kiss that said goodbye.

CHAPTER EIGHT

BRADY WAS NEVER QUITE SURE how he made it through the next twenty-four hours. Somehow he stayed out of sight of the Rocking T guests until he got himself together—and kept them all busy long enough for Tess to put her shirt back on and find a hairbrush. Fortunately everybody was so excited about the "Indian attack" that they weren't too worried about propriety. Nobody even seemed to notice that Tess was gone.

Brady, on the other hand, was acutely aware of her subdued presence every moment of the next long day. The normal last day schedule called for a leisurely return to the starting point where the van was still waiting. The guests then unsaddled the horses, shooed them into the makeshift corral, and waved goodbye as Brady and the other men herded them up over the hill to the home pasture, where they had a week to laze about while another group of horses were prepared for the next wagon-train trip.

But when it came time to round up the horses, Brady found himself making excuses to hang around the van. As desperately as he'd tried to avoid meeting Tess's eyes since the night before, he just couldn't let her go without some sort of final farewell.

In the end, he found himself tapping on the window next to her seat, waiting for her to face him from the safe vantage point of the dark interior of the van. Her eyes were dark pools of pain and resentment, devoid of all hope.

He struggled for the right gesture, but nothing came to him. At last he decided to let his eyes do the speaking. For an endless moment he held her gaze. Then he whispered, "Goodbye, Lady G."

She turned away briskly, as though fighting tears, and he strangled an oath as he forced himself to march off. Of all the stupid things he'd ever done as a wagon master or as a man, last night had to take the cake. Except, of course, for selling the ranch and trailing Claudia to New York City.

He was still kicking himself when Joe Henderson showed up the next morning at about six o'clock. Brady, half-awake but not yet out of bed, staggered to the door when he heard the familiar knock.

"Good God, Joe, it's the middle of the night," he groused. "I know you get up with the chickens, but you had roll out of the sack at three or four to get here by now!"

Suddenly his own words hit him, and he realized that Joe *had* done exactly that. Not for fun, surely. So...?

"What's wrong, Joey?" he asked, the cobwebs of sleep quickly clearing from his mind. In the old days, he and Joe had always shown up at each other's homes at odd hours and savored the unspoken kinship that merited such unscheduled visits. But all that had changed once Joe had married Mandy. Brady still spent a lot of time at Joe's place, but he was a guest now, even though Mandy referred to him as a member of the family. And as for Joe's visits to the Rocking T since his marriage... well, they were few and far between. There had to be a powerfully good reason for him to show up at this time of day.

A sudden jab of fright cut his heart as he asked sharply, "Is my dad all right?"

It was always the first fear that crippled him. Not just because Jake was getting on and not just because the family had consisted of only the two of them for most of Brady's life, but because he'd been frightened, ever since Claudia left, that his dad would die while there was still bad blood between them. And no matter how angry he was with his father—how certain that he'd betrayed him—absolutely nothing Jake Trent could ever do would kill his son's powerful love for him.

"Your dad's just hunky-dory," Joe declared sarcastically as he pushed his way in through the patched screen door and headed straight for the tiny kitchen. While he began to rummage around for coffee-making supplies, he dropped the bombshell. "He just turned down another refurbishment loan."

"The church?" Brady rubbed the last grains of sleep from his eyes. "I was afraid of that."

"It's more than the church," Joe answered, dropping two pieces of white bread into the bunged-up toaster Brady had picked up from a garage sale. Actually most of his furniture had come from garage sales, except for some hand-me-downs from Joe after he'd married Mandy. The little house was clean but spare, and the only thing in it Brady truly valued was his collection of western artifacts and barbed wire.

Joe was staring at the barbed wire now as he declared crisply, "Harold needs help this time."

Brady felt a nudge of true panic somersault within him. "What kind of help?" he asked, slowly coming to grips with what had propelled Joey out of bed in the middle of the night. "How much money is he asking for?"

Joe grabbed the half-cooked bread out of the toaster, slathered on some butter and jam, and plunked himself down at the tiny chipped Formica table that filled the kitchen and half of the so-called living room. "He's asking for enough to redo the wiring, the foundation and the roof. And refurbish the interior while he's at it, since everything will be a mess, anyway." Joe crammed most of one piece of toast into his mouth, chewing nervously as he gazed at his friend. After he'd chewed and swallowed, he said slowly, "The hotel failed a state safety inspection last month, Brady, but Harold never let on. If he can't fix the place up, it'll be condemned. Without a rehabilitation loan, he just can't carry on."

Brady got it then. All of it. Suddenly, he felt light-headed, and he slowly lowered himself into the only other chair in the house, an old rocker by the front window and the wood stove. He found his hands trembling as he gripped the wooden arms.

Somehow he managed to ask, "What are you trying to tell me, Joey?"

"I already told you. I told you every damn thing I know. Except for the fact that Jake's the one who let the cat out of the bag. He came to see me two hours after Harold first approached him. He seemed to feel it would make a difference to you. I mean, the fact that he tried to let you know."

Brady felt dizzy. He was still reeling from his farewell to Tess, and he was in no condition to withstand this gut-punch at the first crack of dawn. Joe knew as well as he did that his wagon-train business couldn't carry on without the Redpoint Hotel. If it went under, it would take the Rocking T with it.

For a while—for a long while—the two men just sat there, staring glumly at each other, or at the pair of purring cats that lay curled on the old rag rug, or at the sunrise. Brady wasn't sure what Joe was thinking of, but he was mentally recapping his financial situation, which had looked so promising only a week before. With the hotel, he could continue to eke out a living that allowed him to make his monthly payments to the bank and, next summer, start sharing halfway decent profits with Joe. Without the hotel, visitors to Redpoint would have nowhere historic to spend the night before and after the long ride out to the Rocking T, no reason to do more than make a whistle stop at the Slow Joe if they happened to be on the road to somewhere else. The chances of people camping out the night before the Rocking T van picked them up were minuscule. The chances of them paying for lodging in Montrose or Grand Junction—at least or an hour away—were less likely yet. The chances of his business surviving without the Redpoint Hotel were virtually nonexistent.

As dawn's golden fingers gentled the rough land, Joe finally asked, "Somebody punch you in the nose?"

"What?" It wasn't the question he'd expected Joe to ask.

"Your nose is purple."

Brady flushed. He didn't want to think about what had happened to his nose...or what *hadn't* happened with Tess. "I ran into something," he said shortly. He did not look at Joe.

Another silence, more awkward this time, filled the tiny cabin. Then Joe stood, stretched his long legs and asked almost tersely, "So what do you want to do?"

"You mean, besides hold up a bank?"

"Any bank in particular?" Joe asked grimly. "You thinking of robbing Trent Savings and Loan?"

Brady rolled his eyes. "It's not a bad idea, actually. Might give us some great publicity. We could saddle up the horses and wear bandannas. Storm the place and—"

"Brady, for God's sake! This is no time for jokes! I'll do the legwork in town if there's anything you want done, but you've got to give me some direction. Mandy and I were up half the night trying to think of something. I raked Harold over the coals for keeping this a secret, but all he did was blubber that he was sorry and there was only so much he could do. Your dad won't help us, Brady, and I'm not sure I can press John Carleton into doing me any more favors."

Brady assumed that Joe was referring to the Rocking T loan John had authorized based on Joe's credit, but something in Joe's tone made him wonder if he'd done Joe other recent favors as well.

Before he could pursue the subject, Joe continued, "The most we can expect is sympathy from some of the shopkeepers. They're behind Harold, but they don't have the kind of money it would take to bail him out. And God knows we don't, either."

Brady stood and crossed the small room to stand by the bigger window, the one that dominated his postage-stamp-size living room. It opened on to his favorite view of the Rocking T, a huge shaggy butte that separated the ranch headquarters from Silvergold.

The memory of his last trip there swam over him and pinned him down. Why did his bad luck always run in relays? Why did his father always manage to kick him when he was down?

For a moment he let his memory wander, let Tess's laughter fill the solemn space. He tried to picture her as she'd stood in the jail, ridden on Calypso, sat on his lap by the lake. And then, abruptly, he saw her eyes warm with sympathy as he'd lamented the loss of so many historic buildings in downtown Redpoint, heard her saying, "Have you ever really tried to save them in an organized fashion?"

The words echoed in his mind for a long, thoughtful moment before he said slowly, "Joey, I think maybe we're having trouble seeing the forest for the trees."

Joe stood and crossed the room to stand beside him, morosely staring out at the landscape. "I don't see any forest, Brady. I don't even see one lousy tree. Symbolically or otherwise."

Brady shook his head, trying to recall the heart of his conversation with Tess. "The problem is, we're fighting this war one battle at a time. A building needs rehabilitation, somebody tries for a loan, we say he won't get it, he *doesn't* get it, we moan and groan. Isn't it time we went beyond that kind of piecemeal after-the-fact thinking?"

Joe turned to study him oddly. Then, very cautiously, he smiled. "You've got a plan." He tapped Brady's forehead with his index finger. "There's something stewing up there, isn't there?"

Brady grinned. *Thank you, Tess. Maybe there was a reason we met after all.*

Out loud he said, "In some cities, the downtown area—or whatever section was settled first—has been declared an historic district. Nobody can bring in a new shopping mall unless it looks like the old stuff—in Boston it's seventeenth-century New England architecture, in parts of California it's mission-style. Here it would be early mining camp."

Joe continued to stare at him, but he did not interrupt.

"Any renovation has to fit with the designated period, and the banks are required to give the same loan opportunities to restoration in the district as they would to new buildings."

Now Joe's eyes narrowed as he asked, "So what are you suggesting, Brady? You want to declare the hotel some kind of historical monument? Do you really think that will help?"

"It's a bit more complicated than that." He wasn't sure he could explain Tess's idea as well as she could. After all, it wasn't just a spur-of-the-moment notion on her part. It was part of her job. "One of my guests on the last tour is in the business of historic preservation and suggested that we ought to get the whole downtown area declared a historic district before it's destroyed by 'encroaching twentieth-centuryism.'" He grimaced as he quoted Tess, recalling how he'd laughed at the phrase. He'd expected her to be angry, but she'd taken it in good humor. In fact, she'd been a good sport about so many things that he'd expected her to squeal over. Time after time she'd surprised him. Especially when she'd said nothing—nothing at all—when he'd found the courage to tell her goodbye.

Let her go, Brady, he ordered himself tersely. *Just put her right out of your head.* He knew it was ridiculous to think of her, absurd to even imagine he could take the risk of seeing her again. And yet he still remembered the flow of that long blond mane around his face, the pressure of her thigh half wrapped around his own.

"Brady! Have you gone deaf?"

He blinked as he realized that Joe was staring at him impatiently.

"I said, why don't you get in touch with him and see what direction he can give us? Or I can call him when I get back to town. Give me a phone number, address, something."

"Him?" Brady repeated blankly.

"Your guest. The historical preservationist. You've got records on all those tourists. If—"

"No." The word was quiet, but final.

Joe grimaced impatiently. "No, you don't have his address, no, we don't need a phone number or no, you won't do it?"

"No, he's a she. Yes, I have her address. And no, I won't get in touch with her to ask her anything. And I don't want you to do it, either."

Joe leaned back on his heels and studied Brady thoughtfully. "I see." His eyebrows raised. "Do I see?"

Brady didn't bother to beat around the bush. Turning back to stare out the window he said simply, "She's from New York."

"So are seven million other people, Brady. They can't *all* be just like Claudia."

"Close enough."

Joe groaned. "For Pete's sake, Brady, if you're interested in the woman—or if she can help us—get on the phone to New York!"

"She's not in New York. She's in L.A."

Joe smiled kindly. "Claudia never lived in L.A."

"Dammit, Joe, this isn't funny! The Rocking T is at stake here!" *And also my heart,* he might have added. Instead he said bluntly, "There ought to be some state or federal agency of historical something or other we can call. I bet if you ask your friend who runs the museum in Grand Junction we can get a lead on it."

For a long, searching moment, Joe stared at him. It made Brady itch. It had been a long time since Joe had looked like that...as though he wanted to say something crucial and just couldn't bring himself to do it. The last time had been when Claudia was six months pregnant and having trouble, and Joe had hemmed and hawed for fifteen minutes and finally told Brady that if he didn't let his wife move into town for the winter, her death—or the death of the baby—would be on Brady's head.

Now his best friend said softly, "We don't have a lot of options, Brady, and we don't have a lot of time. Harold's scared. He's depressed. He says he's too old to fuss with all of this, and he's about ready to chuck the whole thing." His tone dropped as he added the obvious. "The Slow Joe can survive without the hotel, Brady. I don't know about the Rocking T."

"I'm holding my own, Joe," Brady snapped. "I don't eat a lot some months, but I've never been late on a payment."

That look—that strained, awful look—darkened Joe's eyes again. It made Brady long to shout, "What is it, Joey? What the hell are you trying so damn hard not to say?" But suddenly he realized that he didn't want to know. Not yet. Not now. Ever since Tess had left the Rocking T he'd been off kilter, and now he was reeling with the news that the hotel's trouble could cost him the ranch. He couldn't cope with Joe's problems right now. Maybe the next time he went into town...maybe then he could cope with it.

How selfish can you be? he chided himself. *Your best friend might be in trouble, and you're too damn chicken to lend him a hand.*

But suddenly Joe was saying, "Your guest can't be the only preservationist west of the Mississippi."

"No, I reckon she's not," Brady replied with some relief.

"If push comes to shove, we can hire somebody else."

"Of course we can."

He met Joe's eyes for a moment, as though to underscore the notion. Tess was replaceable. Tess was irrelevant. Tess was a memory. A memory he desperately longed to forget.

"I'll call my friend in Grand Junction and see what I can do. At least we've got an idea to work with. That's the important thing."

"Yes." *That's what's important. Not that Tess is the one who thought of it; not that she could tell us what to do. Not that I can't bear the idea of seeing her again, pretending that all I want from her is information.*

Joe crossed back to the kitchen, rinsed out his coffee cup and marched back to the front door. "I've got a long drive back, Brady. Sorry I can't stay. But I've got an engine on the fritz and I've got to get it running before that big tour group from Japan rolls in or they're going to have to walk the rails."

"I thought you had an extra engine for emergencies like that."

Joe licked his lips uneasily. "I do, but it's down, too."

Brady was surprised. Joe was a very astute businessman, and he loved the old train as though it were his child. It was rare that he let anything slip by him. "What lousy luck to have them both break down at the same time," he offered sympathetically.

Joe's eyes met his for just a moment—a long moment—that made Brady uneasy.

"Lousy luck," Joe agreed. "I'm sure I can get her running, but I'll need some time."

Brady nodded. He understood. Time was money, and none of his other friends could spare the time to drive so far out to see him. One or two asked to bring their families camping on his land once a year, but that was hardly the same as a personal visit.

Only Joe regularly made the trip out to see him. Only Joe took his calls, gathered his mail, shipped his packages and stored his food. And only Joe had gone out on a limb to get a loan to save the Rocking T. Joe who seemed to be carrying some kind of burden this morning, a burden that a worthy friend would have chosen to share.

"Joey?" Brady called out just as Joe began to move off the wooden step outside the door. "Is there something else you wanted to tell me? Is there something else wrong?"

Joe stopped, turned around, met his eyes. "Wrong?" he repeated slowly.

"Is Mandy okay? The girls? You worried about Ira spending the summer out here again?"

The old warmth, the trust, the unspoken understanding that had always linked the two men now filled Joe's eyes as he shook his head and offered Brady his classic Joey Henderson smile. "Everything's fine, Brady. I'm just worried about the hotel. And we'll straighten that out, too. You can count on it." He glanced at the dirt, dug at a nonexistent hole with his toe. For a moment he was silent. Then he met Brady's eyes and slowly promised, "Brady, I won't let you lose the Rocking T."

He didn't add the words, "No matter what it costs me" but Brady heard them in the quiet angst of his low tone.

For the first time he wondered just what saving the Rocking T had already cost Joe Henderson, and this time he realized that he really couldn't bear to know.

TESS WAS NEVER QUITE SURE how she made it to work the Monday morning after she left Colorado. Never had a vacation left her less refreshed. She felt as though she'd been strapped into a tilt-'o-wheel at a traveling carnival for a good seven days, and by the middle of the week she was still struggling to find her sea legs.

It had all happened so fast! One day she'd been happily living in L.A., going about her work with competence and she hoped, a fair degree of grace. Then she was galloping off to the middle of nowhere to play cowboys and Indians with Roberta. And now Roberta was back in Arizona, regaling her friends with all of her dramatic recreations of historical speeches and events, while Tess was sunk in the blackest depression she'd experienced since the first time she'd realized that her marriage was truly over.

The worst of it—if she could actually separate out all the painful strands of the fabric of this disaster—was that she'd never been entirely certain just how Brady truly felt. In her darker moments she suspected that she'd just been a game to him, an interesting way to pass the time. At other times she was certain that he was head over heels in love with her and would realize it in time. But sooner or later she always returned to a steady middle ground that braced her with the sad reality. Brady wanted her, but not enough to make any adjustments in his primitive life. And there was absolutely nothing she could do about it but forget him and go on.

I'm going to do it, she vowed each morning when she struggled to look bright and eager as she faced her friends at work. *I'm going to do it,* she promised herself as she drove down to San Diego to study an old schoolhouse whose owner was seeking landmark status. *I'm going to do it,* she started to believe by the time she'd survived two whole weeks since her return from Colorado.

But that was before she came home from work one night and found a letter in her mailbox from Brady Trent.

CHAPTER NINE

"LETTER FOR YOU," said Mandy the next time Brady came in to the Slow Joe with the van. "Joey says it's important. Something to do with the hotel."

He snatched the envelope from her feminine hand, wishing to God he could keep his jaw from clamping at the news. He'd known she would answer. Hadn't he? Tess Hamilton was too professional to let a few kisses and the memory of a man's hands on her breasts interfere with the great love of her life—historical preservation. He'd written her a straightforward letter explaining his problem with no hint of what had passed between them. It hadn't been easy, and he'd done it only out of desperation when Joe's Grand Junction friend had reported that the government agencies involved, concerned and helpful though many of them were, had such heavy backloads that they weren't likely to get around to discussing Redpoint's situation for six months to a year. And Brady knew, long before Joe pointed it out to him, that the situation just couldn't wait that long.

Now he ripped open the letter, crossing the Slow Joe lobby to Joe's office, where he made himself at home to read Tess's words in privacy. He wouldn't blame her if she told him to stick it in his ear, and yet he knew he'd be keenly disappointed if she did.

She'd written to him on Historic West Preservation letterhead, which should not have surprised him. After all, he'd written to her on stationery imprinted with the words "Rocking T." But he kept no other mail supplies at the ranch, and he was certain that Tess had personal note cards in abundance.

Dear Brady:

Of course I recall our discussion regarding the status of the historic Redpoint area during my pleasant week on the Rocking T Wagon Train Adventure. The sort of project you describe is precisely the focus of H.W.P., so naturally we will do our best to assist you and the other historically minded citizens and business owners in your area.

Enclosed please find a selection of materials that outline the basic program of community organization and legal considerations that we recommend to interested citizens. If you have any further questions, feel free to contact my assistant, Cheryl Morrison, who generally handles inquiries of this nature.

Yours sincerely,
Elizabeth Tess Hamilton
Assistant Director
Historic West Preservation

Brady slumped down in Joe's swivel chair feeling as though he'd been slammed in the belly with a two-by-four. Never, in his wildest imagination, had he expected to feel like this. He'd written to Tess; she'd answered. He'd asked for help; she'd given it. He'd hoped to keep things professional, with no hint of what had happened between them, and she'd crisply followed his lead. So why did he feel so ill?

He was still sitting there, fiddling with Joe's desktop pictures of Mandy and the kids, when Joe himself barged in a good ten minutes later.

"Well?" he demanded almost gruffly. "Can she help?"

Without a word Brady handed him the letter, along with the packet of information he hadn't even glanced at yet. Joe grabbed it, flipped quickly through the pages and gave a shout.

"All right! We're in business. I think we can organize a group like this. We can get a petition going, drum up support . . . all kinds of things as long as it doesn't cost any money. Our Congressional rep brought his family to the Slow Joe last summer and made a point to tell me how much his kids enjoyed it. I could contact him as a political backer and—"

He stopped abruptly when he noticed that Brady was staring glumly at a blank space on the wall.

"Brady? Am I missing something here? Isn't this good news?"

Brady shrugged. "Sure. It's just what we wanted."

Joe perched on the edge of his desk. "Which is why you're so thrilled, right?"

Brady didn't move. After a long, morose moment, he asked, "Did you read the letter?"

"Sure. She said she'd help. Gave us somebody to contact." He glanced at the note again. "Even said she had a good time on the Rocking T. What more could you ask for?"

Suddenly all Brady could see was Tess's endless blond hair covering her supple breasts. He could feel her arms around him, hear her screams when she was covered with leeches, hear her cry when she thought he was dead.

"Two weeks ago," he said dully, "that woman wanted to make love to me. She begged me to forget she was a city person and try to work something out." Slowly, sadly, he met Joe's eyes. "I told her she'd forget me in time. I guess I hoped it would take her a little bit longer."

JAKE FELT downright morose when he slouched into the house after work early one August evening. Arleen, his wife of nearly five years, hurried to his side and gave him an especially tender greeting kiss.

"Hard day, honey?"

He shook his head. "Hard lunch. Ran into Oscar Reynolds."

Arleen's kind brown eyes opened in surprise. Jake recalled telling her how strained things had been between Oscar and himself since he'd denied the church a restoration loan, but he figured she knew as well as he did that Oscar wasn't one to carry a grudge.

Still she asked, "Is Oscar still upset with you?" as she followed Jake into the kitchen. He sat down at the table while she busied herself with the pots and pans.

"Oscar is upset with me *again*. And when Brady hears about our chat today, he's going to hit the roof."

Arleen made a sympathetic clucking sound, which he took as encouragement to continue.

"Believe it or not, Brady's got some damn fool idea in his head to pass some kind of law making the whole downtown area an historic district, which would lock everybody into holding on to these archaic buildings or rebuilding in the same damn way. Apparently some gal who took one of his wagon train treks is a big honcho in a preservationist organization and plans to help him. Joey's all gung ho and so is Oscar. I guess they had a meeting and elected Oscar president and Brady V.P.

Joey's going to be the secretary and they want a *banker* to be the treasurer." He grimaced. "Guess who those turkeys had in mind?"

"Oh, dear," said Arleen.

"Oh, *hell* is more like it. I told Oscar he was off his noggin, and he said that if he was nuts, so was half the town. I guess they've already got a long list of folks who like the idea. Linda McCray's all hot for it, and since she's on City Council, she could really get the ball rolling. There're a lot of other folks who like the idea too...folks who won't lose any money either way. I told Oscar that the only one with a lick of sense is Harold Dobson, because he's decided to sell out regardless. Oscar said not to be too sure of that, because the historic district might give Harold the boost he needs."

Jake stared morosely at the coffee, sugared and creamed, which Arleen placed before him. "The trouble is, it'll give Brady a boost, too. A false sense of security. All this fuss over the historic district could postpone the inevitable for years."

Arleen clucked again and started to rub his shoulders. "Your son is a very determined young man," Arleen quietly observed. "You must be terribly proud of him."

Jake swallowed hard. He could not reply. He *was* proud as hell of his boy. Proud of his determination, his hard work, his thriftiness, his ethics. But pride couldn't recapture the closeness they'd once shared, and it couldn't justify tossing good money after bad. And it sure as hell couldn't change the writing on the wall.

Sooner or later, the Rocking T would fall of its own weight, and poor Brady would once again get crushed beneath it.

It was only a matter of time.

AUGUST WAS A BUSY MONTH at H.W.P. Tess was doing a detailed study of a tiny town in southeastern Utah, which required three separate trips to the area. Each time she realized how terribly close she was to the Colorado state line she thought of Brady's frosty letter and felt hot all over as she realized that he'd written to her only out of desperation. If there had been any other way to protect his ranch from disaster, she was certain that she would never have heard from him again.

As it was, she'd had indirect contact with him a dozen times since he'd first written. Although most of the correspondence between Redpoint and H.W.P. had taken place between Cheryl Morrison and one of the Hendersons, Cheryl had kept Tess posted and frequently asked for her advice. And twice, Mandy had called to ask a question when Cheryl was out of the office, and Tess had taken the call.

The first time neither woman had mentioned Brady. Tess had answered Mandy's questions about the historic district, then chatted with her about more casual things—her favorite niece's achievements in college, Joe's youngest daughter's braces, her honeymoon with Joe on the Silverton-Durango railroad. The second time, Tess had suggested that Cheryl might come make a supporting presentation at the first Redpoint public meeting scheduled for early August. Mandy had asked Tess outright if *she* might like to come instead.

"Well, I don't see any point in that," she'd answered awkwardly. "Cheryl has been handling things and I'm . . . only marginally involved."

To her surprise, Mandy Henderson answered, "I think that's the problem. Your involvement has been so distant, Tess. I think it would be better if you came here yourself."

"Is there a problem?" she'd asked, confused. "Cheryl seems to feel that things are going very well. And she's one of my most trusted people, so if there's—"

Suddenly Mandy interrupted with a blunt statement that knocked Tess over backward. "Brady's not in love with Cheryl."

"Pardon?" she blurted out, at a loss for any other words.

"You heard me," Mandy said bluntly. "I know this man, Tess. I told you when we first met—he's family. I know what's wrong with him even if he doesn't. The only thing I don't know is what he means to you."

Tess swallowed hard. She couldn't begin to think of anything safe to say. She had said goodbye to Brady in her heart the night he'd cloaked her breasts with her hair. She could not bear to see him again. Not unless . . . well, not unless he had a drastic change of heart. And even then, it was already much too late.

Wasn't it?

"SHE'S WHAT?" Brady barked when he heard the news. "She's coming *here*? Why isn't H.W.P. sending Cheryl?"

"Apparently Cheryl is getting married and taking three weeks off for her honeymoon," said Joe. "Either Tess fills in for her or we postpone our meeting until she gets back. Mandy and I felt that time was of the essence. We need to strike while the iron is hot."

"I don't believe it. I think Mandy set her up to this."

Joe shook his head. "No, she didn't. She tried once, as I understand it, and Tess told her that whatever had—or hadn't—happened between the two of you was none of her business. The next time I talked to Cheryl, she was gung ho to come, but when she mentioned the date to her fiancé, he pointed out that they'd already rescheduled the wedding because of an illness in the family and she'd have to postpone it again."

"I don't buy it. Mandy's playing matchmaker. She's always wanted to set me up with somebody. You must have told her about Tess and—"

"Whoa, now! Let's not get carried away with accusations. In the first place, I don't ever confide your secrets to anybody, not even Mandy. In the second place, she'd have to be deaf, dumb, blind and just plain stupid not to notice the change in you whenever Tess's name comes up. Any fool can see you're dying to see that girl again, Brady. The only one who can't see it is you."

"I see it. I see it!" he snapped. "But it's stupid. It's dangerous. It would be a mistake for Tess and it would sure as hell be a mistake for me."

"Okay," Joe relented with surprising speed. "It's your call. If you want me to postpone the meeting till Cheryl can come, I'll do it."

Brady took a deep breath. "No, that's too risky," he finally relented. "We can't afford to drop the ball." Then a new thought came to him as he suggested, "Maybe I could just . . . skip the meeting. Stay on the ranch. That way I wouldn't have to see her at all."

"Sure," agreed Joe. "Slink away like a yellow dog. That's the way I'd handle it."

Brady glared at him. "That was low, Joey."

Joe grinned. "I know."

THE NIGHT BEFORE Tess left for Redpoint, she curled up in her beloved leather recliner and quietly pondered her living room. She had decorated it herself in a western motif, and she was especially proud of the Remington prints that lined one wall. The cowboys were all strangers, of course, but she talked to them anyway. She'd even given them names. One of them was black haired and blue-eyed, but she'd resisted the urge to dub him Brady. Still, she wouldn't have minded hanging a picture on that wall of Brady himself.

"I can't do this," she told the nearest cowboy, who was busy breaking a bronc. "I can't fly into Grand Junction and ride off to Redpoint with Joe Henderson as though I don't give a damn if I see his best friend. I can't keep from asking about him. I can't keep from going nuts. And if I see him, and he's anything but thrilled to see me..."

Mercifully the phone rang before she could follow that thought too far down the road. As she picked up the receiver with trembling hands, she found herself hoping that they were canceling the meeting. Or that Cheryl could go, after all. Of course she knew that was impossible. She'd been to Cheryl's wedding last Saturday, and she'd already gotten a postcard from Hawaii.

"Heydee-hey, Tess," Roberta's cheery tone greeted her. "I thought you might need a little last-minute advice."

Tess gripped the phone tightly, powerfully grateful for the understanding of her off-the-wall friend. Tess knew that under all the splash and drama was a sensitive soul.

"Oh, Roberta, I don't want to go," she confessed.

"Nonsense. You're dying to see him. Panting at the thought."

"Well, he's not panting to see *me*."

"You don't know that. He might be thrilled. He's had plenty of time to realize what a jerk he was when you were on the tour. I bet he might like a chance to do some things differently this time around."

"Roberta, he knows where I am. He's never once tried to contact me. He doesn't even call Cheryl if he can help it. This meeting is going to be as awkward as hell for both of us. I suspect he'd get out of seeing me altogether if he could. I'd sure like to avoid him!"

"Would you really, Tess?" Roberta asked, suddenly sober now. "If I could whisk you away from Colorado and promise you that you'd never have to see Brady Trent again, would you really be happy?"

BRADY SHIFTED UNEASILY under the Arrivals sign as the passengers from Flight 236, Los Angeles to Grand Junction, began to deplane. He didn't know how he'd let Joe goad him into doing this when his friend found himself "unexpectedly" overwhelmed with station work. After all, Tess was expecting Joe. She might not be happy about a substitute chauffeur. She might not even want to see him again.

Ah, hell, I didn't give Joey much of a fight, he had to admit as his pulse picked up the instant the first passenger stepped into the building. *I was damn eager to have some time alone with her.*

He did not know what he planned to say to Tess. All of the business of the historic district meeting had pretty well been covered by mail and phone—mostly by Joe and Mandy—and there wasn't a great deal he could add. He felt both frightened and elated at the opportunity to share another tiny chunk of his life with Tess. Despite his determination to keep his feelings for Tess at bay, he realized, as he waited tensely, that if he hadn't needed her advice on the historic district, he would have found some other way to see her again.

A claw in his belly tightened when he first spotted the exquisite blond woman marching down the steps of the plane. It was the claw that made him certain it was Tess; she didn't *look* at all the way he'd seen her last.

Her hair was swooped up in a fancy knot on top of her head. Despite the tiny escaping tendrils that framed her heart-shaped face, the look was sophisticated and businesslike. It was a big-city coiffure, far from a ranchwoman's practical braid.

She was wearing makeup—lots it it. He had never noticed whether or not she wore war paint during the wagon-train trip; he had only noticed that she looked beautiful. And while the effect of today's painted artistry was striking, too, the formality and skill of the application reminded him of the other world Tess lived in. The one where his well-worn jeans—clean but tired-looking, nonetheless—would definitely be out of place.

In his mind, Brady always thought of Tess in blue jeans as well, but this afternoon she wore a crisp suit—matching navy skirt and jacket—with a blue silk blouse that only hinted of femininity in the subtle lace collar and cuffs.

She carried a garment bag over her left shoulder and a small piece of luggage in her right hand. A briefcase was tucked under her arm. Despite the burdens, her stride was smooth, polished, self-assured as she looked up to read the signs, then veered confidently to her right, toward the curb.

Brady followed her with a lively step. He didn't want to holler her name, but on the other hand, he didn't want to trail her all over the airport like a lovesick puppy dog. He caught up with her in about fifteen feet, laid one hand on the nearest handle and tossed out casually, "Need some help, ma'am? Free of charge. No need to tip."

He prepared himself to give her his best wagon-master-greeting-the-arriving-guest grin, but the instant his fingers brushed her own—and her eyes met his—he felt his smile fade, and his confidence ebb.

God, I'm an idiot, he told himself harshly. *I never should have come.*

It was the blank stare in her eyes that did it—the expression that was half-confused, half-afraid, and entirely resistant. For a moment he wasn't even sure that she recognized him.

"Brady Trent," he joked, releasing the suitcase handle to quickly tip his hat. "Courtesy of the Redpoint Historical Preservation Committee."

Tess squared her shoulders but slowly set her luggage on the ground. She was staring at him as though it had been years since they'd been apart. As though she'd never expected—or hoped—to see him again.

"I'm in no danger of forgetting you, Brady," she declared frostily. "I was simply expecting Joe."

She might as well have slapped his face. Somehow he stood his ground. "Sorry to disappoint you, but Joe got held up at the station. Not all our visitors are so choosy about their reserved chauffeurs," he growled, deciding that it was time to bring it out into the open. It was obvious that she was still angry with him—bitterly angry—and while he couldn't really blame her, he couldn't bear to let her fury fester any longer. One way or another, he had to lance the boil.

But suddenly Tess retreated. A stiff, courteous smile edged up on her face. "I'm sorry if I appeared ungracious, Brady. It was very kind of you to drive up here to get me. I was simply... taken aback. I thought I'd have more time to... get ready."

"Get ready?" His startled glance took in her formal attire. "My God, Tess, if you looked any more slick you'd stick out like a sore thumb in Redpoint. How do you usually dress?"

She reddened, which surprised him. For a woman of her sophistication, a blush seemed out of character.

"I generally dress appropriately for a given situation, Brady. And I do not generally have to explain my choices to volunteer taxi drivers," she snapped. Abruptly she thrust her suitcase in his direction. "Are you planning to help me with my luggage or just stand there and criticize my clothes?"

"Tess, the last thing I want to do is—" He stopped, suddenly realizing why everything was going haywire. It was no accident that her hair was lacquered and sprayed, no accident that she was keeping herself as rigid as a post. Surely she was hollering at him to keep from revealing that he'd shredded her soul.

Brady took a deep breath as he faced her again, read there the uncertainty—the anguish?—in those beautiful blue eyes. He took the suitcase she'd shoved at him, then set it on the floor.

"Maybe we should start over again," he suggested hoarsely, vaguely aware that the other couples greeting one another all around them were jubilantly sharing embraces. "We haven't had a lot of practice at hellos and goodbyes. I always wished we could do our last farewell over. Maybe we can improve on this hello thing if we do it twice."

And then he stopped talking. He let his eyes say it all. He gave up trying to hide the pain, the hope, the loneliness that had haunted him ever since their last parting. He let her see right into his heart.

Tess swallowed hard. She closed her eyes, patted her stiff hair, then straightened resolutely. Still, her voice seemed very small when she said, "Hello, and thank you for coming to get me."

He intended to say something like, "It was no trouble at all. It's the least we can do to help the historic district get off the ground." But as he watched her tongue nervously trace her lower lip, he suddenly knew why his first hello had come out all wrong.

He'd tried to greet her with words.

An instant later he was gripping her shoulders as Tess clutched his waist with tight, desperate hands. Their bodies touched, pressed, surged against each other as Brady's lips sought the side of her neck, her soft throat, the sensitive lobe of her ear.

"Oh, Brady," Tess whispered huskily as she gripped him even harder, "when I left Colorado I never thought I'd see you again. I cried for three straight days."

His fingers slid up and he tenderly fanned them out across her lovely face. Her breasts were crushed against his chest. Then his lips found hers—or maybe vice versa—and from that point on there was nothing else to say.

CHAPTER TEN

IT TOOK A FEW MINUTES of tears and kisses before Tess became aware of the hustle and bustle of the airport all around her, aware that she'd surrendered totally to Brady.

By then he was saying hoarsely, "Let's get out of here, Tess. We can talk in the truck."

He broke away from her and grabbed her things, suddenly taking on the chauffeur role again. His eyes were dark as he avoided her questioning glance, and he said nothing else as he steered her toward an old pickup that had little to commend it except that it appeared to have been freshly washed.

Brady talked about the weather—"hot as the underside of a saddle blanket after a hard ride"—as he loaded her things in the back and covered them with a clean tarp. Even when he unlocked the passenger door, plucked out the seat belt for Tess and waited until she was securely nestled inside, he did not look at her. By the time he climbed in the other side, she knew he was angry with himself for yielding to his instincts where she was concerned. He'd already begun to retreat.

Tess could not bear to lose him again. Not when she'd just felt his arms around her once more, heard the anguish in his voice when he'd groaned her name. When he slipped the key into the ignition, she lightly touched his wrist. "Don't, Brady. Please. Not until we talk."

He stopped, defeated, his jaw tightening as he stared at the street. Still, he loosened his grip on the keys, wrapped his fingers around Tess's and rested their intertwined hands on his knees.

"Tess, I promised myself I'd keep you at a distance this time around. When you left here last time, I never intended to contact you. I wouldn't have if there had been any other way. If we hadn't been desperate, I would have let things take their natural course."

"You mean you would have forgotten me," she clarified softly.

At last he met her eyes. "Dammit, girl, I would have tried."

She could not hide her pain. "Could you have done it, Brady? Really?" She paused for a moment, then said softly, "If it really would have been that easy for you, then what just happened was a mistake."

His grip on her hand tightened, and he looked positively gray as he dropped his gaze. "I'm not denying that I have strong feelings for you, Tess," he admitted in a low, husky tone. "I'm not denying that I wish . . . I wish things were different. I just don't see how they can ever be."

Tess lifted their interlocked hands and kissed his knuckles. "I care for you, Brady," she confessed. "I care for you in a way I haven't allowed myself to care for a man in a very long time."

At last he glanced up at her, sighed painfully, then leaned across the stick shift to kiss her gently on the mouth. A long moment later he whispered, "If feelings were all that mattered, Tess . . ."

"They're all that matter to me."

He kissed her again, but he pulled back when she would have deepened the kiss. "Just for the sake of argument, let's pretend we get involved. We follow this trail wherever it leads. How much good do you think those feelings are going to do you in midwinter when you haven't seen me in four or five months and can't even reach me by phone or mail? How much good do you think they're going to do me when I'm snowlocked and dying to see you, knowing you'd rather live in the southern California sunshine than winter with me?"

Tess closed her eyes and tightened her grip on his hand. "I don't think we have to plan the rest of our lives right now, Brady. All that matters is that we want to be together."

He pulled back, then—though he didn't quite let go—and straightened edgily in the truck's tape-patched seat. "That's what Claudia said when we first got together. 'I love you, Brady, and you love me. That's all that matters.'" He stared bleakly at Tess. "That wasn't all that mattered to her after a few months on the Rocking T. And after I sold the ranch and followed that woman to New York, it wasn't all that mattered to me."

This time it was Tess who glanced away, Tess who tasted the bitterness of defeat. She wasn't prepared to tell Brady she could give up everything for love and move to the Rocking T, even if he'd been asking. She liked his ranch just fine, and if they could have lived somewhere else and kept it as a vacation retreat, she would have been happy. But she knew that Brady couldn't give it up, and he'd hate her if she ever asked him to.

"There must be a compromise of some kind we can reach if we're . . . still together long enough to need one. Surely the important thing right now is that we have a few days to spend together."

Now he looked at her directly. His jaw looked stiff. "I don't want to compromise, Tess. I've done that already. I compromised my values, my dreams, my home and my business for a woman who hadn't the slightest intention of compromising anything for me. I will *never* do it again."

Tess stiffened. "That sounds pretty final."

"It is."

"It also sounds like you think you're talking to Claudia," she snapped, unable to conceal her hurt. "You really don't have any idea how a compromise might turn out with me. In fact—" she was a little angry now, and made little effort to conceal it "—you don't have any idea how much compromising I've had to do in the past. You don't know how many times I had to give up a good job to follow my husband after another farfetched dream. You don't know how hard it was to put off having children, to—"

She stopped abruptly as she watched Brady's face grow pale. Too late she remembered that Brady had lost a baby of his own . . . a loss that was somehow tied into his first loss of the ranch.

"I'm sorry, Brady," she whispered, appalled at her heedless words. "I forgot about your . . . little one."

He blinked. "You know about that?"

She nodded. "I never meant—"

"I can't believe Mandy!" Brady burst out. "She said you two had gotten chummy over the phone, but I never thought she'd started blurting out—"

"It wasn't Mandy, Brady!" Tess stopped him quickly. "It was Ragweed Willie. And I didn't push him for any information, either. He mentioned it on the ride out there the first day, before you and I had even met."

Brady glowered for a moment, not at anyone in particular, before he conceded, "It's hardly a secret. You could have heard the story from anyone in town. It's just that I don't see any point in parading my losses or shortcomings to every eligible female who strolls through town."

He stroked her hand with his fingers as he spoke, as if to soften any harsh words. "She didn't lose the baby because she was living on the ranch," he insisted, as though Tess had accused him of such. "She'd moved in with my dad six weeks before she miscarried. It wasn't anybody's fault. The doctor said it just wasn't meant to be."

Sensing the pain beneath the strident explanation, Tess said softly, "I guess that doesn't really make it much easier."

His eyes met hers with a spark of surprise. "Not too many people realize that, Tess. They always say, 'Well, at least you don't have to feel guilty.' Of course I would have felt guilty if we'd lost the baby because I couldn't get Claudia to a doctor in time. But guilt is . . . a different kind of hell."

For a long moment he was silent, and the silence convinced her, as no eloquent words ever could, that losing the baby had hurt Brady Trent as much as the loss of his wife. She was ready to forgive him for almost anything by the time he finally said, "Don't you see, Tess, that nothing has really changed? If I ever married again, and my wife, or my child, had any kind of medical complication and I couldn't get help in time—I *would* blame myself. A hundred years ago, proximity to a doctor probably wouldn't have made any difference, so I could have lived with the risk. But nowadays, I know what I'm asking of a woman, let alone a son or daughter, and I won't ask it of anybody but myself."

Tess couldn't argue with him. She couldn't say she'd be brave; she couldn't say that she wasn't afraid to live hours from civilization. She couldn't say she wasn't afraid she'd go stark, raving mad in such primitive conditions, as too many pioneer women did, and she couldn't say she'd be willing to raise her children under such conditions or give up giving birth altogether. All she could say was, "Maybe there's a way, Brady. Some kind of middle ground. If we put our careers in the background for just a minute—"

"I can't put mine in the background. If I take my eye off it for a moment, it will slip away." This time a different tone filled his voice, a tone that held a passion even greater than she'd felt when he'd first took him in her arms. "The Rocking T is my *life*, Tess. If I don't fight for it tooth and toenail, I could lose it again." Slowly, carefully, he released her hand and moved it gently back to her own lap. Then he patted it, just once, as though to say goodbye. "I can't be your lover, Tess, but I'm begging you to be my friend. I need your help tonight. All this time we've been talking about saving the hotel, saving the old buildings, saving the historic downtown for tourism and good business and community cohesiveness." His eyes were bleak. "But you know that's only the surface, Tess. You know that's not why I risked hurting you all over again."

He turned to face her squarely, as though to deliver the most important words he'd had to say since her arrival. "I care about the town, Tess, but I could live without it. And I care about the Slow Joe, but it'll carry on no matter what." His eyes darkened and his voice dropped. His next words left her with no doubt that he'd contacted her out of desperation, and for no other reason. "But the wagon train won't last another season if the hotel folds, Tess. I'm begging you—no matter how things stand between us—if I mean anything to you at all, help me save the Rocking T."

Defeated, she promised gravely, "I'll do my best, Brady."

He kissed her one more time—too quickly for her to pretend it meant anything but thank-you—and started up the truck.

IN THE END, Brady did manage to carry on a normal conversation with Tess as they drove to Redpoint. It was, he reflected silently, the first complete conversation they'd ever had. It almost felt like a real date. He learned about her family, her college years with zany Roberta, her long-term vision of her career. And she told him openly about the gradual disintegration of her marriage as she'd painfully realized that her ex-husband was using her financially—repeatedly ignoring her personal and professional needs as he moved from place to place—relying on her income as he followed his own course. Brady had already told Tess everything about his own life that really mattered, but he answered her questions about his schooling and his mother's death, surprised that she'd figured out, by what he hadn't said, that the only woman whose picture hung on his bedroom wall had been gone a very long time.

By the time they reached the parking lot adjoining both the Slow Joe and the Redpoint Hotel, he was feeling a little less tense, but he knew he didn't dare carry her bags up to her room. Normally he had the greatest of self-control where women were concerned, but with Tess he just didn't trust himself. Worse yet, he couldn't even count on his normal friendly banter with Harold to ease the tension when they entered the lobby. Ever since he'd learned that Harold wanted to give up, things between the two of them had been terribly strained.

"I'm not a coward, Brady," Harold had told him just a few days ago, though Brady had never used the term with him. "I'm just an old man who wants to make sure I have enough to live on when I can't work anymore. I've got a wife to take care of. Someday you'll understand."

But Brady certainly didn't understand at the moment, and he didn't want to talk about it in front of Tess. So he kept the conversation light as he delivered her to Harold and promised to meet her for dinner later at the Hendersons'. Then he hurried on over to Joe's.

Nobody was home. Mandy, he presumed, was still out at work, and it was too early to expect the kids. To his surprise, Brady found himself a little disappointed. Ira, of course, was still out at the ranch, but he'd been looking forward to seeing Lynne. As for the little one, Sally...well, she was his special buddy. Just a little older than his own little girl would have been. The little girl he'd seen only after death, the one he'd still named for his mother.

He used the key that hung on a nail in a nearby tree to let himself in, then changed for the meeting and kept busy paying bills for the next hour. It occurred to him that he might have used the time to drop by to see his father, but he knew he just couldn't be cordial at the moment. How was he supposed to greet his dad with a hug in the afternoon when in the evening they'd be meeting with daggers drawn?

He suspected that by six o'clock, he'd consider his father the least of his problems for the evening. And when Tess arrived at Joe and Mandy's—looking incredibly classy and distant in a royal-blue silk blouse and matching skirt that mirrored the color of her sorrowful eyes—he was sure of it.

BY SIX O'CLOCK when Mandy ushered Tess into her kitchen—cheerfully responding to Tess's offer to help by plopping a hunk of lettuce and a knife in her hand—she realized how Brady survived his solitary existence. This was his family. This was his second home.

Walking in the door, she'd found him helping a fourteen-year-old girl with her homework while a smaller one—armed with a mouthful of braces—perched on his lap. Despite the disconcerting flush that had darkened his face when he'd spotted Tess, it was obvious that he thoroughly enjoyed playing uncle to his best friend's children, and he probably longed for kids of his own.

She was still assembling the salad when the tiny one—Sally, she'd heard Joe call her—sauntered into the kitchen and stared at the new guest. "Uncle Brady says you're gonna help save the Rocking T," she declared as a conversation starter. "You gotta do it, 'cause Uncle Brady's the best."

Tess smiled. "I couldn't agree with you more," she assured the child. "And I promise you that I will certainly do my best to help him."

Sally grinned, then skipped over to Mandy and lifted her arms up for a hug. Mandy gave her a kiss on the cheek, then turned to Tess after the sweet child left the room.

"We're all doing our best to help Brady," she said rather seriously. "But frankly, I'm not sure it's going to be enough."

Tess raised her eyebrows. "What do you mean?"

"I mean," she answered pointedly, "that the men in this family—and by 'family' I mean Brady, too—are not realistic about certain things."

Tess waited while Mandy licked her lower lip, as though she had something crucial to confide. Ultimately she must have thought better of it, because finally she said, "I'm just telling you, Tess, that no matter how desperately Brady wants to keep the ranch, the time may come when he has to sell it again. And if his stubbornness about living on the Rocking T is the only thing that...well, that interferes with your friendship with him, you might want to remember that someday, the ranch may set him free."

Her words jolted Tess. She had not expected Mandy to be so bold and forthright, nor had she realized, until this moment, how precarious Brady's hold on the ranch really was. But even as she realized that if he lost the Rocking T, he might be free to love her, she turned away from that skewered hope and staunchly shook her head.

"I don't want him that way," she confessed. "As much as I wish there were some common ground Brady and I could find, I'd never pray for him to lose his ranch. He just wouldn't be the same man without it."

Mandy blinked once or twice. "I knew it," she said softly. "I knew he'd found a woman who truly loves him, a woman who truly understands."

"Oh, I understand." Tess shook her head. "For all the good it'll ever do me."

It was precisely at this moment that Brady marched into the kitchen, looking like a stranger from a western wear advertisement in his trim black western suit.

"Ah, have I interrupted some sort of women's talk in here?" he asked, his voice a mixture of teasing and suspicion.

Mandy laughed as she darted past him, quickly leaving the room. "Of course. We females take advantage of every opportunity to gossip about you men."

Tess managed a feeble grin. "It's true," was all she could say.

And then she was alone with Brady, alone in a home that tingled with such joy and warmth. *We could have a family life like this, Brady,* she longed to tell him. *Neither of us have to keep living alone.*

But he didn't speak at first, and neither did she. A rush of warmth seemed to fill up the room, a rush that had nothing to do with the sweltering weather. Brady's eyes were on her face, watching, waiting, *willing* her to make the next move. Or was he begging her to keep her distance?

"I like the kids," she finally said, unable to bear the silence that vibrated between them. "They seem awfully fond of you."

He nodded. "It's mutual."

And then, because she could not help herself, she added, "I'm awfully fond of you, too."

He swallowed hard. "It's mutual," he repeated, his voice thick with frustration.

"I spent the afternoon walking through the downtown district, getting the lay of the land. I could have used a tour guide."

Slowly, Brady crossed the room until he stood beside her, leaning against the sink.

"I can't stay near you, Tess. It would be even harder than . . . staying away."

It was hard to tell whether or not he counted this encounter as staying close or staying away. His body now lingered maybe six inches away from hers, so close she could almost feel the heat of his hunger. Her heart was doing cartwheels as she struggled with a fresh wave of desire.

"I won't be coming back this way for a long, long time, Brady," she whispered now. "If there's ever a chance for us to be together, it's now, tonight, this weekend."

Brady closed his eyes. She watched his fists tighten. "It's bad enough already, Tess. Don't make it worse. Don't tease me."

"I'm not teasing you, Brady Trent. If you don't know by now that I want you, then you're—"

"Don't!" It was a single word, whispered in a tone that almost shattered her with its tender angst. He opened his eyes, met hers with a desperate, anguished plea. "If you care for me, Tess, I beg you. Let it be."

TESS WAS STILL REELING from the urgency in Brady's eyes when he ushered her into the conference room at the hotel an hour later. If Brady was feeling likewise, he gave no sign. He'd kept the conversation light and upbeat around the Hendersons, and nothing had changed now that they had a few moments by themselves.

It no longer mattered to Tess. She had given up. At some moment during the evening—maybe in the kitchen, maybe afterward over dessert—she had realized that Brady was determined not to take the risk of loving her, and there was nothing she could do to change his mind. The most loving thing she could do for him was to grant him his freedom without shackling him with guilt. It would not be easy, but she'd decided that she had to do it. If not for herself, for him.

"I thought it would be better if we got here early," he announced as she put down her briefcase and surveyed the ancient room. "It's always better to get the lay of the land before your enemy does. Gives you the advantage."

Tess caught his eye. "We're talking about your friends and neighbors, Brady. Are you sure they're the enemy?"

He glanced away. "We're talking about my father, too, and nobody's more dead set against this historical movement than he is."

"Will he be here tonight?"

"Of course. And he's likely to be your most vocal opponent, so watch yourself." Brady eyed her unhappily. "I hate this," he suddenly whispered. "I just hate knowing he's on the other side."

Tess laid one hand on his arm and gently squeezed. "I'm so sorry, Brady. I wish there was something I could do to help."

He shook his head, then stepped away, dislodging her platonically comforting hand. "I told you once before that this was hard to explain. If I fell off a horse and broke my back, my dad would close up shop, follow me to a hospital in Timbuktu, and camp out in the lobby day and night for the next fifteen years if he had to. If I decided tomorrow to sell the ranch and go into banking—or any other career of which he approved—my dad would roll out the red carpet, loan me a fortune, even *give* me a fortune, and invite me to move back home." He shrugged uncomfortably. "But as long as I belong to the Rocking T, he won't lift a finger to help me."

Tess studied him quietly, then bravely took a step forward and lifted one hand to touch his face. Her fingers fanned out to stroke him, to warm him only with her concern, but she feared he'd misunderstand her touch and pull away.

To her surprise, he closed his eyes and leaned a fraction of an inch closer, until his cheek rested trustingly against her palm. "I'm not a child, Tess. I've learned to live without a lot of things that I desperately wish I could have. My dad's respect is just one of them." He opened his eyes and gazed into hers with a powerful surge of longing that reflected what he surely saw in her own. Then he added hoarsely, "Tess Hamilton is another."

THE MEETING WAS already underway when Jake arrived. Oscar Reynolds, looking terribly official in his best black suit, was explaining the purpose of the forum and introducing the gal from California. Tess Hamilton, he called her. She was a beautiful young woman with layers of blond hair wrapped severely around her head in a fashion that enhanced her aura of grace. She looked a trifle too sophisticated for Redpoint, but then again, most outsiders did. She also looked tough enough to take on any comers, and Jake suspected that she'd have a slick answer for any opposition to her point of view.

As he found an empty chair near the back, his glance fell on Brady, who was sitting at Miss Hamilton's side. The boy looked uneasy, which did not surprise his father. The fact that he was wearing a western suit for the occasion did. Jake didn't even know Brady owned a suit anymore, let alone that he could be persuaded to don it in public. His awareness of the importance of the evening sharpened.

So did his guilt. It was bad enough that he'd refused to loan Brady or Joe any money in the past and had turned down both the church and Harold Dobson just last month. What made things worse was that he'd been asked, on several occasions, to voice his opinion regarding the proposed historic district, and each time he'd said plainly that he thought that Redpoint's commercial success lay in the future, not in the past.

Tonight it would be worse. Tonight, if he spoke out loud, his lack of support of his son would be obvious. Brady would never forgive him.

But then again, Brady had never forgiven him for lots of things—even things that were not his fault. Claudia would have left Brady no matter what his father had done. And sooner or later, loan or no loan, he would have lost the ranch. Just as he was going to lose it again, no matter how valiantly he tried to save it. It was just a matter of time.

Jake briskly turned his thoughts to other things. Mentally he checked out the room, trying to gauge the mood of the crowd. Most looked interested, a trifle excited. One or two looked scared. Poor Harold Dobson looked bowstring taut this evening. Oscar looked on edge. Mandy Henderson's sister, Ruth, looked frisky and determined, and her daughter, Karen—who was home from college for the summer—positively bloomed with the fresh beauty of her youth.

"Thank you for inviting me here this evening," Tess Hamilton began, rising to stand in front of the city hall podium. "As some of you know, my first visit to Redpoint was purely recreational. Like many out-of-state tourists, I was drawn to the historic quality of the town by word-of-mouth advertising regarding the enchanting hotel in which I stayed, the charming old train I got to ride, and the marvelous slice of the old west I experienced on Brady Trent's Rocking T Wagon Train Adventure."

A smattering of applause swept the room.

"Business enterprises of this nature have done extremely well in most of the areas that I have visited on both personal and professional journeys. In fact, some communities, such as Virginia City, Nevada and Tombstone, Arizona, have converted entire towns into western tourist attractions, to the great benefit of those merchants involved. While this is no longer a feasible option for Redpoint, the downtown section, which I have observed and soon hope to study, still retains some classic centenarian buildings that provide the groundwork for a historical district composed of a partially preserved, partially reconstructed 1860's mining camp."

The applause grew greater after that. Tess Hamilton began to speak on the general trends of historical preservation, financial resources Redpoint could draw upon, and the various kinds of benefits the town could derive from creating a historic district. She was affirmative, forceful and unerringly optimistic. If Jake had not been well aware of the other side of the picture, he would have followed her anywhere.

As he glanced again at his son, he had the uncanny sense that Brady was prepared to do exactly that. And though the woman's words on a subject so near and dear to his heart might have justified the rapt attention with which he studied the woman, something in Jake's fatherly soul registered a greater intensity in his son's expression than the situation called for.

Jake wondered, for a moment, if the thought of the Rocking T ever made Brady look quite like that. And as he thought of it, he remembered when he'd last seen that expression of passionate intensity on his son's face. It hadn't been when Brady was talking about the ranch.

It had been first the time he'd introduced his dad to Claudia.

CHAPTER ELEVEN

BRADY WAS SWEATING by the time the meeting broke up, and not just because of the lingering evening humidity. Although Tess had held her own under fire, he wasn't sure that she'd really made the necessary impact on the Redpoint merchants. And though his father had, mercifully, said nothing to sabotage the operation, his silence had nonetheless been damaging to Brady's cause.

"You want to go back to the Slow Joe and have some coffee?" Mandy asked when Tess finished answering questions and joined her, along with Brady and Joe, in front of City Hall. "I think there's some ice cream in the freezer if Joe and the kids haven't devoured it since three o'clock."

"Hey, I'm innocent!" Joe insisted, raising one hand as though to swear it in court. "I haven't even *been* in the kitchen since three o'clock."

Mandy tossed him a teasing smile. "I saved you some dinner, Joey," she sweetly assured her husband. "If you're nice to me I might even whip up a sundae for dessert."

Brady knew the look on her face, the one that always made him tighten with envy. He didn't want Mandy as his wife, but sometimes he longed to have a woman of her devotion who would drive him nuts by fussing over him when he came home. Instead he had nobody but his horses and half a dozen dogs to greet him in the evening . . . and Ragweed Willie, who holed up in the bunkhouse until November, at which time he began visiting old friends in sunny Arizona, using the holiday season as an excuse. Brady knew he was really only interested in free places to ride out the harsh Colorado winter. At the moment, when Brady felt so estranged from his father, it was as though Joe and Mandy were all the family he had in the world. And sometimes, their intimacy was so intense that he felt excluded. Never unwelcome, just . . . unnecessary.

Tonight was one of those times.

"Brady? Tess?" asked Joe.

Brady shook his head. "I think I ought to get back to the ranch," he replied, not daring to glance at Tess. "I've got a new wagon train starting out in a couple of days and I want to repair a harness first."

Mandy shot him a disapproving glance, then turned to Tess. "Just because Brady's going back to his cows doesn't mean you have to call it a night, Tess. Joe can walk you back to the hotel if it gets late and—"

"That's okay, Mandy," Tess said softly, the faintest hint of a tremor in her tone. "It's been a long evening and I think I'd just like to go to bed. Maybe I can come over for a cup of coffee with you in the morning before I go."

"Do that," Mandy urged. "By tomorrow morning we'll know how it really went tonight. Everybody and his brother will stop by this evening to let us know."

Joe then turned to Brady. "Why don't you come in early when you come back for the next group of tourists and I'll bring you up-to-date."

Brady nodded. "Sounds good. See you folks in a couple of days." Slowly he turned to Tess, afraid to take the risk of telling her goodbye without Joe and Mandy as inadvertent chaperones. "And I guess I better say goodbye now because I don't know when I'll be seeing you again."

Slowly her eyes met his. *Never,* they said mournfully. Pain mixed with anger in the beautiful lines of her face. *This is goodbye, you coward, and you know it.*

For a moment Tess did not speak; neither did Joe nor Mandy. Brady tried to look away, or say goodbye, or do anything at all to break the hold of that solemn, hopeless expression on Tess's face. But he couldn't seem to move.

Vaguely he heard Mandy murmur, "Good night, then." Quietly she and Joey seemed to vanish.

Tess still stood before him on the sidewalk, her spine erect, her arms perfectly still. She waited for what seemed like an interminable length of time, but still he said nothing. He wanted her desperately. *If I so much as lean in her direction,* he realized with sudden panic, *I'll have to take her in my arms.*

"Good luck, Brady," Tess finally told him. Defeat and sorrow painted every word. "I truly hope things work out for you. I hope that the historic preservation committee can help you save the ranch." She held out one slim hand to shake his. Her tone was distant now, as though her heart had said farewell, as though she really had given up on him at last. "You know that the services of H.W.P. will always be available to you."

Brady responded automatically, but there was nothing automatic about what happened to him when his fingers touched her palm.

He felt it again, the double-whammy of her silky skin rippling across his calluses. It happened every time she touched him. He felt that soft tremble of a woman struggling desperately to hold back a dam of turbulent feelings; he remembered the feel of her in his arms.

Remember Claudia, he ordered himself. *Remember the hell that waits for you down the road.*

"Goodbye, Tess," he said hoarsely. "Thanks for your help."

She nodded. She licked her lower lip. She tightened her grip on his hand.

"Goodbye, Brady." It was a whisper, a promise . . . a breathy trio of syllables that sounded a lot more like hello than goodbye.

It took all the strength he had to disengage his fingers, but he did it. He even managed to look away.

"Goodbye," he said again.

For a moment Tess just stood there on the sidewalk, her face uncertain, disbelieving. He knew she couldn't believe he really had the strength to let it end like this. He couldn't believe it, either. But somehow he managed to stand there, holding his ground, mute, broken, drowning in hurt and desire.

And then, abruptly, the woman he cherished turned without a word and walked away.

He did not decide to follow her. In fact, even as he frantically scrambled the half dozen paces it took to catch up, a voice inside was saying, *Of course you're not going to walk her to her room, Brady. You're too smart to take a chance like that.*

But suddenly he was hurrying along beside her, holding her hand. Her fingers gripped his tightly as she quickened her pace, almost tugging him along beside her. She did not look at him directly, but he could see silent tears coursing down her face.

They did not speak as they crossed the street, slipped through the Slow Joe parking lot and took the steps two at a time up to her room. Tess released his hand only to find her key and slip it into the lock. An instant later Brady slammed the door behind her and took her in his arms.

He felt her body, warm and throbbing, crush against his chest as her arms fiercely wrapped around his neck. Her mouth lifted eagerly—searching, begging, commanding—as he claimed it with his own. There was nothing tentative about this volcanic embrace, nothing that allowed for questions or rules or logical restrictions of emotions and desires. All time for hesitation was past.

He didn't ask if he could stay. She did not invite him. They simply moved, kiss by kiss and touch by touch, from the doorway to the bed. In a matter of moments they were stretched out on it, lying hip to hip, thigh to thigh. Tess buried her soft lips in the hollow of his throat, stroking the sensitive area with her hot, moist tongue.

"Tess," he moaned into her hair, which was already starting to spill out of the cluster of pins that had crippled his fantasies all evening. "I want you so much. I've wanted you right from the start."

She kissed him fiercely, rolled him over and slipped one knee between his thighs. Her skirt flipped back, helped along by Brady's hand as it traced a path from her knee to her waist beneath the smooth fabric. Her body was fenced off from him by her pantyhose, and he tugged at the waistline impatiently.

He'd never meant for it to be like this. He'd never meant for it to happen at all. But he cared deeply for this very special woman and he belonged to no one else. He could not remember any reason why he should put her from him, any reason not to meet her own urgent needs and quell his own desire.

The feminine knee between his thighs was moving now, caressing his most intense erogenous zone. He stiffened, swelled, rose under the sensual pummeling, groaning as she edged more fully on top of him. Suddenly it was hard to think, hard to concentrate on the project undertaken by his own fingers.

Defeated by the pantyhose, he slid his hands up over Tess's breasts. His searching fingertips blazed an exploratory path across her bare collarbone, then slid under her blouse, deep inside the fortress of her bra. Gently they nudged the stiffening peaks still concealed from his view.

He heard her moan, sharply at first, then with a deep, ongoing kind of desperation. Still fully dressed, she locked her knees around his thighs and pressed urgently against him. In an instant his own desperate moan matched hers.

"Oh, Brady," Tess whispered fiercely, nipping sharply at his shoulder as her hair cascaded over his face. "Don't you dare change your mind again. Don't you dare make me wait."

It was faster than he'd ever imagined.

They clenched each other with an urgency so intense, that he felt as though they'd been engaged in foreplay for hours or even days. Ever since he'd kissed Tess hello in the morning, he'd been aching for this. And he knew that she had been aching for it, too.

He released her breasts and tried to pull down the pantyhose again, but Tess was ahead of him, tugging them off along with her panties in one fell swoop as she kicked her shoes to the floor. A moment later she was unhooking his belt, and he lifted his hips to help her as she tugged his pants down to his knees. At the same time Brady slipped both hands beneath the skirt and silky slip that still adorned her lower half. Bracing her backside with one broad palm, he slid his other hand down her smooth abdomen until his broad fingers could explore the secrets of her woman's nest of hair. Gently he teased the tiny ridge of pleasure he found hidden there until Tess began to moan. His searching fingers rotated in tiny, tingling circles as he desperately tried to make up for all the other times he'd aroused her, filled her with hope, and left her aching for something he'd never believed he could give her.

He waited until her gasps were rhythmic, urgent, almost beyond her control. Then he plunged two fingers deep inside her body, leaving his thumb to continue the erotic massage he'd already began, as he stroked her ever more urgently toward the peak of ecstasy.

By now Tess was thrusting against his hand, crying out her need for release. Brady longed to pull her down on top of his upthrust, swollen organ, but somewhere in the back of his mind he knew that he couldn't risk getting her pregnant, for her sake as well as his own, and somehow it didn't seem like the right moment to ask her if she'd taken any precautions. He tried to ignore the painfully urgent throb of desire in his own body and concentrate on the task at hand—meeting the immediate need of this beautiful woman who was nearly astride him. He was determined to satisfy Tess first, then he'd worry about his own needs. Surely he could restrain himself for just a little while longer.

And then her hands seized his naked masculinity. Small, skilled fingers rubbed and ever so lightly scratched the flint-hard tip. Brady gasped. Every inch of his body seemed to tingle and surge. Concentration vanished; so did control. When he thought he couldn't possibly take another moment of pleasure, Tess lowered her mouth as though to swallow him in the hot moist cavern, lashing him mercilessly with her tongue.

A moment later he was lost. So was Tess. She shuddered against his hands as he shuddered into her mouth, the two of them rocking the bed as though it were mired in an avalanche. He heard her cry out with unabashed urgency, then moan more hoarsely in fully met need. She whimpered again and again as he continued to caress her, each stroke more gentle now. Still breathing hard, he relished the soft heat of her tongue.

In the quiet moments that followed, Tess lowered herself to rest on his chest, and Brady tenderly wrapped both arms around her, trying to remember why he'd fought this beautiful bonding for so long. In the afterglow, he could not find one scrap of regret. He loved this woman—dammit, he did!—and he knew without hearing the words that she loved him, too.

He stroked her endless hair, now cloaking his body just as he'd always fantasized that it would. Tenderly he dropped a kiss on her temple. She nuzzled his throat, then kissed him in a different way than she had kissed him before. It was not a frantic kiss, a kiss of urgent desire. It was a kiss of promise, of bonding, of willingness to forget all the pain they'd caused each other before.

"You're not sorry?" he heard her whisper.

His only answer was a fierce and potent hug.

TESS WOKE at first light, as she always did, but she knew in an instant that there was nothing commonplace about the day's awakening. She felt deeply, richly satisfied and yet aroused—a paradox to her sleepy mind—and though she was in a strange bed where she'd never awakened before, she did not feel as though she were far from home.

Gradually, through the dawn mind's fog, she sensed another body touching hers. In fact, her limbs were so totally intertwined with those of the other body—a very lean, very male body—that it was hard to tell where hers stopped and his began. But as the night came back to her, she recalled distinctly that their bodies never had quite joined, though their lovemaking had been deliriously complete in every other way. During the long, sensuous night Brady had richly, creatively satisfied her... not just once but two or three or—how many?—glorious times.

She snuggled closer, listening to his steady heartbeat as she laid her head on his chest. It felt so good, so utterly right, to feel Brady's warmth, the intimacy of his arms loosely draped around her. Not once, from the moment he'd surrendered outside her hotel room, had he mentioned or even hinted at regret. Still, after all the times before last night that he'd told her that their situation was hopeless, her body tightened now as she waited for him to wake up. Waited for him to apologize or tell her that their magnificent, inevitable night together had been a mistake.

As if he could read her mind, he suddenly asked, "What time is your flight?"

She had assumed he was sleeping, and the abrupt sound of his voice took her off guard. It was not exactly the "Good morning, darling, let's pick up where we left off last night" sort of hello she'd been hoping for.

Without moving from his languid embrace, she replied, "Ten o'clock. But—" she just couldn't help herself "—I don't have to be back at work until Monday."

For a moment Brady said nothing; she heard him inhale sharply. His arms tightened around her shoulders ever so slightly, and one hand lightly caressed her sensitive spine.

"How long does it take you to get ready?"

It wasn't the question that threw her—Tess had her routine down to a science. It was the fact that he asked it at all. Surely he didn't *want* her to leave, did he, when they could have the whole weekend together? It might be their last rendezvous in months.

"About an hour if I'm going to the airport."

Suddenly the hand on her back stopped moving. In fact, Brady held completely still. Then he asked, "If you don't have to go to work until Monday, I assumed you'd want to spend the weekend at the Rocking T."

Tess lifted her head to face him, read the aching tenderness in his eyes. "Oh, Brady," she confessed, "I was afraid you wouldn't ask me."

Brady closed his eyes. He lifted one callused hand to touch her face.

"You said you didn't want this to happen. You made it so clear that—"

He stopped her with a quick kiss, then pressed her face against his shoulder as he lightly stroked her hair. "I said it would be a mistake for us to get involved. I said we'd pay for it down the road." He kissed the top of her head. "And we will. But right now—" he kissed her ear "—this feels so right to me, Tess. So right for you to be with me."

She pressed against his chest, her arms tightening around him.

"I just asked how long it took you to get ready because I've got some errands to run while you pack. I've got to get some grain and pick up some stuff I left at the Slow Joe. And then—" he lifted her chin so she could watch his face as he grinned "—I've got to stop at a drugstore before I lay a hand on you again." He kissed her, clearly holding back, then tacked on, "Although you realize that everybody in town will know about it in ten minutes flat."

Tess giggled. "Would you rather I go? Then they could wonder what cowboy I fell for while I was in town."

He nuzzled her neck. "I reckon they'd know the truth soon enough."

He kissed her again, stood, stretched slowly, then pulled on his jeans, which he found in a pile of clothing on the floor. Tess didn't move as she watched him dress, just enjoyed the view as she told him the brand of contraceptive sponge she liked best. He gave her a wink and an intimate pat on her behind, then told her he'd be back in half an hour.

At the door he stopped and stared at her.

"What?" she asked, suddenly uncertain of his intentions.

He glanced at the carpet, then at the walls and far drapes of the room as though the archaic interior decorating was suddenly of grave importance to him. Slowly he shoved both hands into his pockets, looking strangely young and ill at ease.

"I just want you to know that I've never done this before, Lady G. Taken a woman to bed in town. Taken her back to the ranch. In fact, since Claudia left the only female who's ever laid eyes on my house is Mandy, and she's only come twice. She's been too kind to say anything, but I'm sure that if she had time to warn you, she'd tell you to expect a log cabin or a soddy." Suddenly he looked almost shy. "It's a long way from a modern house, Tess. It's clean inside, but it's... primitive."

She heard the fear in his voice—no, the absolute certainty—that she'd hate his small home, reject the rough-hewn choice of accommodations he'd built himself. And she knew, from everything she'd heard, that she *wasn't* going to like it, at least not as a full-time abode. But she vowed to think of it as a summer vacation cabin, a welcome alternative to sleeping on the ground. And she also vowed to conceal her feelings from Brady. No matter what she thought of his hand-built home, she would not insult him. On Sunday night she would leave him convinced that there was room for Tess Hamilton on the Rocking T.

IT WAS EASIER said than done. The ride out was pleasant enough—though it was hotter than it had been in June—and every bit as scenic. Brady insisted that his old truck had not hit *every* pothole—there were just so many that it was inevitable that he'd hit one "now and again." Tess tried to concentrate on the joy of his company and the majesty of the surrounding red buttes. He held her hand during most of the ride, wrapped her in his radiant smile. She'd never seen him so happy, so ready to put all his cares aside.

And then, almost suddenly, they topped a ridge on an old dirt road and came upon an old miner's cabin. At least that was what it looked like to Tess.

"Civilization," she chirped, ready to make a comment on finding another ghost town so close to Silvergold. But then, in the nick of time, she spotted an old horse trailer between the barn and bunkhouse and half a dozen horses grazing in a nearby pasture.

There was nothing dingy about the barnyard. Chickens squawked, cats meowed, and black-throated swallows' nests lined every inch of the eaves of the huge barn.

The whole scene looked like a marvelous painting out of Currier and Ives. But the main house, if she could even call it that, was about the size of a studio apartment, and she had a sinking feeling that the old planks that served as the outer walls served as insulation and wallpaper as well.

A dog started to bark, then another, until half a dozen or more were yelping as they gamboled up to the old truck. A horse whinnied in greeting, and a wind vane lazily moved about an inch.

As a scene in a book of yesteryear, it would have been charming. And as a vacation cabin, it would have been fine beside a calm lake or a fast-running brook. But here in the middle of nowhere—with no air conditioning, no heat, no phone, and no women friends, copy machines, computers, grocery stores or mail service nearby—it was a sentence to a lifetime as a miserable hermit, a life Brady Trent had chosen for himself.

Tess was still trying to make sense of his decision—and trying to come up with something flattering to say—when Brady, his voice dark with disappointment, broke the silence.

"I warned you," he said softly, covering her hand with his own. "It's no good pretending you could ever make this your home."

SHE TRIED. He had to give her credit for that.

She didn't lie, exactly, but she did heap praise on everything she could think of—the size of the barn, the sturdiness of the corral fence, the majesty of the front window's view. She called the kitchen "orderly" and the wood stove "authentic." She grew a bit pale when she saw the twin bed tucked away in one corner of the living room, but she managed to comment on the beauty of the handmade quilt that Mandy had made for him.

For the first time in years Brady looked at his house with fresh eyes, and he wasn't impressed with what he saw. Mentally he started counting the pennies in his savings account, wondering how much it would take to finish off the interior walls with paint or even wallpaper...what it would take to make the place appealing enough that Tess would want to stay.

It would take a fortune, he realized glumly. *And even then there'd be no guarantee. Besides, if she doesn't love it the way it is, she'd never be happy living here with me.*

"I want the whole tour," Tess declared as soon as she'd run out of feeble compliments. "Do I get to see the bunkhouse and the barn?"

Brady smiled, grateful for her pluckiness. "I'll show you the barn and I'll even let you take a carrot to Calypso. But if I brought a woman into the bunkhouse, neither Willie nor the Jenson boys would ever forgive me. And nowadays, good help is hard to find."

Tess laughed and tossed back her ponytail. "I hope they respect your privacy with equal determination. At least while I'm here."

He nodded. "They'll be stunned, no doubt, but I don't think they'll be stupid enough to bother us once they realize I've got company."

He took her hand, as though it were a natural thing to do, and led her through the structure he and Joey had built with their bare hands. He had a mare with a four-month-old filly in a small corral near the barn and a caged baby bobcat, which he'd found orphaned on a recent tour and hadn't quite figured out what to do with. She was fascinated by the chicken coop and helped him collect some eggs.

"But Brady, don't you have a cow?" she asked when he'd finished the tour. "No predawn milking?"

He shrugged. "No, it's not worth the trouble. Cows need cowboys with very regular schedules, and during the summer mine's a bit too crazy. During the tour somebody always comes back here twice a day to check on the animals, but the times vary. We don't like to make it obvious to the tourists."

Suddenly Tess was studying him with a sweet and knowing grin. "It was pretty obvious to me when you slipped off to Silvergold."

He tugged on her ponytail. "Of course it was. I wanted to show you my etchings."

Tess chuckled. "It would have served you right if you'd permanently injured your nose on the bars of that jail. You broke my heart when you abandoned me in that cell."

He remembered the afternoon vividly... not to mention the following night of ripe frustration with which he'd paid for his determination to keep Tess at a distance.

"It's the Rocking T's policy never to leave a guest dissatisfied," he teased, "or *un*satisfied, as the case may be. Would you like to plan an afternoon picnic to Silvergold to see if I can do better this time, or would you rather have your money back?"

Tess laughed, then tugged him closer and gave him a very provocative, promising kiss. "I'd rather go to Silvergold. But I'll be monitoring your performance very closely this time."

As it turned out, Tess had nothing to monitor during the first hour they spent at Silvergold, because the mechanics of finding a good "table" near the abandoned hotel and eating without swallowing red dust took a good deal of time. As they sat cross-legged on the old blanket Brady had produced, they compared notes on ghost towns each had visited in the past.

"I was overwhelmed by the one near Cody," Tess informed him. "This couple has spent twenty-five years or so collecting every famous building they could get their hands on. They've got the original house of Butch Cassidy and the Sundance Kid, an old jail, a schoolhouse, you name it."

"You mean they didn't rehabilitate a ghost town that was already standing?"

"No, they made their own. Then they gathered up all the artifacts they could find to furnish the buildings. They created a museum with the leftovers."

"I could create a museum with my artifacts. I've been collecting them all my life. Not all of them fit in with the wagon-train tours."

"Your collection is amazing, Brady," Tess praised him, and he knew she was telling the truth. She'd spent a good half hour studying his old furniture and cooking utensils, and she'd been particularly impressed by the number of samples in his barbed wire collection. She'd also oohed and aahed over some old pictures he'd collected and asked for one of him riding Buck to enlarge and hang on the wall of her condo. "If there was some way you *could* set up a paying museum, you could really increase your revenues."

He sighed. "I've thought about rehabilitating old Silvergold, but I'm not sure I could bear to have strangers tramping through here. Besides, it would cost a fortune, even if I knew how to do it, and I surely don't have a penny to spare."

Tess grinned. In fact she absolutely glowed. "I'd give my eyeteeth to rehabilitate a whole ghost town, Brady!

I'm always falling in love with some wonderful little school or bank or old library, always planning how I'd love to fix it up. But as soon as H.W.P. is done with the preliminary investigation, it's back to L.A. I never get to see how the restoration comes out." She gazed longingly at the cluster of weathered buildings around them. "Nothing would be more fantastic than bringing a ghost town back to life."

"You mean like Tombstone, where they stage the shooting at the O.K. Corral every Sunday?"

She laughed. "Well, you'd probably enjoy the shoot-out more than I would. But to create a place with everybody in period dress—"

"We could hire Roberta!"

"And set up an opera house and dancing girls in an old saloon! Oh, Brady—" her eyes glistened "—wouldn't it be wonderful!"

For a moment he shared her pleasure, but then he remembered it was only a daydream. Planning anything with Tess beyond this weekend was surely a fantasy, a fantasy as distant as his vision of Tess riding Calypso down the streets of Silvergold wearing only her hair.

Suddenly he realized that she was staring at him.

"What?"

"What are you thinking, Brady? You've got the strangest look on your face."

He shook his head, embarrassed. "It doesn't matter."

"Of course it matters. I'm curious," she pressed.

He shook his head with more energy. "I was just mulling on another fantasy. One that involves you in a charming state of undress."

Tess, currently clad in snug jeans and a new Slow Joe T-shirt, smiled at him provocatively. "Tell me," she beguiled him. "Maybe I can help."

"No," he insisted, turning red.

Tess moved one hand on his thigh, grinning devilishly. "Yes."

He gave up. He knew where she was headed, knew where he wanted her to go. He offered her an embarrassed, apologetic smile as he admitted, "Lady Godiva." He glanced at the empty Silvergold main street. "On a horse."

She grinned. She laughed. Then she slid her hand back and forth on his thigh, each time edging closer to his groin and further from his knee. "Really?" she prodded.

Again he flushed. By now he was too aroused to deny his fantasy. "Really, Lady G."

Suddenly Tess abandoned him, leaving his body aching for her departing hand. Still laughing, she was scampering back toward the shade where the horses were tied. Over her shoulder she called back, "Clean up the dishes, will you, Brady? I don't think you'll be in the mood when I get back."

He grinned, savoring the provocative sashay of her hips as she sauntered away from him. Then he did as she'd suggested, clearing their picnic lunch off the blanket and trying not to think about what Tess was doing out of sight behind the jail. He concentrated on the antics of a rock squirrel and a whip-tail lizard, listening to the incessant squawking of a pair of pinon jays. He glanced at the blue and white columbine twisting in and out of the weathered boards of a half-collapsed saloon; he studied the clumps of serviceberry in the distance. He loved the land and every spark of life in it, but he drew no peace from his perusal of it now. His body throbbed for his woman.

She made him wait for almost ten minutes, and by the time he heard Calypso coming, Brady was certain that he'd lost his mind. He was still sitting at the edge of the now-empty blanket when he first caught sight of horse and rider, but one glance at the rider and he forgot about the horse.

Her hair, brushed to perfection, was draped over her cheeks, her breasts, her thighs. Only a few strands cloaked her naked back, and despite the curtain of hair, a fair amount of midriff was visible, not to mention the darker curls between her legs that bore little resemblance to the long blond tresses.

Slowly she rode toward him, one knee locked around the saddle horn as she feigned a sidesaddle pose. There was something intensely provocative about that position on horseback, one that spoke of feminine beauty. The sidesaddle, after all, had been created to keep a woman looking chaste when she rode in a long dress. Yet there was nothing chaste about the naked woman riding toward him now, her enticing, entrancing, alluring blue eyes beckoning to him with an unspoken urgency that was downright primeval.

The night before, Brady had been certain that he'd never been more aroused in his life. But nothing could compare with the fire that gripped him now. He waited endlessly while Tess drifted toward him. As the breeze ruffled her long tresses, her lovely breasts protruded ever more fully, and the intimate joining of her legs was exposed.

Suddenly Brady couldn't stand it any longer. He bolted to his feet and ran the last few steps to reach her, tugging the reins from her hands to ground-tie the horse.

A moment later his hands circled her back and lifted her off the saddle.

The bewitching smile on her face told him she wasn't going to make him wait.

TESS TRIED to cook dinner for Brady that night, but he insisted that it was easier to take care of everything himself. She knew he hadn't meant to brush her off, but his comment solidified the point he'd been making since the day they'd first met: he was used to taking care of himself. He had no room in his life for a woman.

Since the first moment he'd taken her hand outside the Redpoint Hotel, she'd been too deliriously happy to worry about the future. Brady was finally beside her, sharing his small home, giving her a glimpse into his real life. It was more than she'd ever dreamed of. All the rest was gravy.

She was not surprised at his passion as a lover. She'd known they would sizzle right from the start. Still, she was thrilled to discover that the reality was even more terrific than her imaginings. And never in her life had she made love with a man who worked harder at meeting her own sexual needs. Clearly he did not think that sex was a one-way street—a feminine obligation to a man. In fact, despite her obvious desire for him, he'd gently asked her this afternoon if all their sexual activity in such a brief period of time might be making her body a little tender. If she needed to back off a bit, he insisted, she should feel free to tell him so.

Tess didn't want to back off. She wanted to fill every moment of this weekend with memories to cherish after she left, memories that could counteract the past month of angst. But as she watched Brady carve a roast chicken and serve it on his best chipped plates, she knew that the real pain—now that she'd known the magic of his loving—was yet to come.

"DO YOU HAVE EVERYTHING?" he asked softly as he stood in the shadow of the open door on Sunday morning.

It was an exquisite dawn. A bright, shimmering host of sunlight was welcoming the new day. Just beyond the barn a horned lark was winging toward a distant clump of blackbrush, and far to the east, where the juniper-studded cliffs speared the clouds, two bald eagles cruised sky-high.

"I think so," Tess said softly. "If I left anything crucial, you can always send it to me."

As soon as the words were out, her face darkened, and Brady knew she was fighting tears. He wanted to go to her, to put his arms around her, but he knew she'd break down if he did. They'd both gone into this weekend with their eyes wide open, knowing the price they'd have to pay for it down the road. The bill was due and payable as soon as he put her on the airplane. He didn't want to start paying interest now.

She stood in the center of his tiny home and glanced around it, as though memorizing every inch for the long months to come. Then she turned to him slowly, her long, loose hair flooding her shoulders in the brilliant desert light.

"I don't want to leave, Brady," she whispered.

His eyes met hers. "Then stay."

Tears glistened. "I can't. You know I can't. Even if you were sure that you...that you really wanted me for...for—"

"Forever?" he finished for her.

She nodded. The tears were streaming down her face now.

"I'm not sure of that yet, Tess," he told her honestly. "At the moment the idea sounds like heaven on earth. But we both need some time apart to gain some objectivity about this, you know. We need time to think, time to plan."

"Are we going to plan, Brady? Are we really going to plan a future? Or am I going to get a letter from you in a week or two saying, 'It was swell, kid, but you know it'll never work'?"

He crossed the floor then, in two quick strides. He cupped her tear-moistened face with both hands and tenderly kissed each cheek. "I won't break up with you by mail. I promise. And I'll call you whenever I'm in town."

"Even if it's during work hours?"

"Yes. If that's what you want."

"Of course it's what I want. I'd tell you do to it if you were traveling in a foreign country, Brady. And you are, aren't you? At least, you will be when winter moves in."

Slowly, reluctantly, he nodded. "You've got to remind yourself that not hearing from me is different from not hearing from any other man you've ever known. It doesn't mean I've forgotten you or I've changed my mind. It just means I can't get to a phone."

The tears were flowing freely now. "I miss you already. I missed you the last time I left here even when I knew there was no hope. This time—"

He stopped her with a quick kiss, then pulled her fully in his arms. He felt sick inside, weak, powerless, and he didn't know how to take away her pain. Everything she feared might come true.

"All I can promise you is that until you hear me say it's over, then nothing has changed. Okay?"

He felt her nod against his throat.

"Unless—" he swallowed a great lump "—you're the one who decides that this long-distance courtship is not for you."

He didn't know where that word "courtship" came from. He didn't know where it would lead. All he knew was that he desperately wanted to find a way to keep Tess with him on the Rocking T for the rest of his life, and the chances of that were about as good as building a snowman outside his barn in July.

CHAPTER TWELVE

TESS WAS SO QUIET her first day back on the job that at least three people asked her if she was ill. Her supervisor suggested that she go home and take the next day off. But the last thing she wanted to do was face her empty condominium...a home that featured everything in the world she wanted, except for Brady Trent.

Brady's little cabin, of course, was at the opposite end of the spectrum. It featured *nothing* she wanted—except the man who'd built it with his own bare hands.

It wasn't a bad little hut, she admitted in the privacy of her heart, and she knew that if she'd been a pioneer woman who had just finished four months of wagon-train travel across the plains, she'd simply adore it. And, for a week in the summer now and again, she could pretend just that. But for a lifetime? Not a chance. Brady knew it and so did she.

She understood why Claudia had left him. She could never admit it to Brady, of course, but if Tess had found herself battling a difficult pregnancy in deep winter, she probably would have gone to New York, too. Or Redpoint, at least. Anywhere where there was central heating, a doctor and a telephone. Why was that so difficult for Brady to understand? He was a mature, highly educated man. He'd spent time back east as a young man and his father, who had been very polite when Brady had introduced him after the meeting, was a banker of some standing in the tiny town. Brady's insistence on total isolation somehow didn't ring true to Tess. She understood his love of the red-rock land—she loved it, too—but she could not accept his refusal to consider living anywhere else . . . even part-time.

Nor could she accept the alternatives—living without him altogether, or living on the Rocking T.

BRADY SHIFTED UNEASILY in his seat in Harold Dobson's big hotel dining room, surrounded by the other key players on the Redpoint Historical Preservation Committee. It was obvious that everyone was getting jumpy and losing heart. Tess's presentation last month had been the high point of their battle, but now they were running out of steam.

"The problem, as I see it, is still money," said Harold Dobson, glancing pointedly at Brady. "Linda McCray told me last week that she'd really like to support us, but she has grave reservations about tying the merchants' hands. If nobody will give us loans, then she doesn't think it's fair or feasible to require refurbishment."

The problem, as I see it, is you're losing your guts, Brady wanted to reply. Councilwoman Linda McCray was a good soul, and Brady could see she had a point. He also understood, without Harold stating it explicitly, that Linda—and maybe some other key figures—could be swayed if even one crucial Redpoint banker gave his support to the historical district concept. Harold, along with several other merchants, blamed Brady for failing to win his dad's support.

Before Brady could come to his own defense, Joe said softly, "I think maybe we need to broaden our scope." His tone was tense, edgy . . . almost protective. "Just because we've traditionally gone to Redpoint bankers for this kind of thing doesn't mean we can't go beyond our local sphere of interest for financial assistance. I suspect that Tess Hamilton could give us the names of a dozen institutions in L.A. or back east that would be glad to approve restoration loans or become equity partners just for the tax credits."

"An out-of-town bank would charge us an arm and a leg for a loan," maintained Oscar Reynolds, rubbing his double chin. "I've already checked that out for the church. Joey, you know as well as I do that Redpoint bankers have always undercut the interest rate by a point or two to help us out."

"Have they?" Brady asked bluntly. "Or have they done it just to keep local business?"

Several pairs of eyes turned on him in surprise. At that moment, he was certain, people were staring at Jake Trent's son, not Brady Trent, businessman-wagon master. Brady felt a twinge of guilt for making a comment that could be construed as disloyality to his father. But he thought he'd made a valid point. The door of local business support could swing both ways.

"Let's face it. This local bank stranglehold is what's keeping us from making a go of this historic district. Personally, I'm not willing to see this committee fold just because three stubborn old men won't consider another way of looking at our situation. We've all approached them, singly and en masse, and failed on each occasion. I say it's time to find some other avenue of financial assistance for those of us who may need it from time to time."

The committee tossed the idea around for a while before Joe brought up another subject. "While Tess was here she mentioned a historic preservation conference in

Las Vegas that I think one of us ought to attend," he suggested. "There are workshops for professionals, of course, but there is one whole series of presentations for do-it-your-selfers like us. It's the first weekend of September."

Several people asked questions, the most crucial being, "How much does it cost?" In the end there was a general consensus that somebody ought to represent the group and everybody would chip in.

Brady had little to say during the discussion. Personally he couldn't see how he could spare a penny, and if by chance he could, he'd spend it to rendezvous somewhere with Tess. She'd been gone for two weeks already—make that two and a half—and he was still haunted by the scent of her hair.

I knew right from the start I'd pay for this, he'd told himself every day since she'd left the ranch. *But even then I never knew it would hurt this much.*

It wasn't their current separation that was so terrible. If he'd known he would see her in a week, in a month, even in a long year that would be the *only* year they'd be apart, he could have weathered it with grace. But all he could see was a bleak future of awkward calls and clumsy letters, gradually moving further and further apart until it grew too embarrassing to write anything at all.

At the moment he had three letters in his pocket, which he'd brought into town to mail—the first romantic, the second sad but hot, the third already showing some signs of embarrassment for the first two and written with more restraint. He hadn't yet decided which one to send, or whether he'd be smarter not to send anything at all.

TESS HAD BEEN HOME for three weeks on the Friday night that she found Roberta, clad in an old plaid shirt and blue jeans, sitting on the front step of her condo with her nose in a book called *Women's Suffrage in the Old West*.

"Roberta!" Tess greeted her with delight. "I wasn't expecting you this weekend, was I?"

Roberta gave her a toothy grin. "Of course not. But you should have been."

Tess gave her a quick hug and unlocked the door. "Why is that?" she asked.

"Because the letter I got from you yesterday made it clear that you were feeling like death warmed over. I thought you might need a shoulder to cry on." She shrugged, looking almost embarrassed by her compassion. "If this isn't a good time, Tess, just—"

Tess shook her head, fighting fresh tears, and hugged Roberta again. "It's a wonderful time. I need to see you more than anybody else in the whole world."

"Almost anybody," corrected Roberta gently.

A tear or two did spill over before Tess got a hold of herself. "I don't want to talk about Brady. There really isn't anything to say."

"Maybe not to me, Tess, but I think you ought to talk to *him*. The man told you he wouldn't be able to get word to you very often. Just because it's been a couple of weeks—"

"Roberta, he promised to write to me right away. One of his men comes into town at least twice a week in the summer to collect and deliver the guests if nothing else. And I, fool that I am, have already written to him several times, with naked honesty about my feelings, I might add." She swallowed the hurt, the absolute conviction that despite Brady's promises—and whatever feelings he possessed for her—he'd been right all along. It just wasn't going to work. "Not a word in three weeks, Roberta. I don't think he could write anything that would be more articulate than that."

This time Roberta didn't argue with her. Instead she suggested stoutly, "Pioneer women had to go months without mail, Tess, and they survived it. So will you. After all, if you're going to fall in love with a man from another century, I guess you're going to be bound by some of the constraints of the time."

Tess wiped away the last tears, ordered a home-delivered pizza for their dinner, and fixed her friend a cold soda with ice before she settled down on the couch. "Enough about me. What have you been doing with yourself?"

At once Roberta's eyes took on a glow. "I've been whipping up a wonderful idea for my Women of the West class that you won't believe. It came to me on the way home from Redpoint, actually, and it's sort of been stewing in my mind ever since." Her grin grew broad. "You remember when I jumped up on the wagon tongue on the Rocking T and gave my favorite Susan B. Anthony speech?"

Tess nodded. The memory was indelibly printed on her mind.

"Those other guests—forgive my lack of modesty—but they were enthralled, Tess, weren't they?"

Tess managed to smile. "Stunned is more like it."

"Well, they did listen intently. I got their attention long enough to get across the gist of my lecture. Right?" For Roberta, she sounded uncharacteristically hesitant, and Tess dragged herself from the fog of her own miseries long enough to realize that Roberta wasn't just trying to get her mind off Brady but actually sharing something important with her.

"Roberta, they loved you," she assured her friend. "You were the hit of the week. I'm surprised Brady didn't hire you on the spot."

The toothy grin returned. "Don't I wish! But he never mentioned it." She leaned a bit closer, eyes aglow. "But he did give me a wonderful idea. He asked me once how my students liked my presentations, and I told him I'd never done one in class. He said I was missing the boat. At the time, I thought he was kidding, but the more I thought about it, I think he's absolutely right."

Tess was intrigued. "I'm not quite sure I follow you."

"How do you think the students would react if I showed up dressed as Susan B. Anthony the first day? I could give them her speech, word for word, and then get them to talk about it. Then when I give them a related reading assignment, it might mean something." She was so delighted she was glowing. Her inner beauty rose to the surface and splashed like sunlight across her strong face. "And after that maybe I could try another character. Maybe I could even have *them* come as different characters. A different role-playing episode every day. Or every week, at least. Instead of a term paper, they pick a suffragist, dress and act the part as they give her speech!"

Tess loved the idea, and she tried to put aside her own misery long enough to applaud Roberta's creativity. "I think it's terrific. But what about the men? Are you going to put them in dresses, too?"

"Great idea, Tess!" Roberta teased. "The women's rights movement in this country has always had a few enlightened male supporters. It might take a little more research for my male students to uncover their speeches, but I could give them a little hint here and there." She looked intently at Tess, then asked, "So what do you think? Should I go for it when school starts next week?"

"Absolutely," Tess concurred. "Strike while the iron is hot."

They talked some more, but before Roberta could go into a great deal more detail, the doorbell rang and the pizza was delivered. It was a great pizza—except for the anchovies Roberta had insisted on—and Tess relished it as she enjoyed Roberta's conversation. It wasn't until the pizza was finished and both women were full to the gills that Tess realized she'd been so excited to see Roberta's car out front that she'd neglected to check the mailbox. By now she had little hope for word from Brady, but she excused herself anyway to check the mail just in case.

The box was stuffed with mail-order catalogs, the latest copy of *American History Illustrated* magazine, a letter from Tess's parents and a telephone bill.

Sandwiched between the bill and the letter was also a postcard with a picture of a single, lonely wagon wheel. On the back was scrawled boldly:

> Lady G—
>
> I've written you half a dozen letters and torn up every one. I miss you like hell. What else is there to say?
>
> B.
>
> P.S. I'm sorry.

Tess read the card a dozen times before she tucked it back into the pile, and even then she wasn't sure whether to be wounded or relieved. What did he mean by "I'm sorry"? Was he sorry he hadn't written, sorry he felt so lousy...or sorry he'd have to say goodbye?

IT WAS A SWELTERING August day when Jake spotted Brady's old truck across the street at the Redpoint Feed and Seed. He waited, for almost twenty minutes, to see if his son might drop by the bank to see him, but when Brady finally appeared—mired under a hundred-pound sack of grain—he never even glanced in Jake's direction. He dumped the sack in the back of the truck and retraced his steps inside, and by the time he returned with another burlap sack, Jake was waiting for him beside the truck.

"Good afternoon, Dad," Brady said civilly, without a trace of filial warmth. "What brings you outside this time of day?"

Jake tried to swallow his hurt, but he knew his voice was gruff as he said, "I just spotted your truck and thought I'd say hello."

Brady dumped the heavy sack in the back, then hopped up on the bed of the truck to straighten it. "So how's everything at the bank?" he asked stiffly.

"Fine," said Jake.

"And Arleen?"

"She's fine, too. Been after me to get you over for dinner. She hasn't seen you in a while and she worries that you're not eating right. You know how women are."

Brady shot him a suspicious glance. "I haven't had a woman cook for me on a daily basis since I was ten, Dad, and nobody's ever thought I was underfed."

It was true; Brady was thin and lanky, but firmly muscled and incredibly robust. Nobody who so much as glanced at him could have any doubts about the state of his health. Whatever combination of food and exercise he chose these days obviously agreed with him.

"I guess . . . I guess she'd just like to spend some time with you, son." In a smaller voice he tacked on, "So would I."

"Maybe after the tourist season, Dad. Right now I really can't spare the time."

Jake glanced at his watch. It was eleven forty-five. More bluntly he asked, "Well, it's almost noon. Why don't we get caught up over a bit of lunch?"

Brady hopped off the bed of the truck in a single, graceful bound. "Sorry. I'll be loading up here for another fifteen minutes and then I've got to get back home. I've got three horses to shoe before tomorrow."

Jake looked him straight in the eye and called his bluff. "Surely a half an hour for a hamburger wouldn't hurt."

"Time is money," Brady answered coolly. "Isn't that what you always taught me?"

"I also taught you that family comes first," Jake snapped back. "All those years that we were alone together, Brady, all that mattered was that we had each other."

Brady's eyes darkened. "You gave me a good childhood, Dad, I'll give you that. But all that 'we had each other' stuff sure didn't warm the cockles of my heart when you persuaded my wife to leave me. And it sure didn't offer me much comfort when you cheered that my ranch was going belly-up."

Jake felt a keen rush of color to his face. "That's not fair, Brady, and you know it! I had nothing to do with your divorce. Claudia would have left you regardless of my advice about where she spent that last winter."

"Maybe, maybe not. But I didn't have to lose the ranch. All it would have taken was a pittance of what you've got stored in there—" he pointed toward the bank "—which you used to say would all be mine someday, anyway."

"It *will* be yours!" Jake insisted, wondering if he dared mention the piece of perplexing information he'd recently acquired regarding Brady's own financial picture. "It looks like I'm going to have to die first, since you won't become my partner, but as long as there's enough for Arleen—"

"I figured you'd leave it all to her at this point," Brady snapped. "Or maybe to charity. Or even to some organization you hate. *I'm* sure as hell not counting on it. After all, haven't you rewritten your will to say I can only inherit if I give up the ranch?"

"Brady, you know I'd never do—"

"Isn't it enough that I lost it once and you didn't lift a finger to help? Are you determined to undermine the livelihoods of half the folks in this town to make sure I fail again?"

Jake loosened his tie; suddenly he was having trouble breathing. "You can't believe I wanted you to fail, son. All I've ever wanted was your happiness."

"Of course!" Brady's tone was rich with sarcasm. "That's why you let Claudia see another man right under your roof without telling me till half the town found out! That's why you let me lose the ranch sooner than loan me a lousy extra hundred bucks a month!"

"I didn't know she was having an affair until the very end!" Jake burst out, feeling sweat pool on the bald spot on his head. "I swear it! And even then, if I took an extra day or two to tell you, it was only because I couldn't bear to be the one to break your heart!"

"But I suppose breaking my heart didn't bother you when you told Oscar you couldn't possibly lend your support to the historical committee?" Brady countered fiercely.

Jake had no answer for that blow. While he struggled for words, Brady ploughed right on.

"Look, Dad, here's the way I see it," growled his son. "You've never given up this pie-in-the-sky dream of yours that someday I'll take over the bank. Trent and Son Savings and Loan." He drew a line in the air with his thumb and forefinger as if to make a sign of the words. "It's not a bad dream, but it's not *my* dream. For a long time I tried to pretend that it was because it was so important to you. But finally I realized that I had a dream of my own."

"A child's dream!" Jake croaked. "A little boy's fantasy, playing cowboys and Indians!"

Brady straightened the Stetson on his dark hair and squinted against the sun. "Look at me, Dad. Really take a good hard look." He waited while Jake did. "I'm not a child anymore. I've given up all my dreams. I'm never going to pretend that I'll find a woman who's willing to give up everything to share my life on the ranch. I'm never going to pretend that I can start a business, work hard, and never have money problems again. And I sure as hell won't ever believe that I can count on my father to stand beside me through thick and thin."

Jake winced.

Before he could defend himself, Brady charged on. "All I've got—all I'm sure of in this world—is that I own the Rocking T. And whether you like it, or understand it, or even admit it, Dad—" his expression was positively fierce "—the Rocking T owns me."

BRADY PUT TESS out of her agony three days after she got his postcard.

The phone rang around three o'clock on Tuesday afternoon. "Tess Hamilton speaking," she declared as soon as she picked up her extension.

A deep male voice on the other end said simply, "Tess."

It was the first time she'd ever talked to Brady on the phone, but she knew his voice instantly. Joy and fear cycloned through her as she remembered his promise never to break up with her by mail. If it was too far to come in person, she knew he'd resort to the phone.

Trembling, she replied, "Hi, Brady. It's wonderful to hear your voice."

She heard him sigh heavily. "I'm no good on the phone," he answered. "I just... I was in town, and I didn't get a letter this time, so I thought I'd... well, see how you were doing."

She realized that he was trying not to say, "I miss you," which was a thousand times better than what she'd feared he'd called to say. The fear began to subside; a new kind of trembling took its place. Surely everything was okay?

Still cautious, she warmly confessed, "I felt silly writing all those letters to somebody who never wrote back. I didn't know... well, how you were feeling."

He swore softly, then spoke with a firmer tone. "I do write you, Tess. I write you all the time. I just can't bring myself to mail the letters. They're so stupid. So...gushy. Every time I think about anybody seeing all the sentimental slop I've written down my ears turn pink."

Tess closed her eyes. How she ached for a single word of that "sentimental slop"! "Brady, you don't have to feel embarrassed about sharing your feelings with me. How could your letters possibly get any gooeyer than the ones I've sent to you?"

He exhaled again, clearly frustrated with himself. "Tess, I warned you this was going to be terrible. God knows, I warned myself. Even so, I never imagined—" he broke off and breathed deeply once again.

"That it would be this hard," Tess finished for him.

There was a long silence before he said, "Yes."

"Please send me your letters. All of them. Tell me about the bobcat and the horses and the silly things the tourists do. Tell me what you had for breakfast and how you sleep at night. Let me in, Brady. Let me share your life even if it's long-distance. I can stand the separation if it's just . . . miles between us. I can't bear it if you shut me out."

He swore again, softly but insistently. "Dammit, Tess, I want to see you. I want to touch your hair. I want to hold you in my arms."

Tears suddenly filled her eyes. "Brady, let's start working on a plan to get together," she begged him. "If we knew for certain there was a time we could look forward to, maybe it wouldn't be so hard."

Again he sighed. "Tess, I don't have a penny to use for traveling. And I can't justify leaving the ranch during tourist season even if I could. But anytime you can come back here—"

He broke off as a childish shriek exploded in the background.

"The girls are home," he told her, not needing to explain that he was at Joe's. "I can't talk much longer."

It also went without saying that he couldn't keep talking in the same intimate way. Suddenly the conversation shifted to more prosaic things. He'd received a sweet letter and a hundred-dollar contribution to the historic committee from plucky old Trudy Lincoln, who'd apparently learned about the situation from her mail subscription to the *Redpoint Register*. Other contributions had also come in, but the support was too little, too late, for Harold Dobson, who'd put the hotel on the market yesterday anyway. Oscar Reynolds, Joe and Brady had spent half the night trying to get him to change his mind to no avail. Without a bank loan for renovation, he maintained, the situation was absolutely hopeless.

Brady guardedly expressed his concerns about the Rocking T. If the hotel's buyer had the money and the inclination to refurbish it, the wagon-train business would probably carry on as before. But if the hotel were leveled and replaced by any other enterprise, his ranch was in serious jeopardy.

"Joe wants somebody to go to Vegas to that convention you mentioned," Brady also informed her. "But we'd all have to chip in and I, for one, just don't have the money to spare. I've got a tiny savings account built up, but I need it for emergencies. Otherwise I'd spend it on a vacation with you."

The idea filled Tess with such hope that she almost proposed a specific weekend plan, but before she could make her suggestions, the noisy little voices in the background made conversation impossible.

"Hey, Uncle Brady!" Tess heard the girls call out. "When did you get here?" She could ever hear some welcoming kisses.

What I'd give for a kiss from him, she secretly mourned. *What I'd give to come home and find him waiting in my kitchen!*

But when he hung up a few moments later without making any effort to plan a rendezvous, she struggled to accept the fact that it would never be.

CHAPTER THIRTEEN

IT WAS ONLY DUSK when Brady's plane touched down in Las Vegas two weeks later, but the city was already awash with signs of nocturnal life. Flashing neon signs advertised everything—gambling, wedding chapels, famous comedians and singers for every hotel's show. In some other time and place, the excitement of seeing Dolly Parton live might have appealed to Brady, but at the moment there was only one woman in Nevada who held any appeal for him, and he'd booked her for a private show.

It was Joe who had eventually pointed out that Brady could represent the Historical Preservation Committee as well as anyone, especially since the conference was sandwiched in between wagon-train treks. It was, he insisted, crucial that *somebody* from Redpoint attend the event, and if Brady could cut the group's cost by splitting a room with another conference attendee, so much the better.

Tess had been ecstatic when he'd called her back with the news. She'd also raved about the half dozen letters he'd mailed since their last awkward telephone conversation. His missives were clumsy—not because he was inarticulate on paper, but because it was so hard to share his feelings with Tess when he wasn't really sure of them himself. Most of the time he tried to write about the weather and the livestock, because it was easier to share with her the more prosaic parts of his days. But sooner or later his loneliness would creep into every letter. The kind of loneliness he remembered keenly from his married days...when his wife had chosen to live so far away.

He hadn't mentioned his last fight with his dad to Tess, but it was weighing heavily on his mind. She knew a little bit about the strain between them—and had surely sensed it when Brady had introduced the two after the Redpoint meeting—but he wasn't sure that anybody but Joe could understand the subtleties of their particular situation. He was as mad as hell at his father, but only because he loved him so terribly much. If they hadn't once been close, their current distance wouldn't have troubled him. Somehow, being angry with his dad in Redpoint was easier to bear than being angry with him on an airplane to Las Vegas; if anything went wrong, his hurtful words would be Jake's last memory of his only son.

Brady had dressed for the flight in cotton twill pants and an old but respectable blazer and felt that his attire was appropriate. But when he paid the cabbie and marched into the hotel reserved for the conference, he realized that he'd grossly underestimated the swankiness of the place.

The carpet was an impractical shade of pink, and the lobby furniture was largely white and pale green silk. A water fountain splashed continuously in the center of the reception area, giving the illusion that it wasn't as hot as Hades outside. The mere sight of it had Brady longing for the sight of the Rocking T's natural, leech-ridden spring.

After dumping his duffel bag beside two fine leather suitcases in the room Tess had reserved for them, Brady hiked down sixteen flights of stairs—out of sheer recalcitrance more than a desire for exercise—to the conference registration area on the third floor. Restlessly he glanced at the posted schedule of activities to figure out his best bet for the first evening session following the keynote presentation, which he'd already missed. He noted a workshop in the "Do-It-Yourselfers" series entitled, "Saving Your Favorite Landmark from the Bulldozer." He was about to leave for the specified conference room when he saw "E.T. Hamilton" listed as a presenter of another workshop.

In an instant he knew that he could not possibly wait for two more hours to see Tess when the opportunity was so close at hand. And, strangely, he also realized that he wanted to study her anonymously for a while before they found themselves alone. Their last meeting, in Grand Junction, had been awkward and strained. Here in Las Vegas—where everything felt odd to him—he needed time to get a grip on himself so that he didn't do anything to upset Tess.

He double-checked the number on the schedule, then hurried down the hall and slipped into the listed conference room. "Recreating Historical Ambience" was the title of the workshop, according to the sign by the door, but Brady would have attended it if the subject had been "False Eyelashes—Status Symbol of Soiled Doves" or "How Pioneer Women Used Cactus Spine Needles to Darn Woven Agave Socks." Suddenly he was absolutely desperate to see his woman's face.

But when he slipped in and took a chair in the back of the room, he couldn't find that fetching female anywhere. Oh, there *was* an attractive blonde behind the podium wearing an H.W.P. name tag, which would surely say "Tess Hamilton" when he got close enough to read it, and she did, in a fleeting sort of way, bare a passing resemblance to his Tess. But she did not look like the woman who'd ridden bare bottomed through a ghost town just a month ago. She didn't look like a woman who could ever be at home on the Rocking T.

Even in Redpoint, when Tess had dressed quite formally for her speech, she'd chatted with the locals with a charming brand of small-town friendliness, which she obviously considered out of place in this lecture to several hundred people. Tonight she wore a crisp black suit with a small scarlet puff in her vest pocket. She was armed with three-inch spike heels, and her hair was pulled straight back in a dignified bun. Every word that came out of her mouth was precise, formal, and laden with the sound of New York City.

She did not see him. He made sure of that. The last thing he wanted to do was unnerve Tess while she was working. He had hoped it would make him happy to be able to stare at her from a distance, to rejoice in their imminent reunion; he hadn't counted on catching this glimpse of Tess in her role as a very skilled and professional career woman, a woman who presented herself so well that there was absolute silence in the room. Tensely he waited for her to make a joke or crack a smile, or even make a tiny error. He longed for some recalcitrant curl to pop loose from her corseted hair, but it was pinned up so tightly that she might as well have had it trimmed an inch from her head.

Brady tried to think of her in the saddle as Calypso galloped across the Rocking T. He tried to imagine her perched on the front step of his house or trapped inside the Silvergold jail, dreaming of ways to refurbish it. In desperation, he tried to fill his mind with his favorite Tess Hamilton memory—Lady Godiva on the horse—

but here, in this sterile setting, even that sensual fantasy failed.

He wondered, with a sickening lurch in his stomach, which Tess Hamilton was planning to spend the night with him.

TESS FOUND BRADY standing by the bedside window, long sleeves rolled up to his elbows, unknotted tie draping his neck, unbuttoned shirt revealing the coarse curls on his chest. His hands were jammed stiffly in his pockets, and his eyes held a distant, almost frightened look as he ever so slowly shifted his glance from the flashing neon street below him to her.

She stood in the doorway, her briefcase in one hand, waiting for him to greet her . . . or rush to give her a hug or a kiss. But he seemed to be waiting for something.

Carefully she closed the door.

"Hello," she said softly, shaken by the sudden crashing of her heart against the walls of her chest.

"Good evening, Tess." There was no warmth in his voice. He did no move toward her.

"How was your flight?" she asked, not certain how to start the conversation.

He shrugged. "Can't complain. How was yours?"

"Fine."

His eyes looked dark and troubled. Nervously he licked his lower lip.

"I got here around six," Tess continued. "I barely had time to grab a bite to eat before I started my first presentation."

He nodded. "I caught part of it. Very smooth. I was impressed."

There was something wrong with his voice, but she wasn't sure what it was. He wasn't being sarcastic, exactly, but he wasn't particularly proud of her success.

"Why didn't you wait for me? I never knew you were there."

He glanced away, back at the chaos below the window. "I didn't want to interrupt. You were surrounded by—" he seemed to struggle for the right words "—others of your ilk."

She got it then. It was Las Vegas, it was her suit, it was... his entire attitude about her world in L.A. and New York. It was the reality of the situation that faced them at every turn.

Slowly he began to cross the room, his twill slacks doing little to camouflage his bowlegged stride... or his hesitation. When he reached Tess—an eternity later—he reached out ever so subtly to take her hand. She gripped his fingers fiercely as he leaned down to briefly graze her lips with his. It was not the kind of hello kiss she wanted, and she let him know it in the way she kissed him back. She offered him a deep kiss, a hungry kiss, a kiss that sought reassurance... and something more.

The strong male fingers around her own tightened, and Brady's free hand crept up to the side of her neck. He took a deep breath and kissed her again, more slowly this time, and his hesitation—reluctance—seemed to ebb. Still, there was a tension in his body that did not vanish, even when he finally wrapped both arms around her, pulled her closer and slowly rocked her back and forth.

Her relief was monumental, but short-lived. The embrace was sweet but brief before Brady released her and stepped back, continuing to hold on to her hand. His eyes were tense, uneasy.

"You must be tired," he said almost solicitously. "I guess you've had a long day."

She nodded. She was weary, but more from the excitement and fear of meeting Brady than anything to do with the conference. She was accustomed to making presentations and was not intimidated by them. Realizing that Brady was probably intimidated—or at least irritated—by everything in Las Vegas, she asked gently, "How is everything on the Rocking T?"

He shrugged. "The ranch is okay."

"And the committee? Any progress on getting legislative support for the historic district? Any luck on getting a loan for the hotel or the church?"

"Not much."

After that there was a long silence, accompanied by a gray, distant expression in Brady's beautiful eyes. His sadness tore at Tess, stripped the joy from their reunion.

In fact, as she began to ponder his behavior, his sadness frightened her. Clearly something was troubling him deeply. If it wasn't the ranch or the committee or the loans, it had to be...

She swallowed hard and bravely met his eyes. Gingerly she queried, "Brady, what's wrong? Is it... us?"

"Us?" he repeated blankly, his expression unchanged.

"Yes, us." Her heart was thudding against her ribs, but she knew she had to face her fears head-on. "You promised me you'd never do it in a letter, and if you came here just to—"

Suddenly his eyes narrowed and his grip on her fingers tightened. For a long moment he clung to her hand, then released it as he slipped both arms around her waist.

"I love you," he vowed fiercely, eyes dark and full of fire. "I don't want to, but I do."

Tess froze—thrilled, confused and relieved. For a man who'd just confessed something monumental—something she'd dreamed would never come to pass—he didn't look very pleased with himself. But the fervency of his tone was unmistakable, and the grip on her sensitive flesh was very firm.

She leaned forward, and ever so lightly nuzzled his throat. "I'm sorry, Brady," she confessed, desperately wishing she'd never said a word. "I guess I'm . . . feeling a bit insecure about us, with all that's happened, and you seem so . . . distracted. Unhappy. Almost as though you wished I hadn't come."

"I wish *I* hadn't come," he answered bluntly. "I wish I'd arranged to meet you somewhere else."

"Vegas?" she queried softly, trying to get to the root of the problem as she snuggled closer, relishing his warmth. "Too much like New York?"

"Way too much," he agreed. For a moment he stood there, easing her hurt, gently caressing her back with open, gentle hands. He kissed her temple, just once, before he whispered, "Ah, hell, Tess, it's more than that. Whenever I fly, I think about...well, dying, you know? Not going back. I had a fight with my dad a couple of weeks back, and I haven't seen him since. All the way from Grand Junction I kept thinking how awful it would be if something happened to me and his last memory was having me yell at him like that."

"Oh, Brady, there's an easy solution to that problem," Tess counseled, relieved that nothing more complex was bothering him. "Just pick up the phone and call him. Right now. Tell him you forgive him and you're sorry. He'll be so pleased and—"

"But I haven't forgiven him. I'm sorry that we're... well, at odds... I'm sorry about that a lot. But I still think he's the one who wronged me. He's *still* doing it, damn him! What's it going to take for him to stop beating a dead horse? What's it going to take for him to start believing in me?"

Tess heard the deep hurt in his voice and wished she could have eased it. It was a problem she'd never experienced in her own life. Her parents had always hoped she'd do well in life, but to them that mainly meant that she'd find happiness. They worried about her divorced state, but had never berated her for the failure of her marriage. Career-wise, all they cared about was that she loved her work. They'd never tried to create a blueprint that matched her dreams to theirs.

Gently she said, "Have you ever really told him how you feel? I mean, that you do still love him, that you wish things could be all right?"

He shrugged. "I'm sure he knows that. We were too close for too many years."

"That doesn't mean he wouldn't love to hear you say it."

Brady pulled her closer. His grip was firmer now—confident and tender. "We don't all get everything we want in life, you know. For the past month I've wanted to wake up with your hair tangled up in my pillow, but every time I feel fur in my face it means that I'm sharing the bed with one of the cats."

Tess couldn't stifle a grin. From Brady, that line was almost romantic. "I imagine that's one dream I could make come true for you," she promised him. "At least for the next few days."

At last he smiled back, apparently willing to put his troubles with his dad on hold. For a moment they shared the quiet intimacy of their reunion, the unbridled joy of knowing that for this one precious weekend, they'd really be together again. Then Brady's expression darkened. "It's been damn hard without you, Tess. It doesn't seem right without you on the Rocking T."

"It doesn't seem right without you *anywhere*," Tess answered. She clung to him, pressing her lips against the hollow of his neck as she confessed, "I love you, Brady Trent." The words tasted sweet and hopeful on her tongue. "For the next three days we're going to be together. That's all that matters."

He stroked her neck, then slipped his strong fingers into the bun of trapped hair and deliberately tugged it loose. "It's not all that matters, L.G.," he insisted as he lowered his mouth to hers. "But for right now it'll have to do."

WITH SEVERAL HOURS between the end of the conference and their scheduled flights late Sunday, Brady and Tess bought a fast-food picnic lunch and headed off to Lake Mead for the afternoon. It was outrageously hot, but they found leafy cottonwood near the water and set up camp in the shade. The heat had kept everyone else indoors, apparently, so they had most of the park to themselves.

They spent most of the day curled up together on a blanket, sharing quiet kisses and cuddles and dreams about the good times in some magical moment of the future when they'd no longer have to live apart. Brady noticed that Tess seemed to have more faith in that possibility than he did. She also seemed to think that they had several options open to them. He *knew* that transplanting Tess to the Rocking T was the only one.

"But Brady," she pointed out gently at one point, "unless Harold gets a historically minded buyer for the hotel, it sounds as though you may have no choice but to give up the ranch. I know you'll fight against that possibility tooth and toenail, but if it should come to pass, we might have more personal options."

Brady did not want to spoil their last few hours together fighting over the ranch, but neither did he want to give her any false expectations. Even though the legislative process involved in declaring downtown Redpoint might take years, the formation of the committee had provided a much-needed vehicle for organizing the Save the Redpoint Hotel operation, which had to take precedence right now. And he wasn't about to consider giving up the Rocking T until he'd exhausted every imaginable option. So far, he hadn't even exhausted one.

"I love you, Tess," he said gently, "and I desperately want you to become part of my life. But my life is the Rocking T, and come hell or high water, that's where I'm going to be."

She was quiet for a moment—a long moment—before she suggested warily, "Don't you think you might be acting a bit... unrealistic about your situation? I mean, leaving me out of it altogether?"

I'd like to leave you out of it altogether when you talk like that, he wanted to snap, angered by her insistence. Instead he said evenly, "It's all a matter of determination. Have you ever been to the Silverton railroad?"

Tess shook her head. "I've heard of it. Isn't it the biggest tourist line in Colorado?"

"Probably the biggest in the southwest, according to Joe. He and Mandy honeymooned there and they just loved it. They keep telling me I ought to go." As he said the words, he realized that neither had urged him to visit the Silverton or anywhere else lately. In fact, ever since the news of Harold's trouble, they'd been pretty quiet whenever anything that cost money was mentioned. Several times in recent weeks Brady had had the feeling that something was troubling Joey, something he hadn't yet shared. Was it a money problem? No, Brady decided. That was crazy. He and Joe had no secrets. At least they never had before.

"The point is," he explained to Tess, "a few years ago the Silverton was on her last legs. The owner had no money to fix her up. Had to sell. A group of local citizens got together—without H.W.P. but maybe some other official group helped them—and formed some kind of 'Save the Silverton' committee."

"I guess it worked," Tess said with a smile.

"Of course it worked. They were *determined*. They found a fellow in Florida who loved trains as much as Joey does *and* he was rich. He bought the line, fixed it up and made it the smash hit it is today."

Tess eyed him quietly. He saw new hope in her eyes. "You're going to find that kind of buyer," she said simply. It was not really a question; it was a statement of fact. "You're going to comb the face of the earth."

Brady nodded. He smiled. "Joey and I think there's no other way. We're already getting unsolicited donations from people who've heard about Harold's situation or read about it in the *Register*. A lot of people are closet preservationists. Surely there's at least one of them out there who's rich."

Tess gently touched his face. "If I may put on my H.W.P. hat for a moment, I'd like to suggest that you send out specific notices to everybody on your mailing lists. Anybody who's interested enough in western tourist attractions to take a wagon train, ride the Slow Joe or stay in the hotel might have contacts with an appropriate party. You haven't had any millionaires on the Rocking T lately, have you?"

He shook his head and pulled her close. "Not that I know of. Then again, the atmosphere of a wagon train doesn't really lend itself to bragging about surplus cash. Nobody's going to wear mink coats or drive up in a Masserati."

They talked about the buyer-recruitment possibilities for a while longer, then shared some more private moments from their respective pasts. Tess told him more about marriage and her career plans; he told her how Claudia had cheated on him and disparaged his dreams. He even shared one incident in New York City that had been particularly humiliating, and the quiet understanding on Tess's face made him marvel that he'd ever compared her with Claudia at all.

They returned to the airport with little time to spare, and Brady longed to think of an excuse to avoid going back altogether. But finally Tess's plane arrived—his wasn't due for an hour—and he had no choice but to stand next to the runway and hold her in his arms as she told him goodbye.

Tears were streaming down her cheeks when she finally whispered, "When will I see you again, Brady?" She traced his jaw with a trembling hand. "When will I touch your face?"

He had no answer. Which was just as well, because his throat had closed up, and he could not have uttered a word.

CHAPTER FOURTEEN

BRADY CAME HOME from Vegas with half a dozen good ideas on historic preservation to share with his committee and not so much as a notion about how to improve his situation with Tess.

The first night after he got home, he had dinner with Joe and Mandy, who wanted to hear everything about his trip. They listened quietly while he told them about mailing requests for a hotel buyer, specific fund-raising for the church and the legislative backing they'd need to guarantee the historic district initiative's success. They also listened while he shared some of the more personal details of the weekend.

"It was so strange at first. It was like I didn't really know her. And by the time we said goodbye at the airport, it was like we'd lived together all of our lives."

"I think that's natural when you're apart so much, Brady," Mandy said. "I'm sure it'll get better when you work out a way to spend more time together."

He shook his head. "That's the trouble. I mean, that's been the trouble right from the start. How are we ever going to spend more time together? I'd die before I'd move to L.A.—even if I did lose the ranch—and now that I've seen Tess in action with all the other hotshots, I'm afraid she's too much of a professional to give up her career to come live in the sticks."

"You've seen her in a professional capacity before. She did a fine job for us here," Joe pointed out.

"But that was different. That was Redpoint. I mean, I don't have any trouble imagining her as a professional *here*."

Mandy handed him a piece of homemade peach pie and waited expectantly until he took an appreciative bite. Then she suggested softly, "I've never gotten the impression that Tess was particularly attached to Los Angeles, Brady. I think she's pretty flexible geographically. I imagine there are any number of places where she could live and still carry on her career."

Again he shook his head. "There could be a thousand places and it wouldn't make any difference. She's sure her career would die if she lived on the Rocking T."

Joe and Mandy exchanged glances that made him uneasy. It was rare that the two of them shut him out, despite the thread of unspoken intimacy that ran between them.

"I think," opined Mandy, "that it's time for you and Tess to start working out some sort of a long-term compromise. It doesn't seem to me that this is a passing fling between the two of you."

Brady felt an unexpected flip-flop in his stomach. "It's not, Mandy. To be perfectly honest with you—" he struggled with the words but finally pushed them out "—if I thought Tess could be happy at the ranch, I think I'd ask her to marry me."

Joe said nothing, but his eyes opened wide. Mandy grinned and crossed the room quickly to give Brady a hug. "Oh, Brady, I think that's wonderful! And I really think—woman's intuition and all of that—that Tess feels the same way about you."

He tried to share Mandy's happiness, but he knew that a major barricade still stood in the way. "Mandy, honey, I think you're missing the point. I said 'if' she could be happy on the ranch. And she couldn't be. At least not . . . forever."

For a long, shaky moment, Mandy was silent. Then she said softly, "Brady, you might not be able to live on the ranch forever, either. It would be a tragedy to give up Tess for the Rocking T if you're going to lose it, anyway."

Hot bile filled his throat. It was the first time Joe's wife had ever challenged his dream like that. Through clenched teeth, he answered, "I'm not going to lose the Rocking T, Mandy." Stubbornly his eyes met hers.

Mandy glanced at Joe, then studied the floor. "I hope you're right, Brady," she agreed in a quiet, almost hoarse tone. "But even if it works out, I still don't think it's worth losing Tess."

He couldn't answer that. Nothing was worth losing the ranch. Nothing was worth losing Tess. But how on earth could he ever have both of them?

"Marital compromise means bending here and there so nobody has to break," Mandy told him, her voice taking on a slightly teacherly tone. "I wouldn't want to work at the Slow Joe full-time, but I'm perfectly willing to help Joey out in the summer because we need . . . because it makes him happy."

Again she looked at Joe, but he said nothing. After a moment Mandy sailed on. "I'd never ask Joe to give up the train, because he loves it. But he'd never ask me to sacrifice my career for the Slow Joe, either, because he *loves* me."

"And I love her career," teased Joe, giving his wife a loving wink that belied the fact that her role as an educator had once been an insurmountable block between them. The casual comment broke the unfamiliar tension. "I've always had a thing for schoolteachers."

They all shared a laugh before Brady said solemnly, "All of this theorizing is easy for you guys because you finally managed to work out your differences." It hadn't been easy, of course; he still remembered how they'd both agonized over their memories of that terrible sixth-grade year Joe had spent in Mandy's class. "But it's different for Tess and me. One of us is going to have to give up an awful lot." Slowly he shook his head. "And I'd be lying to you if I pretended that it would ever be me."

FOR THE NEXT SIX WEEKS, Tess lived on memories. She gobbled up Brady's letters, waited for his infrequent phone calls and agonized over her lonely nights. She tried to fill her heart with the essence of his feelings—he had confessed his love for her more than once—but the longer they were apart, the greater grew her frustration. She wanted to feel his arms around her. She wanted to see his smile. And more than anything else, she wanted some sort of proof—any sort of proof—that she meant more to him than fifty acres of red desert sand. But none of her wishes seemed meant to be.

In the meantime she tried to focus on her work, but she found it hard to stay excited about any of her current projects, though each was vital to the people involved. The folks in Cattle Springs, Nevada, were involved in much the same sort of struggle as Brady was, and Tess was currently doing a survey of historic sites and buildings for the tiny town. And she'd gone to another tiny town outside Santa Fe twice since she'd left Las Vegas. She knew—and Brady knew—that it wasn't all that far from Santa Fe to Redpoint, and with a little finagling they could have tacked on a weekend to her business trip. The trouble was she never could give him enough notice of her plans to arrange anything by mail. Once she wrote to him a good ten days before departing, and he still didn't get word until after she'd returned to L.A. Short of begging Joe or Mandy to make a five-hour round-trip just to deliver a message, there seemed to be no way to communicate effectively.

Bit by bit, week by week, the pressure grew...and the resentment. Tess knew that she had walked into this situation with her eyes wide open; she certainly couldn't accuse Brady of trying to pull the wool over her eyes. But she was slowly beginning to realize that she had deluded herself about the reality of the situation. She had always believed that if Brady truly learned to love her, his priorities *would* change. The separation would not be forever. Sooner or later, she'd fiercely believed, she'd edge out the ranch for first place in his heart.

There was no doubt in her mind that he'd claimed first place in hers. There was not a morning that did not begin without his name on her lips, nor a night that didn't end with the name softly uttered sigh. Other men held no interest for Tess, and those who asked her out were greeted with a quick refusal and a courteous explanation that she was deeply involved with someone else.

By the first of October, after the season's last wagon-train adventure ended and Brady's letters showed every sign that he was planning to hunker down on the Rocking T for the winter, Tess felt the gray dust of defeat settle around her heart. Knowing he was far away had been hard to endure, but knowing that he was busy and happy doing what he wanted to do had made it bearable. But now that the weather was changing, his time was his own—and he admitted, by mail, that it lay heavily on his hands—she could not understand why he would deliberately choose to winter in the middle of nowhere all alone when sunshine and the woman he claimed to love awaited him in California.

Once snowfall began in earnest, her relationship with him would have to go on hold for the winter. Until spring graced the red-rock country, he'd be about as accessible as a hibernating grizzly bear.

ONE BRISK AUTUMN EVENING when Brady had just returned from town, he sacked out on his old couch to reread his last two letters from Tess—which he'd already read at Joe's—and then opened a letter from Trudy Lincoln, the plucky elderly gal who'd taken the same wagon-train trek as Tess and Roberta. To his surprise, Trudy had written to say that she was interested in buying the Redpoint Hotel.

Brady was ecstatic that Trudy apparently had the money—not to mention the inclination—to renovate the old hotel, and he planned to call her just as soon as he could drive back into town. But he wasn't about to put all his eggs in that basket, at least not yet. He never put much stock in daydreams.

Still, he was eagerly mulling over the possibilities an hour later when Ragweed Willie knocked on his door. "Come in!" he called without bothering to get up. He wondered, at times, why he didn't ask Willie to move into the main house with him. It was no warmer than the bunkhouse and considerably smaller, but it had a few hints of hominess, and it was, after all, the boss's place. It was—at least it was supposed to be—a home.

Then again, Willie was a friend, but he was not a friend like Joe, and Joe was the only male friend with whom Brady could imagine sharing his own private space. Worse yet, Willie was transient. Although he always came back to the Rocking T when things got lean, he'd been a saddle bum all of his life and he was proud of his rootlessness. Brady could count on him to show up every spring, but he could also count on him to go south for the worst of the winter. It was, in fact, almost time for him to go.

"Hi, Willie, what's up?" he asked when the old man scraped his boots on the step and limped inside.

"The other fellers . . . they'll be leavin' soon."

Brady nodded. Jeb and L.T. always stayed with him for two weeks after the last tour to help him get caught up on everything he'd been too busy to do during the summer and to make sure that the buildings and tack were ready to withstand the harsh Colorado winter. Then they vanished, like the morning mist on a winter's day, reappearing in March about the time the swallows came back to Capistrano.

"I was wonderin' if maybe I could hang around here this winter. Earn my keep helpin' out with th' stock."

Brady's senses instantly went on red alert. Willie had never wintered with him before. "Willie, I'd be delighted to have your company, but I don't have any cash to spare. You can live in the bunkhouse, but you can't count on drawing pay. You know I'm strapped."

He nodded. "I got a little put by. All I need is enough fer grub."

It's a simple life, Brady pondered. *No bills, no responsibilities, no ties of any kind.* Except, perhaps, some tie to the Rocking T? Willie was getting old. Perhaps, like some aging wild beast, he was looking for a thicket to crawl into near the end.

Suddenly he sat upright, fear clawing at his insides. "Willie, you tell me straight. Are you sick? Are you all right?"

Willie looked surprised. He tugged on his chest-length beard. "Hell, Brady, do I look sick t' you? Th' last time I got laid up was with the stomach flu back in '65. I ain't even been throwed by a horse since then."

Brady stood, walked two paces until he met the old man eye to eye. "Then tell me what's up. Why do you want to hole up here this winter? Why give up the Arizona sun for the Rocking T?"

Willie flinched and looked away. He twirled his hat in his bony, wrinkled hands.

"Out with it."

Willie sighed. "I been thinkin' that ya might need t' do some snowbirdin' yerself this winter. Ya cain't go nowhere without somebody t' take care of th' stock."

Brady didn't know what to say. He was deeply touched. But it had not occurred to him, not even once, to winter in L.A. All of his plans and dreams for Tess were predicated on the dream that *she* would come to *him*. He had forsaken the ranch once before to follow a woman who clutched his heart, and—even if it broke him—he would never do it again.

WHEN TESS GOT HOME from work on Tuesday, she found two packages in her mailbox. Both of them were surprises. The one from Colorado was a framed photo of Brady, a blowup of the one Mandy had taken of him roping a steer on Buck. She'd only asked for it once—and then only for a snapshot—and she was delighted by his thoughtfulness.

The other package was from New York.

Tess didn't need to check the address to know who had sent it; in fact, the address was meaningless to her. But she would have known the heavy black script anywhere. Nathan's address changed on a yearly basis, but his handwriting was always the same.

It was the first time she'd heard from him since the divorce had been finalized, and though they hadn't parted on terrible terms, all things considered, she had not expected him to be an ongoing part of her life. Just the knowledge that he was thinking of her at all left her uneasy.

Carefully she opened the package, a large box tied clumsily with a number of strings. It took awhile to cut through the twine, but inside she found a pile of familiar clothing—two of her old sweatshirts, a comparatively new sweater, and a middle-aged pair of shoes. Inside was a note on yellow legal-pad paper, short and to the point. "Dear T: Found these during my last move. Thought you might want them back. Hope your life is what you wanted. I'm getting married soon."

There was a capital *L*, crossed out as though he'd started to write "Love" and thought better of it. Below that he'd just written his name.

She felt a moment's sorrow for the love they'd once shared. After all, Nathan wasn't a bad man. He'd never cheated on her or abused her, never stayed out all night and come home drunk the next morning. He'd just...put himself first. Always. If there was room in his current play for his wife's happiness, he was glad to oblige. If not...well, he regretted the fact, but he didn't lose sleep over it.

She wondered if Brady ever lost sleep over the unhappiness he caused her. At times he was deeply compassionate, sensitive to her smallest shift in feeling. But other times he could see nothing but red rock and cattle. At times like that Tess almost hated the Rocking T.

She was still comparing Nathan's idea of a relationship with Brady's when Brady himself called her half an hour later. Her analysis of the similarities between the way the two men treated her colored her normal joy at hearing Brady's voice, and she knew she didn't sound particularly warm as she told him about the package from New York.

Brady listened to her lament for a while before he asked, "Did you get the package I sent you? I was hoping it would cheer you up."

"I got it. It's very nice."

He waited, but she did not go on. "That's it? Nice? You ooed and ahhed like crazy about it before."

"Brady, I appreciate the picture very much," she answered briskly, suddenly fighting a wash of tears. "It's just that, tonight, I really need to see you in person. And you might as well be in another country."

He exhaled unhappily. "I'm sorry, Tess. I'm dying to see you, too. I think I would have driven in to call you even if I hadn't had another call to make."

She didn't really care about his other call, but she forced herself to ask about it.

"Remember Trudy Lincoln, the spunky old grandma on the wagon train? Believe it or not, she's sitting on a mountain of money and she's thinking of buying the hotel. Her lawyer husband died two years ago and left everything to her. She told me that she's been waiting to invest it until she was back on her feet—emotionally—and I told her that I'd never met anybody who seemed more firmly planted on the ground. She's all wool and a yard wide."

Tess couldn't stifle a smile at Brady's homespun description of the dear old gal. "I couldn't have put it better myself," she told him. "Is she really serious about buying the hotel?"

"She sounds serious to me. She told me she'd drag her business manager out here to check things over within the week. And apparently she's already talked to Harold."

Part of Tess was deeply happy for Brady, yet she also realized that if Trudy bought the Redpoint, he'd never leave the ranch and she would never be able to marry him. "It sounds...really promising, Brady," was all she could say.

"It sounds terrific!" he corrected her. "I hate to get my hopes up until she signs on the dotted line, but honestly, Tess, I really think this might work out. And the best of it is, I really *like* Trudy Lincoln. I trust her. I think this deal could work out all the way around."

"Yes, it sounds perfect," Tess answered stiffly, resisting the urge to point out that his jubilant solution to the Rocking T's problem would do nothing to solve her own. "It should work out very well for all of you."

There was a long silence before Brady said, "You can be part of it, Tess. I want you to be."

Tess swallowed hard. "Brady, if only it were that simple!"

"It is."

"It *isn't*. If I were a puppet or a milktoast or a mail-order bride, maybe it would all be hunky dory. But I'm a person, too, with my own interests, my own values, my own *life*, and I'm entitled to a husband who believes in me enough to compromise."

Brady's dark, answering silence let her know that she'd struck a nerve. Yet she couldn't say she was sorry.

She'd put off dealing with her true feelings for far too long.

Each time he called, each time she wrote, they danced around the issue. They both pretended that their forced separation was the fault of some uncontrollable, omnipotent third party. War, earthquake, famine. But suddenly she knew who was responsible for her pain, and she was surprised by the sudden flow of resentment his news had unleashed.

"I told you how it was from day one," he now reminded her. "You can't pretend I've pulled any surprises, Tess."

"I'm not saying that you have. But maybe I took on more than I bargained for, Brady. I thought I could live with what you had to offer, but now I'm not so sure. I want more from our relationship than letters and sporadic calls and crying into my pillow at night. I've got all the disadvantages of being married and none of the benefits! I don't go out anymore because even a platonic date makes me feel like I'm betraying your trust. I can't enjoy much of anything because I'm so lonely all the time." She swallowed hard and plunged on. "And I'm angry, Brady! I'm angry at *you*. I'm angry at you for treating me like an old coat you can pull on or toss off according to the weather. You say you love me, but you sure as hell don't act like it. You've made it perfectly clear that you'd rather live alone on that godforsaken ranch than anywhere else on earth with *me*. You can't expect me to take that as a compliment!"

"I expect you to take it as an immutable fact. Besides, you're comparing apples and oranges, Tess. I *can't* leave the ranch. It's not as though I were choosing some other woman over you."

"Nathan was faithful to me, too, Brady, but that didn't change the fact that I came second place in his life."

"Dammit, Tess, I am *not* Nathan and I resent being lumped in with him!"

"If the shoe fits, wear it!" she snapped back. "The only difference I can see is that you *know* you want the Rocking T more than you want me. Nathan never could see the picture clearly. Right up to the end he kept telling me that I was all that mattered, that he desperately wanted to keep me."

"Dammit, Tess, what do you want me to do? I write you almost every day! I call you whenever I can! I'd put everything aside if you could come visit me!"

"I don't want to go visit you! I want *you* to come *here*! You've never even seen my home, Brady. Never even met my friends except for Roberta. I've never even cooked a single meal for you! How can I pretend you're really an active part of my life?"

"I can't come to L.A., Tess." His voice was flat.

"Because it's a metropolis?"

"Because it's far away," he snapped. "I can't take the time and I sure as hell don't have the money. I'm barely making ends meet as it is."

"Only because you're throwing money down a rathole!" she burst out without thinking. "You're the hardest working man I've known in my life, Brady Trent, but what do you have to show for it? Nothing! You're going to age before your time on that ranch. You're going to be an old hermit and look like Ragweed Willie before you're even forty! Is that really what you want? Is it really?"

"What I want," he countered tightly, "is to hang up the phone before I say something I know I'll regret."

Before Tess could answer, the line went dead.

BRADY MANAGED TO HANG UP without slamming the phone, but he swore so viciously at the wall that Mandy, busy cooking dinner across the kitchen, turned sharply to say, "Brady, the girls are here."

He bit off the next hard word and slammed one fist on the table. He wanted to get in his truck and roar off to the ranch, but he knew that if he did he'd have to turn around and come back in half an hour when he cooled down.

And he would cool down. He knew he would. But cooling down wouldn't change a thing. Tess had practically quoted his father. It was obvious that the two of them shared similar thoughts about the ranch.

Suddenly he felt a hand on his wrist—a gentling, female hand. He glanced up sharply as Mandy sat down beside him, her green eyes sympathetic but surprisingly stern. "I love you, Brady, so you know that whatever I say to you is because I honestly think it's in your best interests. I've been biting my tongue for weeks now, and I'm going to have my say."

Brady didn't try to stop her. He'd always known that sooner or later his best friend's wife would somehow get in the way of his friendship with Joe. There were things two bachelors did together—like swearing in each other's kitchens on the phone—that didn't wash when one of them was married. Mandy had put up with Brady coming and going from her house at all hours of the day and night, leaving his supplies, camping out in her spare room, collecting his mail and phone messages and occasional meals as though he paid room and board at the places. He was not surprised that she had finally reached her limit; he knew that a small tongue-lashing was overdue.

But he was surprised at the subject of her harangue.

"You're going to lose her, Brady," she said bluntly, "and when you do, you'll have no one to blame but yourself."

His eyes widened. "Mandy, you don't know all the—"

"Yes, I do. I know everything worth knowing about this situation. I know that you gave up the ranch for Claudia and it didn't do any good. I also know that you gave it up long after Claudia had given up on your marriage, not in the beginning when some sign of sacrifice on your part might have convinced her that you really loved her."

"I worshiped her, dammit!" he burst out. "I followed her to New York! I gave up the ranch!"

"Exactly," concurred Mandy. "Which is why you *won't* give up the ranch for Tess—even during the winter months—and you won't even go to *visit* her where she lives. You're punishing her for what Claudia did to you."

"The hell I am! You didn't just listen to her side of this conversation! *She's* the one stuck in the past! She's mad at me tonight because her crummy ex-husband just mailed some old stuff to her!"

Mandy tightened her grip on his wrist. "Brady, her ex might have triggered some explosion, but Tess isn't mad at you because of Nathan. She's mad at you because you say you love her but you're breaking her heart. If you were injured or at war and simply could *not* manage to see her, she'd miss you terribly, but she'd feel no anger, only pain. What's unbearable to a woman in her situation is that none of this separation is necessary as far as she's concerned. You're apart for one reason and one reason only: you love the Rocking T more than you love Tess."

It wasn't true. He knew it wasn't true the instant she said it, but he also knew that he'd done precious little to convince Tess of the truth. "I'm willing to support any career she wants to undertake on the ranch. She can write or do historical projects, she can—"

"She can't do any of them out there, Brady! Even writers who live in the boondocks have telephones and access to a courier service! Besides, you can't just whip up a career as a historical preservation writer overnight. You have to visit places, meet people, plan research—none of which she can do when she's snowlocked for half of each year. And even if she could do it—and wanted to—*you're still missing the point*."

"I never thought you'd be recruited to the 'Get Brady Trent Off the Rocking T Committee,' Mandy," he said harshly. "But I'm beginning to see a pattern here. And I don't like it one bit!"

She stood up angrily and released his hand. "I only want one thing for you, Brady. Your happiness. Until you met Tess, you were happier on the Rocking T than off of it, so I hoped you could keep it. But now your allegiance to the ranch is crippling your chance for a loving marriage to a wonderful woman who adores you. I'm not sure you have to give up the ranch to marry Tess, but I do think you have to make some sort of rearrangement in your priorities, or pretty soon you won't have any decisions to make. She needs a sign, and she needs one soon, or she's going to leave you, Brady. Not because she doesn't love you—but because she does."

JAKE FIDGETED in his seat at Peggy's Diner, surreptitiously watching John Carleton's face. Although John was a few years his junior, he was also a bank president, so the two had become close friends over the years. Jake knew that as a banker he had no business doing what he was about to do, but as a father, he could do nothing else.

He had known, from the first moment he'd heard that Joe had made a down payment for the Rocking T and cosigned Brady's loan, that his son would be hard-pressed to meet the payments and would have no cushion whatsoever. But he had not expected Joe to imperil either his own family or his own business, which is why he'd been startled when he'd run into Joey coming out of John's office last month looking downright sheepish. When Jake had casually joked to the young receptionist that most banks probably didn't have too many men in engineer's stripes slipping in to chat with old friends over lunch, she'd replied indiscreetly, "Oh, Joey didn't come in to chat today. He talked to John about taking out a loan."

He had known, with every banker's instinct he possessed, that Joe was in trouble because of his son. And he also knew, with every father's instinct he possessed, that Brady did not know that Joe had dug himself into a hole. The only thing he didn't know was how deep it was and whether or not he was going to need help to dig out.

Once he pumped John for all the details, he'd have to tell Brady. And then, for Joey's sake, Brady would have to sell that damn ranch.

CHAPTER FIFTEEN

THE PHONE RANG almost two hours later, long after Tess had given up hope of patching up her fight with Brady. She did not, in fact, expect to hear from him again for several days, and even then, she was afraid he'd only call to say goodbye.

"Hello, sweetheart," he greeted her gingerly. "Are we still friends?"

She took a deep breath, grateful that he sounded so conciliatory. "Of course. Always that. No matter what."

He was silent for a moment. Then he said, "I'm sorry I was so short with you earlier. I'm sorry about . . . a lot of things."

Tess battled futilely at a rush of tears. "So am I, Brady. I didn't mean to go crazy. I just miss you so much."

Another long silence washed between them before Brady continued, "Mandy says we're chewing each other up because we're frustrated with this long-distance stuff. She agreed with you. Says a weekend rendezvous is definitely in order."

"I'm delighted," Tess said warily. "And I'd love to see Mandy some time. But right now I'd rather see you."

He didn't laugh, but he did say, "Joey and Mandy have always wanted me to take a trip on the Silverton-Durango line, and from what I've heard, I think you'd enjoy it, too. Joey pulled some strings with a railroad buddy to get me tickets on such short notice. There's air service to Durango from L.A., and I can drive there in a few hours." He waited a moment, then tacked on, "I'm sure I can get Willie to take care of the stock for a few days. Joe says he'll do it himself if Willie can't."

Tess closed her eyes and battled tears. He was trying. She'd said the worst possible thing to him in her despair, and he hadn't given up on her.

"I'd be delighted to meet you in Durango." Her voice was thick, undisguised yearning. "When did you have in mind?"

"Tomorrow night," he declared with a smile in his voice, causing a ferris wheel of joy to swing loops around her heart. "I hope you haven't made any other plans, because I've already made our reservations."

THIS TIME Tess didn't even have time to look for Brady once she entered the tiny terminal. His arms closed around her before she even cleared the open door.

She dropped her luggage, wrapped her arms around him and clung to him, fighting a mist of tears. He rocked her fiercely as he edged her out of the path of the other passengers, pressing urgent kisses of reassurance against her cheek and trembling jaw.

She didn't know how long they stood there, hugging, crying, ignoring the world at large. Finally Brady pulled back enough to meet her eyes and wipe away the tears with his broad, square fingers. "You stop that now," he ordered gently. "This is supposed to be a happy time."

That only made her cry harder. "Oh, Brady," she wailed. "I've missed you so much. I felt so helpless. It was as though some big tornado had swallowed you up and dumped you halfway around the world. I didn't know how to reach you, how to make you see how—"

He kissed her softly, blocking the flow of regret. "Let's go check in before we get into all of that, okay? I agree that we need a long talk, but I think we ought to start it where we know we won't be interrupted."

She nodded, then shed a few more tears when he kissed her again. It occurred to Tess that for the first time ever, Brady was actually more dressed up than she was. He was wearing a suit again—not a western suit but a three-piece yuppie type—and she wondered where and when he'd gotten it . . . and why. In her slacks and cotton blouse, she felt downright shabby in comparison.

"Do you want to go out to eat or just pick something up to take to our room?" he asked genially as he loaded her things in his freshly washed and waxed truck.

She knew he'd cleaned up the vehicle just for her, and that knowledge made her feel both honored and guilty. And—in a strange sort of way—it also made her feel homesick for the ranch. The truck was a lumpy, beat-up old thing, but it belonged to Brady—to Brady's life. It was a part of the Rocking T.

"Let's just take something to the hotel," she requested. "It would be—" it was hard to put into words "—more homey that way."

His eyes met hers, and she knew he was sharing her thoughts. Neither one of them really wanted to keep meeting at exotic locations where they had to act as though they were tourists.

They wanted to kick back and spend time at *home* together, wherever that was.

Home, Mandy reflected silently, ought to be wherever the two of them were together, but to Brady it only meant the Rocking T.

BRADY GATHERED UP their take-out burgers and suitcases and entered the quaint cottage that he'd selected with both ambience and privacy in mind. Tess had not asked him how much it cost or whether or not they were splitting expenses, but this time, he intended to pick up the tab. He didn't feel good about using part of his hard-earned savings so frivolously, but the alternative to this trip—losing Tess—had been too alarming.

"It's charming, Brady," she assured him as she took in the renovated western look. Tiny flowers graced the wallpaper in the style of years gone by, and wood paneling covered the lower half of each wall. Fragile photographs of the Silverton, thundering through the mountains, hung artfully throughout the room, and a freshly oiled saddle perched in one corner much like a sculpture.

As she turned to face him, a look of desperate relief washed over her beloved features. "You scared me," she surprised him by admitting. "For a couple of hours there, I thought I'd lost you for good."

Brady couldn't meet her eyes. He hadn't hung up on her exactly, but for a few hours there he *had* left things between them pretty grim. Quietly he walked across the room and touched her face. She leaned against the palm of his hand and kissed it gently.

"I was scared, too, Tess," he confessed. "Mandy said I was skating on very thin ice."

He felt her tremble slightly, but she did not reply. Suddenly he felt a bolt of sheer terror strike his heart as he realized that Tess wasn't contradicting him. Brokenly he whispered, "I'm not going to lose you, am I, Tess?"

"Oh, Brady!" she burst out, wrapping both arms around him as she melted against his chest. "You'll never lose me. Never. I'll love you till the day I die."

He cradled her tightly, relief and long-banked hunger doing battle with the leftover fear. But she quickly lifted her lips to his, and the moment their mouths joined, he was lost.

"I WANT YOU TO KNOW," Brady said solemnly after they'd celebrated their reunion and the spectacular news that Trudy had made Harold a generous offer for the hotel, "that I came here prepared to negotiate."

"Negotiate?"

"Compromise. I don't want you to spend any more time feeling the way you have the past six weeks. And to tell you the truth, Tess—" for a moment his eyes grew bleak "—I don't want to feel that lousy, either."

Tess, dressed only in a silky robe, took his hand, and he quickly intertwined her fingers with his own. Brady had slipped on a pair of jeans and was now sitting on the floor by the tiny wood furnace, which he'd just loaded up with kindling. She knew he was ready to light a match, but she just couldn't bear to release him.

"Tell me what you have in mind, Brady," she urged him.

His reply buffeted her flicker of hope like a gust of wind.

"I...I don't have anything in mind," he admitted sheepishly. "I don't know how to solve our problems. I just want you to know that I...*do* want to reach a solution. I mean, some other solution than breaking up with you."

She felt as though a sliver of glass had just pierced her stomach. "Is that an option you've been considering?" she forced herself to ask.

Brady's grip on her hand tightened. His eyes, though loving, were bleak. "There have been moments," he confessed, "when I thought it would be in your best interests." Then he leaned forward to kiss her gently. "But every time I tried to imagine life without ever seeing you again, I just couldn't bear it. I'm not that magnanimous a man."

Tess joined him on the floor, sitting cross-legged as she leaned her forehead against his collarbone. He laid his free hand on her neck.

"I've been thinking about Mandy and Joe," he said quietly. "She teaches all year and works at the train during her summer and Christmas vacations. I was wondering if we could do something like that."

Tess sat up hopefully as a fresh swarm of ideas buzzed in her head. "I could live with that, Brady," she answered pensively, thrilled that he was willing to leave the ranch for her even for a little while. "I could probably live without you from April to October if I knew you were going to winter with me. After all, baseball wives do it, don't they? And I could plan my vacation in June or July so I could join you during the wagon-train season, at least for a little while."

Instantly his expression darkened. The hand massaging her bare nape grew still. "That's not exactly what I had in mind," he countered.

Tess realized, with quick hindsight, that of course it wasn't what he had in mind. It was too easy, too logical. It would involve putting her before the ranch—for almost half of each year. "What did you have in mind?" she asked coolly.

"I was thinking that after we were married—" he tossed the casual words out as though they'd discussed marriage a dozen times before "—you'd be happier if you felt free to go off and do one of your studies for H.W.P. whenever the spirit moved you. Sort of work free-lance a few months spread out throughout the year. Or if it made more sense, I guess you could become a consultant and start your own firm." He gave her a tempting smile. "Rocking T Restorations. Something like that."

It didn't sound too bad. In fact, if Rocking T had a phone and was within thirty miles—even an hour—of an airport, it might have been feasible. Assuming that Tess was independently wealthy and only worked to fill up her time.

"Let's assume, for the sake of argument, that I agree to my half of this compromise. I give up my job, my condo, the bulk of my income and most of my contact with the outside world." Her eyes met his boldly. "What do you give up? What is your half of this 'compromise'?"

Brady looked surprised. It was, in fact, his very evident shock that convinced Tess he truly had viewed his shortsighted proposal as a genuine compromise.

"I give up having a full-time wife," he explained impatiently. "That's not an easy thing for me, Tess, but I've reached the point where I'd rather spend half of my life with you than all of my life alone."

She stood up restlessly, gathering the trash from their supper and dumping it in the small basket by the bed. "Brady," she said slowly, "please don't misunderstand what I'm about to say. I'm deeply touched that you want to marry me, and I desperately hope I'll be able to become your wife. But this 'compromise' you've offered is just a variation on the same old theme. As long as you can continue to live your life completely undisturbed, you're perfectly willing to let me endure physical hardships, isolation, career devastation and poverty right along with you. That doesn't sound like a fifty-fifty deal to me."

His lips tightened. "The deal is for better or worse, Tess. If you're ever ill or in debt or unable to work, I'll still be there for you. I won't throw you out of my house."

"That's it. That's exactly it." She jammed both fists on her hips and glared at him. "It's *your* house, *your* ranch, *your* life. There's nothing there for me."

"*I'm* there for you," he countered hotly. "And if that's not enough then what the hell are we doing here?"

"Let's try it another way, Brady. Let's pretend that I'm saying 'Come live with me in my condo. It's my home. I won't move. I won't change jobs. I won't give up my friends or my nice neighborhood. You can go anywhere you like for summer vacation, but the rest of the time you live in L.A. with me." Her voice tightened. "How does that scenario sound?"

"It's not the same," he answered flatly. "The Rocking T is my life. Your condo is just an address. You've told me a dozen times you'd be happy living anywhere. God knows you've lived all over the country. I'd think you'd be happy to settle down. Isn't that why you left your husband?"

It had to be said then; she couldn't pretend that everything was all right anymore. "Brady," she said slowly, "I left my husband because I was tired of taking second place to something else in his life. I want to be heaven and earth to the man I marry. I want him to be heaven and earth to me."

Brady stood up and walked over to face her squarely. "You can be my heaven, Tess, and every star in my sky. But *my earth* will always be the Rocking T."

BRADY WOKE UP feeling irritable the next morning, and the feeling did not abate as he watched Tess sleep. Her blond hair was sprawled all over his chest and pillow, but still he was not happy. The only compromise they'd reached the night before was an agreement to put their problems on hold for the next twenty-four hours. On Saturday, they would enjoy themselves, remind each other why they wanted to spend the rest of their lives together. On Sunday they'd go back to hammering out a plan to make it happen.

In the end they'd gone for a walk, done some window-shopping in quaint Durango, and wordlessly apologized when they'd gone to bed. Their lovemaking had been sweet and urgent, but it had lacked the healing quality that had repaired all wounds between them in the past. Even now, Brady dreaded the moment of her awakening. Knowing he'd promised not to talk about the future would cast a pall over the entire day.

He knew she had a point about his unwillingness to compromise. All things being equal, if she was willing to leave Los Angeles, he ought to be willing to leave the Rocking T. At least during the winters. And if he'd never been married, if he'd never given up his land before, if he hadn't vowed to show his father that he *would* make a living as a modern-day cowboy...

As the reasons snaked through his consciousness, none of them sounded very good. If this were a scholarly debate, he knew Tess would win on points. But there was nothing intellectual about his reasons for loving the Rocking T, nothing intelligent about choosing to live in isolation and poverty. He had to do it. With or without Tess Hamilton.

That was all.

BY NOON a slow, unquenchable sorrow had taken hold of Tess's heart, and neither the exquisite view of the densely wooded, snow-sprinkled San Juan Mountains nor Brady's determined cheerfulness could shake it. He wasn't going to budge. She knew it. In the end she would have two choices, the same two Nathan had given her throughout their marriage. She could give up her own life to play second fiddle to Brady's, or she could give him up to be true to herself.

But she had promised Brady not to discuss the subject this morning. Today belonged to the two of them, to the historic journey of the Durango-Silverton into the past. Despite her concern for their future, Tess could not stifle her excitement with the day's events. The mile-high view and authentically preserved red-and-gold coach cars would have been enough to lift her out of her doldrums, even if she hadn't been blessed with Brady's smile.

As the engineer pulled twice on the old steam whistle and their open-air gondola began to rock gently from side to side, Brady consulted the dog-eared guidebook Joe had loaned him and paraphrased it with a grin. "First stagecoach stop coming up ahead. Think we'll see any horses?"

"Honestly, Brady, you are obsessed!" she teased him. "Can't you live without those four-footed creatures for even a day?"

He grinned sheepishly. "I suppose I can if I have to. But it just seems to me that if they're going to list a stagecoach stop here they ought to have the old station refurbished, complete with somebody's gray-haired granny feeding us chicken'n'dumplings and apple pie."

"And somebody's gray-haired grandpa waiting with a fresh team of horses."

Brady put his arm around Tess and pulled her close. "Exactly." He dropped a kiss on her forehead. "Great minds think alike."

Tess laughed and snuggled closer as the queen of the narrow gauge chugged through the red-striped cliffs at about twenty miles per hour, a speed that allowed them ample opportunity to study an abandoned mine shaft, the remains of a sawmill, and the occasional deer or elk that scampered off the moment the noisy train lumbered into its field of view. At one point they strolled down to the old Alamosa parlor car where they were entertained by a comedic bartender quoting doggerel that sounded as though it had been written by ancient miners. When he pronounced, "The one thing we need more than gold is girls to tumble before we get old," Tess said, "God help that poor man if Roberta ever takes it in her head to take a trip on this line."

Brady chuckled. "Boy, she is a fireball. How is old Roberta doing these days?"

"'Old Roberta' is doing just fine. She's very excited about a new program she's got going for her students. She's having them come to class in period dress delivering chautauquas. Now she's trying to talk the departmental chair into letting her take her act on the road. Officially, I mean."

"Boy, if I had the money I'd pay Roberta to spend her summers on the Rocking T," Brady told Tess. "What I'd give to have her speeches sparking up my wagon-train tours on a regular basis! I've received more enthusiastic thank-you letters from that trip than all my others put together. And nobody, as far as I know, believes that I didn't put Roberta up to that." He sobered a moment, then asked, "Why won't Roberta ride? Something happened to her, didn't it?"

Tess nodded, unable to lie to Brady despite her lifelong vow to keep Roberta's secret. "I'm sorry I can't explain it to you, Brady. But it's her story to tell." She met his eyes a moment, read the quiet compassion she read there, then added, "And just for the record, please don't ever call her 'old Roberta' to her face. She may act like she loves being one of the guys, but inside Roberta's just as fragile as the rest of us. She's just about given up finding a man who can keep up with her, but deep in her heart I know she still longs to get married."

Brady lightly touched her face. "Oh, I imagine she'll find the right fellow someday. Any man worth his salt can admire that gal's spunk. The only reason I didn't find myself attracted to Roberta is that at the very same moment I met her, I was suddenly blinded by somebody else."

He dropped a kiss on Tess's cheek, then chastely kissed her lips. "God, it's good to see you. I don't want this day to ever end."

Tess bit her lip, then hugged him tightly. She glanced away before the embrace could get too personal.

With an uneven tone to his voice, Brady went back to tossing out bits and pieces of information from his guidebook. "Silverton is completely restored and has been declared a registered national historical landmark." He grinned at her. "You think someday a guidebook will list the Slow Joe that way?"

She grinned. "Certainly, if you set your mind to it. Look at the miracle you achieved for the hotel."

He touched her face with the back of his hand. "You're the one who thought of using our mailing lists to send out the word. We couldn't have done it without you." He was quiet a minute, then he asked, "Do you have any other great ideas for building up business? Not just for me but for Joey? You know, the Slow Joe was just as famous as the Silverton back when it was called the Colorado Fireball. Maybe we could make more of that somehow, build up Joey's income."

"Does he need to beef up his income?"

Brady shook his head. "Not really. Joe's a good businessman. But he paid the down payment on my ranch, Tess, with the understanding that he'd start earning a cut after five years. You know I don't give a damn if I'm rich or poor as long as I can stay on the ranch, but Joey's done so much for me that I wish I were making more money so I could make it up to him. At least I won't go under now that Trudy's going to buy the hotel, but I'm not going to be any Rockefeller for a while yet."

Tess pondered his question for a moment. She had already known that he and Joe had a partnership that involved Joe's capital and Brady's sweat, but she had not, until this moment, realized that Joe was wholly responsible for Brady's miraculous repurchase of the Rocking T. No wonder he felt compelled to repay his friend!

"Well, to be honest with you, Brady, the only real difference I see between the Silverton and the Slow Joe is that when you ride the Silverton, you've got somewhere to go. Joe's done a terrific job on his train, but when Roberta and I took the trip after we left the wagon train, we heard several people comment that they didn't just want to go around in a big circle. They wanted to visit a real ghost town, a working ranch or an old mine."

Brady's eyes seemed to darken. "People who visit the Slow Joe get to come out to the Rocking T. It's not as though there's nothing else to do but ride the train."

Tess shook her head. "You're missing my point. Everybody loves *being* on the Rocking T, but they're not too happy about getting there. There's nothing fun about riding two and a half hours in a van over a lousy road."

"We aren't talking about building the Rocking T's business," he stonily maintained. "I asked you if you had any ideas to help Joe."

Sorry that she'd offended him, Tess said, "I'm saying that if the Slow Joe could visit some genuine historic site on its regular run, Joey could improve his business. Especially if there was something to do when people got there. Shopping, you know, or visiting an old opera house like they have in Virginia City."

For another long moment, Brady just stared at Tess, his lips so taut that she was certain he was furious. But then she read another expression in the lines of his face and the wonder of his eyes. He wasn't angry; he was thinking. Thinking hard.

And then he smiled. He smiled as though God had just granted him acreage on some heavenly Rocking T. "Silvergold is a real place," he announced slowly. "It is a real mining camp, a real ghost town. As real as Bodie or Virginia City or Silverton." His tone was triumphant. "Do you think tourists would like to ride the Slow Joe out there?"

"Brady, you know they'd love it!" It was a great idea but an impossible one, and Tess knew she'd have to put the damper on his joy. "But there isn't a track out to

Silvergold, and besides, it's in quite a state of disrepair. You don't have the time nor the money, nor—forgive me but it's true—the expertise to renovate a ghost town."

"No, I don't," he answered equably. His eyes brimmed with joy. "But *you* do."

Tess stared at him blankly. She could see the jubilance in his face, the unmitigated relief in his beautiful blue eyes. Still, she wasn't sure she understood his plan. As much as she'd dearly love to restore Silvergold—it would be the pinnacle of her career!—there was no way she could undertake the restoration of an entire ghost town in her free time, especially at a distance. Brady had offered the town before as a lure to move to Colorado, and the only thing different about his offer this time was the unblemished joy on his face.

"Brady, I don't see—"

"We can do this, Tess!" he burst out as the train rumbled into Silverton, and he gestured toward the quaint western town with one wildly enthusiastic arm. "We can fix up Silvergold, run the train out there, put together an entertainment plan that can't be beat! And we won't be starting from scratch. We've already got the acts—Roberta, Harry Painted Hat, the stagecoach, the mountain man, the Pony Express. We've already got the narrow gauge train and now that we've got Trudy, we can still count on the hotel! We've got the wagon train as a trump card—and a mailing list and word of mouth advertisement that can't be beat! If we can get the historic district legislation passed, it'll build potential even further. We can do it, Tess!" He took her hands and met her eyes. "Would that be enough of a career to get you to leave H.W.P.? Would that fill your professional needs enough to leave L.A. and live with me?"

She heard the desperation in his voice, realized the depth from which his brilliant idea had sprung. On his own, she was certain that Brady would have been thrilled to keep his ghost town private and never let steel rails reach the Rocking T. The wagon train was all he really wanted. But he'd finally come up with a compromise that really would meet Tess's needs. She was still in shock at the speed of his proposition, but her joy was undeniable.

She didn't want to waste a moment being practical; she was not about to look a gift horse in the mouth. "If we can get the money to pull this off, Brady," she promised, her smile as radiant as his own, "you've got yourself a partner." She laid one hand on his face and whispered, "A partner for life."

CHAPTER SIXTEEN

"BRADY!" Mandy squawked when Brady greeted her with a welcome-home hug that nearly knocked her off her feet. "How did it go? Are you feeling better?"

Brady swirled her around two or three times, certain that she already knew the answer to her own rhetorical question. Still, he joyfully confessed, "I'm a new man, Mandy. I was losing her. You know what I mean? We haven't worked out all the details yet, but I know she's mine again."

"I'm so glad!" she whispered, dropping a kiss on his cheek as she released him. "I know it's going to work out, Brady. I know she's the one for you."

He grinned, recalling the last time Tess had said almost the same words. It was just that morning, in fact—a lifetime ago in Durango. She'd only been half-dressed at the time, her eyes still sparkling from their last intimate expression of love. *It's going to work out, Brady, she'd promised him. As long as we just remember that we love each other, that we're a team, that we're partners in everything from now on.*

Partners, he'd whispered back. *Partners on the trail of life.*

She'd giggled then, kissed him once more, and in a matter of moments she'd lost all the ground she'd gained in getting dressed and had to start all over again.

"So, what's the new plan?" Mandy asked as she poured him a cup of coffee and motioned for him to sit down. Joe, she explained, was at a movie with the kids and wouldn't be home for a while yet. "Have you two worked out a practical compromise?"

"Well, we've got a compromise in the works. I'm not sure that it's particularly practical, but it is do-able, assuming I can secure the cooperation of my other partner."

Mandy sat down slowly, lifting her eyes to his. "You mean Joe."

He nodded.

This time Mandy's smile was a little tighter. "Brady, you know we'd do anything for you. But we're already stretched just as thin as we can be. Does this... partnership require additional funds or just enthusiasm for whatever new idea you and Tess want to implement?" This time her smile was more encouraging. "You know we'll support anything you want to try."

Guilt darkened Brady's hope as he faced her squarely. Only for Tess would he press his dear friends any further, and even then it made him queasy. Joe never complained about lack of funds, but Brady knew that he wouldn't even if he was starving...at least not if it meant Brady might have to sell the ranch. Still, he was certain that once his idea paid off, he could repay Joe for everything. Maybe even make him rich beyond his dreams. "Mandy," he confessed slowly, "I want to lay track out to the Rocking T."

Her mouth opened in a perfect O, but no words came out. He knew then that he should have waited for Joey, talked him into it first. Joe would be more willing to take a gamble. Mandy's priorities were different. As a business, the Slow Joe meant very little to her; she defended it tooth and toenail only because it mattered so deeply to Joe.

"We...wouldn't mind expanding if...the cost weren't prohibitive, Brady," she answered slowly. "But we really don't have any money to spare, and Trudy's going to have her hands full just fixing up the hotel."

Forgive me, Mandy, his heart cried out. *Forgive me, Joe.* Fortifying himself with memories of Tess, he forged ahead. "We could get a business expansion loan, Mandy. It shouldn't be the uphill struggle that Harold's had, because we're not going to be rehabilitating anything old—at least not as far as the cash to lay track is concerned. Tess is willing to sell her condo and use the proceeds to develop Silvergold. But realistically, even that will be cutting it close. There won't be anything left over to pay for the track."

Mandy didn't say a word.

Desperately he continued, "She's going to renovate it top to bottom, the way they've renovated Silverton. In the long run we'll be able to do just what they do in Durango—run a historic train out to a historic mining camp with period hotels, restaurants and entertainment. Like Tombstone, Arizona or Virginia City in Nevada. Tess knows how to do it. It's her job, and the love of her life. It's the only way she can continue her life. It's the only way she can continue her career and still live on the Rocking T, Mandy." His joy was starting to turn to desperation as his eyes begged her to agree. "Isn't it a wonderful idea?"

By now it was perfectly obvious from the floury complexion of Mandy's face that she thought his brainchild was anything but wonderful. In fact, she looked downright horrified.

He didn't really understand it. He'd expected her to fuss a bit about the money, but he'd been certain that when she understood how perfect this compromise was—and how miraculous!—she'd wish him godspeed. Wasn't she the one who had urged him to come up with a solution to his problems with Tess before he lost her altogether?

He leaned forward urgently and took her hand. "Mandy," he begged, "it's the *only* way I'm ever going to be able to marry Tess."

Mandy squeezed his hand, but tears filled her eyes as she turned away. After a second she stood up and walked over to the train in the corner of the living room, fussing with one of the engines just as Joe always did when he was upset.

Desperately Brady whispered, "Mandy, please! Don't make Joey choose between us."

She whirled back to face him. "Oh, Brady, don't you understand? I don't want Joe to choose. I love you as much as he does! We'd do anything for you!" She crossed the room again and took his shoulders as she bent down very close to his face. "The problem is that Joe doesn't have a choice."

"Of course he has a choice! He can get another loan."

Slowly she shook her head. "No, he can't. He mortgaged his soul for the last one."

"I know that, Mandy, and believe me, I couldn't be more grateful. But we're making the payments and—"

"And counting every penny."

"I don't mind counting every penny as long as I can live on my own land!"

"Maybe you don't mind, but we do! Joe has kids to support. Have you forgotten? And I have to dress halfway decently for my job. And I need a reliable car to get there! And I've gotten there late because my car has died on the road six times in the past year."

Brady sobered. "I'm sorry about that, Mandy. Really I am. But you can't blame me for your car."

"I can't?" Suddenly her cool demeanor snapped. "Why do you think I can't afford another one?"

"I don't know," he answered honestly. Suddenly he felt a little ill. There was something seriously wrong with Mandy's response. Were she and Joey in some kind of trouble? Something that was using up their spare cash? Abruptly he remembered the moments he'd sensed that Joe was trying to tell him something and just couldn't find the courage. Now he desperately wished that he'd put aside his own selfish needs long enough to find out what was wrong. Now, slowly, he suggested, "I would think between what Joe makes on the business and what you earn as a teacher, you could afford a decent car."

"I'm sure you do, Brady. But you probably don't realize that in addition to living expenses and child support, we're paying for Sally's orthodontist, Lynne's ballet classes and about half of Karen's expenses at Colorado State. When you add that to the monthly payments on the loan Joey got from John Carleton this summer, we don't have anything to spare."

Brady stared at her, fighting the sudden wave of nausea that gripped him. The somersault in his stomach had nothing to do with Tess. This was family business, Joey business. His best friend was in trouble, and he was almost certain it was his fault.

"What loan?" he asked tightly. Surely Joey would have told him if he'd been that strapped! "Joey's always run the Slow Joe in the black."

"Joey always had a savings account for emergencies," Mandy answered coolly, "until he used it up on the down payment for your ranch. He cut every corner he could after that, but without my income he would have had to borrow money long before this. When both steam engines simply died on him this summer, we couldn't keep pretending that we didn't need more cash."

Suddenly tears filled Mandy's eyes as she took Brady's hands. "Oh, God, I'm sorry, Brady. Joe never wanted you to know. He insisted that we'd be okay, that you'd start making a solid profit by next summer and be able to start paying him back. He didn't want you to feel guilty." She choked back a sob. "But dammit, Brady, I won't stand by and let you use my husband any longer! He's done more for you than any friend owes another, but it's never enough. He's actually going into debt to protect your dreams, and all you can think about is how you can sucker him into giving you even more cash!"

Brady released her hands. He stood and turned away, unable to face her. He felt chilled. He was almost shuddering with the impact of her revelation. All this time he'd been scrimping and saving, proud of himself for making ends meet, certain that it was worth any sacrifice to hold on to the ranch...any sacrifice that *he* chose to make. It had never occurred to him that Mandy and Joe were sacrificing, too.

"My God," he whispered, truly nauseated now. "I swear, Mandy, I never had a clue."

"Well, don't say that if you'd known you would have stopped us, because you know it wouldn't have made any difference," she replied, her tone straightforward but not unkind. "Oh, you would have felt more guilty, but nothing would have stopped you from proving to Claudia that you could hang on to the Rocking T."

"Claudia?" He whipped back to face her. "You think I bought back the ranch to prove myself to *her*?"

"You're still trying to prove yourself to her! You measure every move Tess makes to some invisible standard of what Claudia did or didn't do. You lost Claudia because of the Rocking T and you're about to lose Tess to it, too! What does it take for you to get the message, Brady?"

"What you're really saying," he ground out a moment later as a terrible possibility washed over him, "is that the Rocking T is going to cost me you and Joey, too."

WHEN THE PHONE RANG, Tess did not hurry to answer it. Brady had promised to let her know the outcome of his talk with Joey, but it was far too late by now for him to be calling with good news.

"Hi, sweetheart," he said quietly. Sorrow weighted every word. "Sorry to be calling so late."

"It's okay, Brady. I couldn't have gone to sleep without hearing from you anyway."

She had hoped—for a few hours, actually believed!—that they'd finally found a solution to their problems. But their solution had only been a pipe dream; she knew by the silence—the long, aching silence—that twisted her heart into ragged knots. Finally, desperate for some kind of assurance, she told him, "I love you, Brady. No matter what."

His response was a long, weary sigh. Then he said hoarsely, "It's not going to work, Tess. The railroad. It would cost a fortune to run it all the way out to the Rocking T. And I just found out that my nest egg isn't worth a damn. I've got to give every penny of it to Joey." Now his voice was thick with shame. "Joe had to take out a loan to keep the Slow Joe running this year because every penny he's got is tied up in my ranch. He never gave me a clue—in fact, he never intended to—but when I came home with this crazy new notion, Mandy just snapped.''

Tess closed her eyes. She tried to stifle a body-racking shudder but failed. Running track out to the Rocking T wasn't a great plan, but it had been their only hope. She'd really been thrilled about renovating Silvergold. It had bothered the historian in her that they would have had to build a new railroad line instead of reconstructing an old one, but Silvergold was the only ghost town on the Rocking T, and obviously Brady wouldn't consider a ghost town anywhere else.

''How much do you owe him, Brady?'' she asked hopelessly.

When he told her the figure, she nearly wept.

''I'm going to have to find some way to cut corners even more tightly, Tess. God only knows how. When I think of the money I just blew in Durango—''

Abruptly he broke off, as though he realized how ungracious it sounded.

''Do you really think Joe will ask you to pay him back right now?'' Tess asked, feeling his pain as if it were her own. ''Surely he realized how precarious your financial condition is.''

''Of course he does. That's why he never told me what he'd done. I haven't even seen him yet, and when I do, he'll probably tell me not to worry about it, just to pay him when I can.'' He sounded positively ill. ''But I can't do that, Tess. Not now that I know. I can't leave Joey hanging. Even if he didn't need the money for his own family. I just—'' his voice shook with pain ''—can't pretend it doesn't matter.''

Neither could Tess. She understood his feelings, admired his sense of honor and loyalty to his friend. But she also knew that the easiest solution to Brady's problem—a quick infusion of money from some other source—would only complicate things down the road.

"Brady," she said helplessly, "I want to volunteer to help you but I don't think I can. I bailed Nathan out of so many scrapes, and every time I felt a little more used. If I—"

"Dammit, Tess, did I ask for your money? Do you think that's all I want from you?"

"Of course not! But if we're married...if we were sure that we would be someday... it would be natural for me to help you. If the tables were reversed, you'd do the same for me."

When Brady didn't answer, Tess felt an ugly knot fill her heart. What had happened to the joy they'd shared just hours ago? What had happened to the hope, the sense of the future, the majesty of their love?

"This morning," he said tightly, "I recall some discussion of marriage. In fact, I recall that both of us made a commitment to be partners for life. Did I misread the situation?"

Tess's throat tightened. She tried to swallow the lump, but couldn't really manage it. "Brady, please don't try to oversimplify this. I've been here before."

"Not with me, you haven't." Now there was a tinge of anger in his tone.

"Well, dammit, Brady, you haven't been here with *me* either! Sometimes I think you're so damn determined to make me do what Claudia refused to that you're missing the point altogether!"

It was the wrong thing to say. Even over the wire she could sense his fury.

"Tess, I told you from the day we met what I wanted in a wife. I told you every damn way that Claudia failed to meet my needs. You're the one who insisted on getting involved with me anyway. Over and over again you said it didn't matter, that you were different, that—"

"Brady, don't you dump this all on me! I've offered you a thousand compromises! You've never even considered one that involved a single sacrifice on your part. Now I've told you over and over again that I'll live anywhere with you if I can just carry on with my career and feel that I'm a valuable person in my own right! But you won't budge an inch from your original position. All you want is to live on that land—first, last, always. It's cost you your wife, your baby, your father and now it's hurting your best friend. Has it ever occurred to you that there's a pattern here and the only consistent variable is Brady Trent?"

"What's that mean, Tess? Are you trying to find a place in that lineup of losses? Is that what we're trying to say?"

"No, Brady! I'm just trying to point out to you that maybe there's a reason why Claudia left you and maybe you ought to find out what it is!"

The words seemed to hurl through the long-distance line between them, and Tess found herself desperately longing to reach out to touch his face. *It's always this way,* she thought, crushed. *He's a thousand miles away whenever I need him most.*

"Brady, I'm sorry," she whispered. Her tone was so low she wasn't sure he could hear her, but she couldn't seem to lend more power to her voice. "Brady, I didn't mean that. I didn't—"

"Yes, you did. You meant exactly that. And I suspect that you've been wanting to say it almost since we met."

Although his tone was calmer now, there was a dead sound to his voice, which frightened her. With an instinct known to every woman, Tess realized that she'd gone too far. In the past they'd bickered and battled, stormed and wept, but she'd always known that their problems were nothing that a few quick kisses couldn't heal. This time it was different. This time they'd both hit a brick wall. They were out of excuses and compromises. They couldn't keep walking together unless one of them surrendered completely and gave up where he wanted to go.

"I'd like to think that you love me more than you love the Rocking T, Brady," she tearfully confessed. "That's all I want. Is that really so much to ask?"

"I want you to understand that if you love Brady Trent, you love the Rocking T," was his stubborn reply. "It's really as simple as that."

Tess closed her eyes, battled the hot tears and clenched the receiver so hard one fingernail cracked. "I love you, Brady. And I do love the Rocking T. I'd never ask you to give it up if there were any other way we could make a life together."

"There is another way," he said coolly. "Quit your job or take a leave... or bring your work with you if it comes to that. But sell the condo, Tess, and move in with me." There was another long pause before he added tersely, "Keep the money in your own name, Tess, or give it away. That's not what I'm asking for. All I want is for us to be together. I can support you on the ranch." He waited for what seemed like forever before he urged her in a low, hoarse tone, "Marry me before snow flies."

Tess had always known, deep in her heart, that someday it would come to this. Someday the decision would have to be made. All she'd learned from her first marriage—all she knew in her head—would be pitted against the simple truth in her heart. Pride in her own common sense would do absolutely zilch to make up for the loss of Brady.

But if he won't give up the ranch for you, you don't have him anyway, she realized bitterly. *You're no more than a new ranch accessory... a nice harness, a horse or a cow. If he loved you* he'd *offer to move, at least closer in to a town. He'd consider the options... he'd visit you in L.A.... he'd offer to sell the Rocking T in the same breath he ordered her to give up her own home.*

The lines of logic scattered through her mind, doing battle with the aching need to believe in him, to say yes to whatever he proposed, to find a way to ease the terrible pain inside her. And in another life, before she'd married Nathan, she knew she could have forgotten reality and blindly followed love. But she was a woman now, not a lovestruck girl right out of school, and she knew that Brady still didn't love her enough to make a marriage work.

"You don't know how much I wish I could tell you I'm coming, Brady," she confessed raggedly.

"Then do it, Tess! My God, the first snow's already overdue. There's a storm headed here this weekend from Wyoming. If it's a big one, I may not be able to get through to you for months—even by mail! I can't go through the whole winter with things like this between us, Tess. I'll lose my mind out there."

Tess started to sob. She'd vowed not to do it, but she just couldn't hold it back anymore. "Brady, come to me. Spend the winter *here*. Let's get our marriage off to a good start without battling nature, too. Give me some time to find another job closer. Maybe I can commute. Maybe—"

"No! I've had enough of this damn intellectualizing. Even if I could stand to live in L.A.—which I can't—it would end up the same way. I already went to the East Coast to grovel for a woman. I'll be damned if I'll travel west for a replay!"

"Brady, I'm not Claudia! And I'll never marry you until I'm sure you know that in your heart!"

For a long terrible moment, there was only silence. Tess pretended, desperately, that Brady was only pondering her words, considering her feelings, preparing to admit that she was right. Or at least preparing a genuine compromise.

But in her heart she was terrified that he was building up the courage to say goodbye.

Her worst fears were realized when he stated coolly, "I guess there's really nothing left to say."

"I love you, Brady!" Tess yelled at him, suddenly gasping in panic. "What could be more important than that?"

His voice was hoarse and husky as he answered, "I love you, too, sweetheart. I always will."

For just a moment Tess took hope...until he said, "But if you're not willing to spend the rest of your life on the Rocking T, there's still nothing left to say."

CHAPTER SEVENTEEN

WHEN BRADY HUNG UP he planned to slip silently out of the Hendersons' house without disturbing anyone, but Joe, who must have returned while Brady was talking to Tess, ambushed him in the living room.

Mandy seemed to have vanished, though Brady suspected that she'd had time to greet her husband while he was on the phone. At the moment, he didn't want to see a living soul...especially not Joe. It was bad enough that he'd just lost Tess; he didn't want to deal with the betrayal of his best friend. Or was it the other way around?

Joe looked awful. His face was red and his lips were almost white. He could not look Brady in the eye.

For a moment the silence between the two men seemed to fill the room to bursting. At last Brady said harshly, "I'm going to withdraw every penny from my savings account tomorrow. It's not nearly enough, but at least it's a start. Then I'm going to start paying you a hundred bucks a month right now, not next summer." He took a deep breath and made the offer that honor forced him to extend, the offer that he desperately hoped Joe would reject. "If that's not enough, then—"

"We made a deal," Joe interrupted. Still he could not look directly at Brady. "You start paying at the end of five years. You've got ten more months before you owe me anything."

Brady was swamped with guilty relief. Joe wasn't going to ask him to sell the ranch! But that was the only fraction of good news in this entire horrendous scenario. He could still keep the Rocking T . . . but at what cost?

"You should have trusted me, Joey," he accused softly. "You should have told me the truth."

At last Joe's eyes flashed up to meet his. "If I didn't trust you, Brady, I sure as hell would never have cosigned your loan! No businessman in his right mind would believe a wagon-train program would pan out. If anybody else had been heading up that outfit out there, I wouldn't have signed on that dotted line for love nor money."

Brady flopped down in a giant armchair because he suddenly felt too ill to stand. "I'll pay you back, Joey. Every damn cent. I swear it."

Joe ran a nervous hand through his hair. "I know you will. I've never worried about that, and I'm not worrying about it now. What I am worried about is that you're going to get your pride all tangled up with your common sense and do something you're going to regret."

"Like what?"

"Like get so crazy about paying me back that you convince yourself you can't afford to marry Tess."

Brady covered his swirling stomach with both hands. "It's over. It was crazy from the start and this was the only way it could end. The only thing that surprises me is that I lied to myself about it for so long."

"What do you mean by, 'It's over'?" Joe asked tensely.

The spear in his heart blocked Brady's breath. He didn't answer at once. He couldn't seem to speak.

Joe stood up and edged toward him. "You mean Tess? My God, Brady, do you mean it's over with Tess?"

His hands were trembling; all he could do was nod.

"She left you?" His tone was incredulous. "I don't believe it!"

Brady closed his eyes. He didn't believe it, either. "She won't come" was all he could sputter.

"What do you mean she won't come?"

"I asked her to marry me. Now. I asked her to take the chance, to believe in me. To believe in the ranch."

He had expected sympathy from his lifelong friend, but to his surprise, there was none forthcoming. "You mean you gave her an ultimatum. You did the stupidest thing you possibly could have done."

Brady's eyes flashed open, anger flaring amidst the pain. "I did what I had to do, Joey! I couldn't drag it out. I couldn't make it through the winter wondering, waiting, not knowing—"

"So you broke it off instead? What a cowardly thing to do!"

"Dammit, Joe, about the last thing I need right now is you calling me a coward! If all you're going to do is insult me, I think I'll just rev up the truck and go home."

"Oh, no!" interrupted Joe, blocking his path to the door. "You're not going anywhere until you hear a piece of my mind."

"Joey—"

"Sit down and shut up," Joe ordered, pointing at the armchair.

Brady just glared at him. "This isn't really any of your business, Joey. You have no right—"

"None of my business? Like it was none of your business to set me straight when I was blowing it with Mandy before we got married?"

Brady struggled for a retort, but no words crawled out of his mouth.

"Sit!" Joe commanded.

Sheepishly Brady sat. He tried not to listen, but Joe was shouting at him, gesturing angrily above his head.

"All of your life I've stood beside you, Brady. I've backed you up no matter what I thought of what you were doing. I've put my business, my family and my relationship with your dad on the line. I've never tried to second-guess you, never tried to interfere. But dammit, Brady, you've finally gone over the line, and if I don't set you straight, who will?"

Brady said nothing, just stared at his boots.

"Mandy and I are in debt up to our eyeballs because of you. You're barely eking out a living, and you're lonely as hell half of each year. Maybe you're proving to your dad that you can make the Rocking T work in spite of him, but that's not what you're proving to me."

Brady took a deep breath. He didn't want to hear this. He didn't want to believe it was true.

"I always stood behind you because I understand what it means to have a dream, Brady. To fight for it tooth and toenail. But I also understand that there's more than one way to find happiness, and that's something you don't seem to have figured out yet. You're stuck in a rut, replaying old tapes, reliving old failures and making them happen all over again. Claudia, your dad, the Rocking T. I've heard this whole damn story before. You didn't try to rewrite it. You just reread the same damn book."

Joe stopped for a moment and glared at his friend, waiting for some sort of reply. When there was none, he charged on. "Your dream, it seems to me, is attainable. Running a ranch in red-rock country with a woman who's your perfect match, making peace with your dad—you could *have* that dream, Brady. You could buy a ranch closer in, one with a shorter van run or one we could easily connect with the train. There are other ghost towns out here—a couple in the mountains right on the Slow Joe's narrow gauge line—or you could let Tess construct a mock one. You could keep the wagon-train business—improve it, I'm sure, just by being closer in and adding the lure of the ghost town—and still keep Tess. One sign of compromise, Brady, one little sign, and she'll come running. Mandy's sure of it."

At last he seemed to be finished. Brady waited until the silence grew intense, then met his buddy's eyes. "Are you finished?"

Joe nodded. His eyes were grim.

"I wondered if you were going to finish up with a little warning that if I failed to measure up to your expectations you were going to put the ranch up for sale. That is your legal right, as I recall."

Dark, angry red splashed across Joe's face, a reminder of the childhood days when he'd had so much trouble keeping his temper. Now he fairly hissed, "I deserve better than that from you, Brady!"

Shame, the dark and lasting kind, chewed at Brady's heart. He knew it was true; he knew he was too churned up to think clearly, too anguished to say anything right. He'd just lost Tess, and the reality of that angst was just setting in; he felt as though he'd been trampled by a herd of longhorns.

He raised defeated eyes to Joe's. "I'm sorry, Joey. I'm sorry for everything. I owe you everything. I owe you my life."

Joe leaned down and glared at him. "You owe me some common sense. You owe me something besides stupid pride. You owe me the willingness to admit that the Rocking T is no longer the most important thing in your life. Is it really worth losing Tess? Is it really worth losing Jake?" After a tense moment he added fiercely, "Is it really worth losing *me*?"

JAKE, still in pajamas and a bathrobe, was reading the morning paper when he heard the knock on the back door. Only half a dozen close friends and neighbors ever came in that way...and Brady, of course. But it had been years since Brady had dropped by without an invitation.

"I've got it, honey," Arleen called from the back of the house. A moment later she appeared in the kitchen. Joe Henderson stood close behind her.

"'Mornin', Joey," said Jake, surprised to see his young friend at such an early hour. Jake knew that Joe always got up with the chickens, but he usually went right to his office to clear up his paperwork before the tourists showed up at nine.

Joe looked terrible. He had not shaved, and his eyes were bloodshot. It took little imagination to realize that he'd been up most of the night. Jake wondered how long he'd been waiting to come calling.

Jake put down his paper and glanced nervously at Arleen. Her face mirrored his own tension but revealed no clues. Apparently she was in the dark as much as he was.

"I'm sorry to disturb you so early, Jake, but I had to talk to you before you went to work."

"It's okay, Joey. You're welcome here any time, day or night." *Unless you've brought news that something has happened to my boy.* The thought paralyzed him, made it hard to speak. Still, he managed to say calmly, "Have a seat."

Joe sat down on the edge of a straight-back chair, plucking off his engineer's cap to twirl it in his hands. "Jake, I think I've made a big mistake." He licked his lower lip. "Actually, I know it."

Jake stifled a gasp of relief. If Brady was dead or dying, Joe would have told him outright. Any other problem seemed so puny in comparison that he was sure coping with it would be a breeze.

"Brady broke up with Tess last night because she wouldn't move to the Rocking T. I told him he'd blown it with her the way he'd blown it with everybody—Claudia, you, even me."

"Even you?" Jake couldn't hide his surprise.

Joe hung his head. "I didn't know what else to do. It was the only leverage I had. And I couldn't bear to think of him crawling off to that lonely ranch to lick his wounds while this wonderful woman was crying her eyes out in California."

Jake met Arleen's eyes, grateful for the sympathy he read there. "There's no good way to handle him when he's like this, Joey. We've all been here before."

"No," Joe corrected him. "He always had *me* before. Even when he'd lost everything and everybody else."

Jake couldn't meet his eyes. A thousand times he'd wished that he could have comforted his son during Brady's darkest times; a thousand times he'd cursed himself for his failure. He'd even been jealous of Joe, no matter how much he cared for the boy, because he'd been family to Brady when Brady was barely speaking to his dad. How many times had he heard Brady say, "Joe's the only one who understands. He's the only one who'll never turn his back on me."

Now Jake said softly, "It's okay, Joey. He knows. Maybe he didn't know last night, but now that he's had time to think about it, he knows you were only trying to help him."

Joe took a deep breath. "I hope you're right. But I've got to drive out there and tell him myself. He could be snowlocked anytime, and I'll be damned if I'll let him go through the winter with hard words festering between us."

At last Jake met his eyes, wondering exactly why Joe had come to see him this morning. Why wasn't he already on his way out to the Rocking T?

"Then I guess you'd best be on your way, Joey," he suggested gently.

Joe shook his head. "Not yet. I need...I need to take him something. Some fresh hope. I've got to do *something* to make things right for him."

"Joe, you've bent over backward to make things right for Brady all your life. Right now I don't think you can do anything more but apologize for whatever you said last night."

"I've got to do more, Jake. But I can't do it without your help. Brady wants to lay a narrow gauge line out to the Rocking T so Tess can renovate his ghost town. He wants to do a massive historical entertainment deal like they have at Silverton. Mandy was so upset about how much it would cost that she told him that we recently had to take out a loan of our own from John Carleton."

"I know," said Jake, not bothering to explain. He was relieved that Mandy had let the cat out of the bag; now he wouldn't have to be the one to tell Brady. But he also knew how painful the news would be to Brady, and the thought of his boy so unhappy made him feel sick.

"I'm begging you, Jake. For Brady," Joe whispered, his voice eerie in the thin light of dawn. "Make this happen for him. Give us a loan, invest in it yourself, or help us arrange stock to sell, whatever. Brady's got to be able to keep the Rocking T without losing Tess."

Jake stood up, loosened his bathrobe sash and nervously tightened it again. The desperation in Joe's voice was frightening. The thought of Brady going through the same agony that he had after he'd lost Claudia and the baby was almost more than a father could bear.

"Joey," he said softly, "I don't have that kind of money. I can't get that kind of money. And frankly, in good conscience I couldn't ask anybody to invest in such a scheme. I can see some potential for a linkup between the Slow Joe, the wagon train and a ghost town, but not the Rocking T. It's just too far away from everything. If a rail were already laid and just needed to be fixed up a bit, it might make sense, historically and financially. But the cost—"

"Hang the cost, Jake! I'm talking about your son!"

Jake turned, his arms rigid as he faced Joe Henderson. "My son is not a child, Joe. He is a man. And as a man, he must find his own way in life. He would not thank me for whisking away his troubles, and he would not thank you for coming here behind his back. If he can't find a way to marry that woman on his own, he'll never be able to hold her. In a few years she'll abandon him, just as Claudia did, and he'll be even more bitter than he is right now."

Joe stood, his body tense and angry. "Then you won't help me? You don't do one damn thing to help *him*?"

Jake tried to answer the question, but no words came to him. He tried to remember his obligations to the bank, the bank he'd always longed to pass on to his son. He tried to remember the look on Brady's face the first time Jake had seen him gaze at Tess Hamilton, and he tried not to remember the angst in his son's eyes when he'd tongue-lashed his father for refusing to support the historical committee's work. He tried to make sense of the long years of semiseparation between himself and the boy he so desperately loved, but he could find no logic that justified the well of pain.

Abruptly he said to Joe, "You've got a business to run, Joey. I suggest you hustle back to the station." Then he said to Arleen, "Call the bank and tell Lucy I won't be in today."

THE MORNING AFTER Brady's fight with Joe, he marched out to the barn at daybreak, fed the chickens, collected some eggs, then tried to convince himself that his tack room needed to be rearranged. It was a big job that would take all day, and with any luck at all, it would keep his mind on something other than the ugly emotional hole he'd dug for himself the day before.

He was not proud of the way he'd acted. He was ashamed of the way he'd talked to Mandy and miserable over his last parting with Tess. As to Joey, well...that would also take some time to heal. But he had no doubt that his relationship with Joe would survive this latest catastrophe, just as he had no doubt, now that he had time to think about it, that Joe had threatened to abandon him out of a desperate, misguided hope that it might force him to give up the Rocking T for Tess.

He wanted to. It did not seem possible that he could endure her loss. And yet, as he busied himself with the feel of leather and the smell of hay, he wondered if he'd ever really had her love to lose. She could have made the heroic gesture, but she'd refused. He'd asked her to marry him, and she'd turned him down. There didn't really seem to be anything else he could do after that.

When a wild chorus of barking heralded the sound of an automotive engine lumbering along the dirt road near ranch headquarters, he was not surprised. He had known, with the certainty of mathematics, that Joe would drive out to the ranch this morning to apologize. It was unnecessary, but he was glad anyway. He had an apology of his own to make—Joey sure as hell didn't owe *him* one—and Joe's arrival would save him another long trip into town.

He knew that Joe would never ask him to sell the ranch, never stop helping him, never walk out of his life. But he knew that Joe deserved more than he'd been giving him in the past few years. He'd taken advantage of Joe's loyalty, relied on it far too much. Now that he knew what the Hendersons' true financial situation was, he'd have to change all that.

And I'll have to stop aching for Tess, he ordered himself briskly. *I'll have to stop pretending that miracles still happen.* At least that was what he kept telling himself, determined that the jagged hole in his heart would sooner or later start to mend. It was too soon; that was all. Too soon to expect the terrible anguish to pass.

He would feel better, he told himself, after he talked to Joe.

But it was not Joe's old blue station wagon that pulled into view a moment later, nor was it Mandy's white Toyota. Incredibly it was a brand-new gold Mercedes.

Just like the one that belonged to his dad.

CHAPTER EIGHTEEN

BRADY STRAIGHTENED, squinted in disbelief, and then slowly walked out of the barn to greet his father. He wanted to keep working on his tack room and feign total disconcern, but with six dogs on the property who were not accustomed to strangers near the barn, he knew that, without help, his father would not be able to get out of his car.

He called off the dogs, waiting silently while each one joined him, their hackles still raised, and stared down the trail. His father was moving slowly, and in the early light he could see Jake's bald spot clearly. He could also see how slowly he moved on stiffening legs. It had been some time since Brady had noticed that.

The stiffness wasn't all due to arthritis, Brady decided as his father reached the barn and stood facing him, as though they were two gunfighters in a standoff.

"'Mornin', son," was all he said.

Brady nodded. "What brings you out here?" he asked coolly.

"Does a father need a reason to visit his boy?"

"Some don't. You always do." His eyes narrowed. "At least you did when I lived closer in. I don't rightly recall ever seeing you on the Rocking T before." He knew perfectly well that Jake had never been to the ranch; it was one of the things that had always stuck in Brady's craw. It was as though Jake thought that by refusing to see the Rocking T, he could pretend it did not exist.

Jake met his eyes. "I'm here now, son."

"And?"

"And I've had a long drive. You might want to offer me a cup of coffee."

"I didn't think you were planning to stay that long."

Jake winced as though Brady had struck him, and he instantly regretted the harsh words. But he knew he had not a shred of tact left in him this morning. Tess's loss had left him bereft of all human feeling except for grief.

"Do you want me to leave, Brady?" Jake asked solemnly. "Without even hearing what I've come to say?"

Brady lowered his eyes, suddenly ashamed. "No, Dad. I'm glad you're here," he admitted, holding out his hand for a belated shake. "Come on inside."

Jake took his hand, held on tightly, then clapped his son on the shoulder. Brady felt the intensity of his touch, the sense of loss in the man he'd always loved so much. Suddenly alarmed, he asked, "Is Arleen all right?"

Jake nodded. "Sure. Arleen is fine. Everybody's fine. Joey...Joe's afraid you took what he said last night to heart, but I told him you knew better than that. He was on his way out here when I told him that...I was the one who really needed to make the trip."

A curious flip-flop of hope stirred in Brady. This was different. No matter what his father had come to say, he had *come* to the Rocking T; he had admitted that something needed to be said to clear the air between them.

He hurried a little as he hiked up to the house and revved up some leftover coffee and a handful of doughnuts from the refrigerator. His father did not say much as he glanced at Brady's primitive but orderly furnishings. He spent quite awhile studying the collection of western artifacts along the south wall.

They ate in near silence, discussing the weather, the ancient bits and spurs, the cats that roamed freely in and out of the house. Nearly half an hour passed before Jake said softly, "Brady, I was wrong."

Brady almost choked on his doughnut. His eyes grew wide.

"I didn't want to encourage you to do something I was sure was a mistake for you. I didn't believe you could make a go of the Rocking T. I'm still not sure you can, and even if you can, I'm still not sure you should." His eyes met Brady's. "Not for the price you're going to have to pay."

In his darker moments, Brady wasn't sure, either, but he wasn't about to admit it to his father. "You were right when you said you were wrong," he answered. "So what's your point?"

"My point," Jake answered firmly, "is that I never made a clear distinction between supporting the choices you've made and supporting *you*. I don't believe in the Rocking T, Brady. I don't believe you can make a good living from ghost towns and wagon trains and western artifact museums." He stopped, leaned forward, and put down his coffee cup. "But I do believe in you."

Brady stared back, touched and confused.

"I don't have the money to help you run a railroad line out here. I can't in good conscience recommend that anybody else fork out that kind of capital, either. But maybe there's something else I can do."

Brady's hands were trembling. He put down his cup, too. "Such as?"

"I could reverse the bank's stand on refurbishment loans. At the very least I could approve the church's loan application. I could even serve on your committee, lend my name to the historic district enterprise. If you need a loan for some other related project that makes better business sense—even though it's got to do with horses—I won't shut you out the way I did before. I'll do my best to back you up, son. And if you can make things right with Tess, I'll do my best to support your marriage, too." His eyes grew watery as he added, "You would have brought Claudia into town in time. I'm sure of it. If I'd just had more faith in you, we could have shared your loss together, instead of blaming each other for losing that precious baby girl."

Brady didn't know quite what to say. He couldn't say his father had offered him the world on a silver platter, and nothing he'd said was going to help him patch things up with Tess. Still, Jake had taken a massive stride in the direction of reconciliation, and that knowledge lifted one dark shadow from his heart.

"Thanks, Dad," was all he could say.

Jake cleared his throat. "I know you think it's too little, too late—"

"No. It's a beginning. I can't ask for more than that." He shook his head. "And I want you to know that I am developing some business sense. Running a railroad out here doesn't make any sense. I'll have to find some other way to build up business so I can pay back Joe."

Jake nodded, then asked quietly, "Have you found some other way to marry Tess?"

Brady's eyes closed, and he quietly studied the old wooden table. Anguish speared his soul. "This is my home," he said softly. "I've asked her to share it with me. She said no."

There was a long silence before Jake said, "I'm an old man, Brady. You know I was happy with your mother and after she died, I never thought I'd marry again. I just sort of stumbled on Arleen."

Brady nodded.

"You also know that I've spent my whole life building up Trent Savings and Loan. It means as much to me as the Rocking T means to you. But I've got to tell you that if I had to make a choice between the bank and Arleen, I'd walk out the front door of Trent Savings and Loan tomorrow and never look back."

It was the most surprising thing his father had said in the past half hour of surprises. It was almost as surprising as his next words. "If I thought selling the bank would make things right between you and me, Brady, I'd give it up without a second thought. The older I get the more I realize that *things* are meaningless compared to people. If Tess Hamilton really loves you, son, then she's worth a thousand times more than this ranch."

Dear God, I know it, a voice within him answered. *Without her, by December those red-striped cliffs will be prison bars.*

As if he could read Brady's mind, Jake said softly, "That reminds me, I brought your Christmas present out with me in case you're snowlocked through the holidays." He reached into his pocket, pulled out an envelope and handed it to Brady. "It's valid for anytime through next year."

"What is it?" he teased, trying to lighten the mood. "A discount coupon for alfalfa?"

Jake shook his head, and his somber face made it clear that *he* wasn't kidding. "Better. It's round-trip airfare to L.A."

"HELLO?" Tess knew her voice was breathy, almost desperate, as she picked up the phone, but she couldn't help herself. She'd felt nearly hysterical since she'd last talked to Brady—hours and hours before—and she hadn't yet found her feet.

"My God, Tess, what's going on?" Roberta's calm, crisp voice crackled over the wire. "I've got four messages here from you and I've only been gone since yesterday. I was giving a chautauqua up in Santa Fe. The most fascinating—" She stopped herself, then asked again, "What's wrong?"

Tess started to cry. Or, perhaps, it would be more accurate to say she started to cry *again*. The whole night had been a nightmare; agony had gripped her like a bird of prey, its talons embedded in her heart. She tried to tell Roberta what had happened, how Brady had asked him to marry her, told her he loved her...and told her goodbye.

"I feel so sick, Roberta. I can't eat a thing. I haven't slept all night. I'm supposed to be working on that Cattle Springs survey but the words all blur together. What am I going to do?" It was a futile question, one she knew her friend couldn't answer. But she needed to say the words to somebody. She couldn't keep whispering them to herself.

Roberta, ever practical, now asked calmly, "Are you sure it's too late to patch things up, Tess? I mean, it sounds like all he wants is a little reassurance. He did ask you to marry him, after all, and he still said he loved you even when he said goodbye."

"Roberta, how can I patch things up? What he wants is impossible. He wants me to throw away everything for love again. He doesn't care about my life, my dreams or my values. All he wants is some proof that I'm not like Claudia." She stopped to blow her nose, then hit a crying jag again. "And I'm *not* Claudia! I'm *me*! I love the red-rock country, Roberta. She never did. According to Mandy, she intended to go back to New York right from the start. She just figured she could dazzle Brady into going with her." Again she sobbed. "But he wouldn't go. At least not to stay. And now he won't even come to a city long enough to *visit* me!"

For a long moment Roberta didn't answer. Then she said softly, "Tess, has it ever occurred to you that maybe you're punishing Brady with a reverse golden rule?"

"What? This is no time to get esoteric on me, Roberta. If you—"

"It seems to me that the real stumbling block keeping you from giving in to Brady is that you can't bear the idea of being judged by his memory of his first spouse. But I think you're still doing the same thing to him. You don't know if Brady will ignore your career or block your friendships. You're not even willing to find out. All you're concerned about is making sure that Nathan can't make a fool of you again."

"But Nathan is—"

"As real to Brady as Claudia is to you. You're blaming each other for all the rotten things done by the two of them. If you'd just toss them out of the picture and look each other eye to eye, I think your love for each other could overcome this distrust."

For a moment Tess was utterly silent. Roberta, the last of the great feminists, was telling her to give up her career and entrust her heart to a man?

"Roberta, I thought you agreed with me! I thought you understood about Nathan!"

"I do understand about Nathan! And I think you were one hundred and fifty percent right to leave him. But I think Brady Trent is a different kettle of fish entirely. I know it's a gamble, but when you come right down to it, isn't any kind of love? Brady's not a selfish man. And he's not a shallow one like Nathan. There's only one area in his life where there's no compromise—the ranch—and that's because he's had to fight so hard to hold on to it. I've got a hunch that if you'll give in on that, Brady would stand on his head to please you in everything else."

In the far windows of her heart, Tess sensed a tiny ray of sunlight. She savored its warmth, trying to decide if she was so desperate to marry Brady that she was willing to believe anything. And yet, Roberta's theory made sense. Although she and Brady hadn't talked about Nathan much, he'd always been there, lurking in the shadows, stiffening her resolve to fight Brady on the very issue on which he so desperately needed her support.

"As I see it," Roberta continued pragmatically, "the question isn't whether or not you want to marry Brady. It's whether or not you still can. I don't know just how you left things on the phone, but I imagine if you get yourself in gear there's some way you can make it up to him."

Tess swallowed hard. The Cattle Springs survey lay in front of her, needing work... work that she knew she could do a thousand times better in a Colorado cabin than in her modern office while her heart was pulsing through a shredder.

"What's your situation there at work?" Roberta asked. "Are you jammed with appointments, or could Cheryl cover things for you for a week or so?"

"I'd planned to spend the next two weeks compiling data and writing up some reports. I already asked if I could do most of the work out of the office, just in case..."

"So take it to the Rocking T! You can worry about your resignation later if you can't pull off long-distance work indefinitely."

Tess couldn't argue with that logic; she'd already carefully prepared her work for just such a possibility. Still, she asked, "What about my condo? Brady asked me to put it on the market and go to him before the snow flies."

"When is that?"

"There's a storm coming in tomorrow night from Wyoming."

Roberta groaned. "So why the heck are you wasting time talking to me? I'll see you in the spring, Mrs. Trent."

Without another word, Roberta hung up the phone.

If I can just make it till daybreak, I'll be all right, Brady told himself after his father had gone. *I should cash in this ticket and give this money to Joey. Dad would understand.*

But he knew that his father would not understand; for that matter, neither would Joe. They both wanted him to be happy far more than they wanted to be rich. And even though Joe understood how he felt about the Rocking T and his father didn't, they were in complete harmony about one thing: they both believed that he'd never find happiness on the ranch if he had to give up Tess to keep it.

For two long days and interminable nights—ever since their last goodbye—he'd tried to tell himself that they were wrong. Over and over again he'd whipped himself with memories of that terrible winter when Claudia had abandoned him and inadvertently lost the baby. Deliberately he'd dug out some pictures of that awful year he spent in New York. Surely, he'd told himself, it would get better now that he'd made the decision.

Don't lie to yourself, Brady Trent, a quiet, strong voice told him now. *You thought she'd buckle under. You thought she'd come if you gave her no choice. But she probably thinks you're the one who'll fold without her.*

And then he tried to imagine Tess, strong-willed and angry, reveling in his misery, supremely confident that he'd go belly-up and crawl to her. But the face he saw in that imaginary high-rise apartment wasn't Tess Hamilton, the good sport he'd fished out of a leech-ridden pond. It was Claudia who'd gloated in the city, Claudia who'd been certain he would come.

Brady, I'm not Claudia! she'd once railed at him. *And I'll never marry you until you know that in your heart.*

Suddenly he did know the difference. And he knew something else. Tess *would* give up her job and come to him. Maybe not yet, but she wouldn't last the winter in L.A. Not because she couldn't live without him. Not because she couldn't find some other way to be happy in her solitary life. But because she loved him too much to make him suffer. Too much to let her own pride and her painful past stand in their way.

A woman with that kind of loyalty was the opposite of his ex-wife. A woman like that deserved the blind devotion that he'd squandered on Claudia. She deserved a fresh start at a new life.

And so did Brady.

There was only a glimmer of light left in the western sky when he pulled out his boots, tugged on his warmest jacket and tramped out to the bunkhouse that Ragweed Willie—for another week or so, at least—called home. He knocked on the door, then poked his head in, knowing he'd rousted his aging friend from an afternoon nap.

"I'm going away for a while, Willie. I want you to take care of everything."

He heard a muffled oath in reply. "You woke me up t' tell me that? Did ya think I'd let th' stock starve if'n ya didn't show up fer a few days?"

"I'm going to be gone a lot longer than usual," he said softly, trying not to think about the beautiful sunset weaving itself in the sky behind him. "You can move into the main house if you like."

He heard Willie sit up in bed, banging his head on the springs of the upper bunk. "Move inta th' main house?" he croaked. "Good God, Brady, when're ya comin' back?"

"I don't know." The words were hard, but he had to say them. "I may not be back at all. At least not to stay. I'm going to be in California until spring."

Ragweed Willie shook his grizzled head and chuckled. Dramatically he stroked his beard. "Better take Calypso with you. Don't figure that snowbird can ride nothin' else."

Brady tried to laugh, but it was painful. Until he held Tess in his arms again, he knew everything was going to hurt. He had one last thing to say before he left the Rocking T, left his dream buried in the red rock.

"Wherever I end up, I'll need to hire a foreman, so don't you go running off on me," he said in a pseudo-threatening tone.

Old Willie swallowed hard. "Hell, I'm not goin' nowheres till I git my back pay," he groused. But relief warmed his tired old eyes. "I'll be here waitin' come spring."

They gripped each other's hands in silence, then Brady turned and walked away. He stopped at the barn to say goodbye to Buck, then hurried out to the truck.

It took a few minutes to get the old thing started. The engine was cold—the whole southwestern corner of Colorado was freezing—and snowflakes were already falling. He considered putting on his snow chains before he left, because he knew he'd never make it clear to Redpoint without them. But now it seemed more crucial to go, to hurry the leave-taking. He could stop and wrestle with the chains on the road.

He would return to the Rocking T someday, but he knew it would never be the same. No matter what happened now, he'd abandoned the ranch for a second woman. The Rocking T would never forgive him. It would never take him back.

But he had not made a mistake this time. He was sure of it. And he grew more certain with each passing mile. He'd barely reached the first paved road north of the ranch when he realized that the snow was getting so thick, he'd have to stop soon. But just as he toyed with pulling over, he spied another car stopped on the two-lane highway. It was a car he'd never seen before, and the driver—either a small man or an average-size woman—was crawling on denim-covered knees by the edge of the road.

Brady stopped the truck and got out slowly, concerned yet a mite suspicious of a stranger so far out in the middle of nowhere. But as he grew closer to the car, he realized that he had nothing to fear from the driver, who was innocently locking snow chains around the last of the four tires.

Long blond hair flowed everywhere.

If Tess heard him approaching, she gave no sign. She was struggling determinedly with the chains, though it was clear from her clumsy handling that she'd never put them on before. Her gloveless hands were stiff and red. Tears streamed down her face. She was shuddering from the cold.

Brady braced himself on the hood of her car, suddenly too dizzy to stand upright. The true measure of her sacrifice hit him full in the face, and he was awash with shame that he'd ever asked her to give up so much for him.

And awash with gratitude that she loved him enough to do it.

Her teeth were clacking uncontrollably when she finally stood up, but there was a stiff pride in her shoulders, as if she were quite proud that she'd managed the task by herself. When her glance fell on him, she showed no surprise. He was certain she'd known he was there all along.

"I thought I'd get some groceries," she said by way of greeting, gesturing toward the brown bags that filled up every inch of the car. "I figure it could be a long time before we get into town again, and I didn't want you to think you'd been saddled with a wife who couldn't cook." A flake fell on her nose and lingered, but she did not flick it off as she slowly met his searching gaze. "You do still have an opening for a wife on the Rocking T, don't you, Brady?"

Her voice trembled, and not just from the cold. *I did this to her,* Brady realized humbly. *I filled her with fear. I convinced her that I loved this patch of rocky buttes more than I loved her. I convinced her I could actually give her up.*

He tried to tell her he'd been crazy. He tried to offer words of assurance. He tried to apologize. But suddenly the huge rock in his throat made speech impossible, and all he could do was pull off his jacket and wrap it around her, holding it in place with strong arms that would never, ever let her go.

Her arms locked behind his waist as she clung to him, fresh tears streaming, while he rocked her back and forth and let his love refill the terrible emptiness he knew his cruel words had left in her heart. For a long moment they simply swayed there, oblivious to the snow, drawing more strength from each other than either could ever find from any other source.

When Brady loosened his hold enough to lower his mouth to hers, Tess raised her chin and met his lips gently, in promise and joy and leftover sorrow, washing away the terrible hurts of the last few nights. He felt her hands clutch his shirt at his waist, felt her trembling body still under the warmth of his touch.

"Forgive me, sweetheart," he finally managed to murmur. "I'll never test you again. I swear it."

She clutched him more tightly yet. "And I'll never ask you to leave the ranch again, Brady. I've made my decision, and I won't look back."

He shook his head, struggling for words again, but Tess drew him closer and nestled against his neck. For a long moment he simply hugged her, rocking her back and forth, while the snowflakes blanketed them with pristine winter grace.

At last he said softly, "I'd hate to think of all that food going to waste, so we'll drop it off at Joey's on our way back."

"We're going back to Redpoint?" she asked in confusion.

Brady nodded his head. "And then we're going all the way to L.A."

Tess pulled back and stared at him disbelievingly. "Brady, darling, I just got here. I closed up the condo. I put it on the market. I took a leave and—"

"Take it back. We're going to winter at the beach. In *your* world. And after we're married—after we're both sure that *we* come first and *where* comes second—we'll try to figure out a way to come back."

Her eyes were huge. She seemed unable to speak.

"There's got to be a piece of land near enough to town for you to work on and for me to run a wagon train to. Joey says there are lots of other ghosts towns up in the hills, old mining camps that have a legitimate right to claim a historical partnership with the Slow Joe. One of them is surely situated just right for the plan we talked about, just sitting there waiting for restoration. Once we sell your condo and the Rocking T—and pay something back to Joey—we can map out our dreams and choose the right chunk of land *together*."

For another long moment she just stared at him. Then her face crumpled in joyful disbelief, and she began to weep in earnest. She collapsed against his chest again, sobbing from a place deep within her where Brady knew she'd stored up tears for weeks.

At first, he knew, they were tears of unshed sorrow, tears he had to answer for, tears he would always regret. But in a matter of minutes Tess was clutching him in a different way, and her eyes were sparkling with quietly realized hope.

When she started to cry again a moment later, he saw only tears of joy.

EPILOGUE

IT WAS LATE SPRING when the wagon train arrived in Patchwork, the old mining camp that would serve as headquarters for the Double Bar T Wagon Train Adventure. Tess Trent, the ranch's namesake, perched on the bouncing seat beside her husband as he guided the four horses tugging an old stagecoach, the first in a long line of wooden-wheeled vehicles. Behind the stage came six Conestogas, each one stacked to the gills with riding gear, ranch equipment, and a massive collection of western memorabilia, which had once been housed on the Rocking T.

Seven dogs trotted along beside the wagons, and an eighth—a pup that was still too young to make the trip on foot—barked energetically from the back of the last canvas top. "Knock it off!" hollered Jake Trent, the driver of the wagon. "We're all glad we finally made it."

Although Brady did not speak or even turn around, Tess caught the quiet smile that tugged on his lips and lighted up his eyes. It was a smile that had warmed her all winter, a smile that had come to be the sunlight of those joyous snowy days when she and her new husband had stayed with Jake and Arleen while they'd planned their new business enterprise. With Joey's help, they'd examined every possible ghost town attached to the narrow gauge line until they'd found the one that seemed best suited to their long-range plans and financial reality.

It was Jake who had arranged the miracle, Jake who had tracked down the owner of Patchwork and reminded him of how many years he'd been well served by Trent Savings and Loan. Although the gentleman had had no intention of putting the land up for sale, Jake had convinced him that he could spare fifty acres that were currently inaccessible. Jake had even suggested a reasonable price.

Tess eyed the weather-beaten mining town with unmitigated exuberance. Restoring this old western community would be a preservationist's dream! Nothing she'd ever done for H.W.P. had been half as exciting. She already had endless lists of ideas as to how to lure tourists—with period hotels and restaurants, a general store, a real livery stable and even an opera house! Roberta had volunteered to make a splash as a traveling suffragist delivering chautauquas, and her brainstorming sessions with Tess had yielded some marvelous other ideas—greased pig chases, cow-milking contests and camel races like the ones they had in Nevada. Brady would still manage the wagon train and the livery, and help Tess create a museum to house his wonderful collection of artifacts of the old west.

Although Tess and Brady had camped in Patchwork with Joe and Mandy several times already, at the moment she felt as though she were arriving in a thrilling foreign land. Only she and Brady would create this magical world of the past . . . and, like so many western settlers there before them, create a new generation to flourish here. She was already carrying the seed of the first little Trent who would fill the old alleys of Patchwork with childish laughter.

Tess gazed past the half-collapsed buildings to the east, where a piece of old railroad track was barely visible against the magnificent red-and-pink stony cliffs. She swallowed hard as she took in the divinely carved splendor.

And then she looked at Brady, who had one long bowleg braced against the running board as he pulled the team up to the old marshall's office they'd decided to remodel and live in.

"I been thinkin', Miz Trent," he drawled as he grinned at her lovingly, "that we might consider settlin' here."

Their gazes met, locked, held. Despite the rumble of the wagons and the flurry of hooves behind them, Tess felt as though she and Brady were the only two people west of the Animas River. Silently he drew her toward him, their bond so strong that even without their bodies touching, it was as though they sat thigh to thigh.

"I like th' view, Mr. Trent," she concurred softly. "An' I reckon we aint' too far from that fresh runnin' stream down below."

Brady studied her for a moment, as though he had a question to ask. But then he slipped all the reins into his left hand and reached toward her with his right. That dark, callused hand rested ever so briefly on Tess's cheek, then dropped to her waist to stroke the rounded form of his baby, nested deep within her.

Tess covered Brady's hand with her own, clung to it, felt his powerful grip as he wordlessly spoke his love.

"I think it's time this family had a home," he finally whispered, his words almost carried away by the gentle desert wind.

But Tess heard the words—all the words he'd ever uttered and all the words he'd ever held back—as she lifted his beloved hand to her lips.

Then she hopped off the stage and started to unhitch one team of horses while Brady unhitched the other.

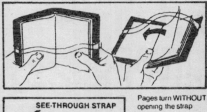

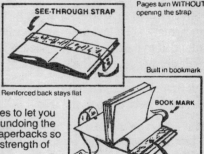

PASSPORT TO ROMANCE VACATION SWEEPSTAKES

OFFICIAL RULES

SWEEPSTAKES RULES AND REGULATIONS. NO PURCHASE NECESSARY.

HOW TO ENTER:

1. To enter, complete this official entry form and return with your invoice in the envelope provided, or print your name, address, telephone number and age on a plain piece of paper and mail to: Passport to Romance, P.O. Box #1397, Buffalo, N.Y. 14269-1397. No mechanically reproduced entries accepted.
2. All entries must be received by the Contest Closing Date, midnight, December 31, 1990 to be eligible.
3. Prizes: There will be ten (10) Grand Prizes awarded, each consisting of a choice of a trip for two people to: i) London, England (approximate retail value $5,050 U.S.); ii) England, Wales and Scotland (approximate retail value $6,400 U.S.); iii) Caribbean Cruise (approximate retail value $7,300 U.S.); iv) Hawaii (approximate retail value $ 9,550 U.S.); v) Greek Island Cruise in the Mediterranean (approximate retail value $12,250 U.S.); vi) France (approximate retail value $7,300 U.S.).
4. Any winner may choose to receive any trip or a cash alternative prize of $5,000.00 U.S. in lieu of the trip.
5. Odds of winning depend on number of entries received.
6. A random draw will be made by Nielsen Promotion Services, an independent judging organization on January 29, 1991, in Buffalo, N.Y., at 11:30 a.m. from all eligible entries received on or before the Contest Closing Date. Any Canadian entrants who are selected must correctly answer a time-limited, mathematical skill-testing question in order to win. Quebec residents may submit any litigation respecting the conduct and awarding of a prize in this contest to the Régie des loteries et courses du Quebec.
7. Full contest rules may be obtained by sending a stamped, self-addressed envelope to: "Passport to Romance Rules Request", P.O. Box 9998, Saint John, New Brunswick, E2L 4N4.
8. Payment of taxes other than air and hotel taxes is the sole responsibility of the winner.
9. Void where prohibited by law.

PASSPORT TO ROMANCE VACATION SWEEPSTAKES

OFFICIAL RULES

SWEEPSTAKES RULES AND REGULATIONS. NO PURCHASE NECESSARY.

HOW TO ENTER:

1. To enter, complete this official entry form and return with your invoice in the envelope provided, or print your name, address, telephone number and age on a plain piece of paper and mail to: Passport to Romance, P.O. Box #1397, Buffalo, N.Y. 14269-1397. No mechanically reproduced entries accepted.
2. All entries must be received by the Contest Closing Date, midnight, December 31, 1990 to be eligible.
3. Prizes: There will be ten (10) Grand Prizes awarded, each consisting of a choice of a trip for two people to: i) London, England (approximate retail value $5,050 U.S.); ii) England, Wales and Scotland (approximate retail value $6,400 U.S.); iii) Caribbean Cruise (approximate retail value $7,300 U.S.); iv) Hawaii (approximate retail value $ 9,550 U.S.); v) Greek Island Cruise in the Mediterranean (approximate retail value $12,250 U.S.); vi) France (approximate retail value $7,300 U.S.).
4. Any winner may choose to receive any trip or a cash alternative prize of $5,000.00 U.S. in lieu of the trip.
5. Odds of winning depend on number of entries received.
6. A random draw will be made by Nielsen Promotion Services, an independent judging organization on January 29, 1991, in Buffalo, N.Y., at 11:30 a.m. from all eligible entries received on or before the Contest Closing Date. Any Canadian entrants who are selected must correctly answer a time-limited, mathematical skill-testing question in order to win. Quebec residents may submit any litigation respecting the conduct and awarding of a prize in this contest to the Régie des loteries et courses du Quebec.
7. Full contest rules may be obtained by sending a stamped, self-addressed envelope to: "Passport to Romance Rules Request", P.O. Box 9998, Saint John, New Brunswick, E2L 4N4.
8. Payment of taxes other than air and hotel taxes is the sole responsibility of the winner.
9. Void where prohibited by law.

 RLS-DIR

VACATION SWEEPSTAKES

MONTH 2 ENTRY

Official Entry Form

Yes, enter me in the drawing for one of ten Vacations-for-Two! If I'm a winner, I'll get my choice of any of the six different destinations being offered — and I won't have to decide until after I'm notified!

Return entries with invoice in envelope provided along with Daily Travel Allowance Voucher. Each book in your shipment has two entry forms — and the more you enter, the better your chance of winning!

Name

Address Apt.

City State/Prov. Zip/Postal Code

Daytime phone number ______________________
Area Code

☐ I am enclosing a Daily Travel Allowance Voucher in the amount of $__________ Write in amount revealed beneath scratch-off

PASSPORT
WIN
1 of 10 Vacations
SEE INSIDE
TO ROMANCE

VACATION SWEEPSTAKES

MONTH 2 ENTRY

Official Entry Form

Yes, enter me in the drawing for one of ten Vacations-for-Two! If I'm a winner, I'll get my choice of any of the six different destinations being offered — and I won't have to decide until after I'm notified!

Return entries with invoice in envelope provided along with Daily Travel Allowance Voucher. Each book in your shipment has two entry forms — and the more you enter, the better your chance of winning!

Name

Address Apt.

City State/Prov. Zip/Postal Code

Daytime phone number ______________________
Area Code

☐ I am enclosing a Daily Travel Allowance Voucher in the amount of $__________ Write in amount revealed beneath scratch-off

CPS-TWO